*'You want me t...
lied to me sinc...*

Client privilege be... ...couldn't let Riane continue to believe the worst. 'I came to West Virginia to see your mother because I thought she might be able to help with a case I'm working on. I have a client who's trying to find someone.'

'A missing person?'

'Not missing, exactly,' Joel hedged. 'The woman I'm looking for was adopted twenty-two years ago.'

'Why do you think my mother can help?'

He hesitated, reluctant to state the conclusion that would crumble all Riane's conceptions about her life. But the fierce determination in her eyes forced his hand. She wouldn't let him continue to evade. More compelling than that, however, was the realisation that he owed her the truth.

'I think you're the woman I'm looking for.'

Available in December 2004 from Silhouette Sensation

Some Kind of Hero

BRENDA HARLEN

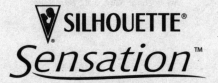

SILHOUETTE®
Sensation™

First published in Great Britain 2004
Silhouette Books, Eton House, 18-24 Paradise Road,
Richmond, Surrey TW9 1SR

© Brenda Harlen 2003

ISBN 0 373 27316 9

18-1204

Printed and bound in Spain
by Litografia Rosés S.A., Barcelona

BRENDA HARLEN

grew up in a small town surrounded by books and imaginary friends. Although she always dreamed of being a writer, she chose to follow a more traditional career path first. After two years of practising as a lawyer, she gave up her 'real' job to be a mum and to try her hand at writing books. Three years, five manuscripts and another baby later, she sold her first book.

Brenda lives in Canada with her real-life husband/hero, two heroes-in-training and two neurotic dogs. She is still surrounded by books ('too many books,' according to her children) and imaginary friends, but she also enjoys communicating with 'real' people. Readers can contact Brenda by email at brendaharlen@yahoo.com or by post c/o Silhouette Books, 233 Broadway, Suite 1001, New York, NY 10279, USA.

A lot of this book is about family,
and I'd like to dedicate this story to mine.

To my parents—
Diane & John and Dan & Marj—
for giving me such a wonderful example of family.

To Shelly and Jim,
whom I am privileged not just to call
my sister and brother but also my friends.

To Robin & Hazel—
for always accepting me as part of their family.

And, of course, to Neill and Connor and Ryan.

I love you all.

PS This book is also dedicated to Ken, who didn't
even blink when his wife said three unknown women
were coming to invade his cottage for a week-long
writers' retreat. (During which time this story took
form in spite of Kate and Sharon and Sheryl.
Thanks anyway, ladies.)

Chapter 1

It took Riane Quinlan half a minute to peg the tall, dark-haired man across the room as an out-of-towner, another thirty seconds to figure him for a cop.

She'd spotted him the minute he stepped through the ornately carved double doors of the hotel ballroom where the Fourth Annual Quinlan Camp Charity Ball was in progress. Part of the reason was that his was an unfamiliar face at this type of event. Another part of the reason was much more basic. Whoever he was, he was an incredible specimen of masculinity: broad shoulders, hard muscles, thick dark hair that was just a little too long for the conservative tastes of the social elite.

Not a departmental regulation crew cut, but some guys took pride in breaking the rules. This man, with the chiseled jaw, strong nose and slashing brows, looked like one of them.

From a distance, Riane couldn't determine what color his eyes were, just that they were dark and intense.

He took a slow survey of the room. Deliberately casual. Too casual.

Definitely a cop.

As the daughter of a U.S. senator, Riane had been shad-owed often enough to recognize the inherent attributes of those in law enforcement. The sculpted physique, the guarded stance, the constant attentiveness. There were security per-sonnel hovering in the background this evening, but she knew this man wasn't one of them. He wasn't hired muscle—just a cop.

Her lips curved in a small smile. *Just* a cop was hardly an accurate description. He was almost larger than life—a real man's man, the type of man she didn't often have opportunity to cross paths with in her social circles.

As he continued his perusal of the room, his gaze collided with hers. The force of the impact literally took her breath away. His eyes narrowed, skimmed over her in a blatantly masculine assessment. She felt her skin heat, an unavoidably feminine reaction.

He held her gaze a moment longer, then turned his head, dismissing her.

Except that Riane wouldn't be dismissed.

She made her way through the sea of rustling silk and black ties, stopping now and again to speak with someone she hadn't caught up with earlier. She smiled at the secretary of state and tried to ignore the fact that her toes were starting to cramp.

It had been a mistake to wear new shoes when she was going to be on her feet for the better part of the evening, but the sling-back sandals were such a perfect match for the silk crêpe dress, she hadn't been able to resist. She'd spent the better part of her twenty-four years in the public eye and knew that image was more important than comfort.

She glanced toward the back of the room again, and her eyes locked with his.

Blue, she realized. His eyes were a startling, stunning shade of blue. And just a little wary.

Her curiosity further piqued, she breached the last few feet that separated them and offered her most winning smile. "I don't believe we've met."

He hesitated a beat before he shifted his untouched champagne glass and offered his hand. "Joel Logan."

His voice was deep and incredibly sensuous, causing her blood to heat in her veins. She disregarded the sensation. She was more than likely overheated from the multitude of lights in the enormous chandeliers, not from hearing this man speak two words to her.

Reassured, she put her hand in his, felt it engulfed by his warm strength. His handshake was firm, his palm wide and slightly callused. There was nothing improper or inappropriate about the contact, and yet she felt a sudden burst of heat arrow straight to her core. She withdrew her hand quickly from his grasp.

"Riane Quinlan," she told him.

"I know."

He said nothing else, offered none of the usual pleasantries.

Riane was intrigued. Her family's wealth and political connections had accustomed her to more deferential treatment. People went out of their way to impress her, never knowing when they might need a personal favor or political ally. But she'd bet every last dollar of the trust fund her grandmother had left her that Joel Logan didn't bow and scrape for anyone, and she couldn't help but admire him for it.

She tried another smile. "What brings you here tonight, Mr. Logan?"

"A desire to support the Quinlan Camp for Underprivileged Children?"

It was more of a question than an answer, and she couldn't decide if he was just unsociable or deliberately trying to annoy her. She should thank him for his support and leave it at that, but there was something about him that made it impossible for her to walk away.

"It must help that your shoulders are so broad," she commented.

He frowned at her. "Excuse me?"

"Your shoulders," she said again. "They must be the reason you can walk upright with the size of that chip you're carrying."

He shifted his champagne glass into his other hand again, his scowl deepening.

Dark, moody, and no sense of humor, Riane decided. She signaled to a nearby waiter, turned to speak with him briefly. When the server disappeared, she plucked the crystal flute from Joel's hand and brought it to her own lips, sipping the cool, bubbly liquid.

"I wasn't finished with that," he said testily.

"I know." Her response was unapologetic.

His mouth opened, then closed again when the waiter returned with a tall pilsner glass filled with amber-colored liquid, a thick foam head skimming the frosty rim.

"Thanks, Jeffrey." Riane took the glass and offered it to Joel. "I thought this might be more to your liking."

For half a second she thought he might refuse the drink, but thirst must have triumphed over obstinacy as he reached for the glass. His fingers brushed against hers and she felt that zing again.

"What makes you think you know what I like?" Joel challenged.

She took another sip of his champagne before responding. "It's something of a hobby of mine—studying people."

"Have you been studying me?"

"I study everyone."

"And what do you think you've learned?"

"You don't like champagne," she said, "and you won't pretend to enjoy it, even though everyone else guzzles it like water at this kind of event."

He tipped the glass of beer to his lips and drank, his eyes still on hers.

"I imagine you suffered through dinner," she continued. "The food and the conversation. You would probably have preferred a nice thick steak, rare, and a discussion about the Yankees' chances at the pennant.''

She saw the corners of his mouth twitch, wondered if he might actually smile. He didn't.

''Medium well,'' was all he said.

''Sorry?''

''My steak,'' he clarified. ''Medium well. I like to be sure it's dead.''

''And the Yankees?'' she prompted.

Now he did smile, and it completely transformed him. With his dark and somber expression, he was dangerously handsome. With those sensual lips curved, he was devastating.

''Absolutely.''

She nodded, but couldn't for the life of her even remember what the question had been. The man had just smiled, and her mind had blanked.

''Is that the end of your analysis?'' he prompted.

''Not quite,'' she said, wondering whether she should pursue the issue or make a tactical retreat. He intrigued her—maybe too much. She was a woman used to being in control of her life and her emotions. But after less than ten minutes in Joel Logan's company, she felt her comfortable world tilting crazily on its axis. It thrilled her. And terrified her.

''What else do you think you know?''

''You're looking for someone. Someone you expected to be here. Whether he is or not, I couldn't say, because I don't know who it is, but I know you haven't found him. Or her,'' she amended quickly.

He pinned her with that deep blue gaze, and she felt as if all the bones in her body had simply melted. When he spoke again, the low, throaty tone was as seductive as a caress. ''Maybe I'm just looking for someone to take home for a quick bout of hot, sweaty sex.''

''I hadn't completely disregarded that possibility,'' she acknowledged, a little breathlessly. ''But I think if that was what you wanted, you would have found her by now.''

"I'm flattered, I think."

"Just an observation, Mr. Logan. So why don't you tell me what it is that brought you to West Virginia?"

"Why do you assume I'm not a local?"

"If you were, we'd have met before now." And she definitely would have remembered. Joel Logan wasn't the type of man any woman would forget.

"I'm here on business," he admitted after a pause.

"What kind of business?"

"You haven't figured that out?"

"I'm still working on it," she said. "But I haven't been able to think of any reason why an out-of-town cop is at my fund-raiser."

"I'm not a cop." He took another sip of his beer.

"Oh." She frowned. Then, in an accusatory tone, she said, "You look like a cop. Standing at the far end of the room, your back to the wall, as if you expect armed gunmen to come charging through the door."

This time his smile seemed to come more easily. "I used to be a cop," he conceded.

"And now?"

He shrugged. "Now I'm not."

Joel tipped his glass to his lips again and drank deeply, wishing for at least the hundredth time since Shaun McIver walked into his office that he'd refused this assignment. It should have been a simple job: to find a child who had been adopted twenty-two years earlier. But four months later Joel had made scant progress.

The few facts he'd managed to uncover so far led him straight to Senator Ellen Rutherford-Quinlan. If the senator had information that would help find Shaun's fiancée's sister, Joel was determined to get it. Which was his reason for coming to West Virginia.

He hadn't counted on crossing paths with Riane Quinlan, though. And he'd been completely unprepared for the quick punch of arousal that struck low in his belly when he'd first set eyes on her.

A smart investigator would turn the situation to his advantage—get whatever information he could from the daughter as the mother was nowhere to be found. But he was having difficulty thinking like an investigator with the subtle scent of Riane's perfume fogging his brain.

Which meant that the wisest thing would be to establish and maintain a safe distance from Riane Quinlan. He needed answers, and he wasn't going to get them if he allowed himself to be distracted. The senator's daughter was quite a distraction.

"Riane, darling—"

Joel exhaled a silent sigh of relief as she was forced to turn her attention to the stocky woman who descended upon them in a cloud of sweet scent and glittering sequins.

"Margaret," Riane said, exchanging air kisses with the older woman. "I'm so pleased you could make it."

The woman looked vaguely familiar to Joel, but it took a moment to search his memory banks for the reference. When it clicked, he wondered that his jaw didn't hit the floor. Margaret Cassidy. The attorney general of the United States.

The upper echelons of political society had turned out for this event—all the way from Washington, even. A reminder of how much political clout the Rutherford-Quinlans wielded. As if he needed any reminders. He'd tangled with them once before, and that encounter had cost Joel his reputation and his career.

He was clearly out of his element here, even if no one else seemed to realize it. He didn't fit in with these people; he didn't want to. He'd attended this gala event because his client was paying all incidental costs—including the thousand-dollar ticket for dinner and the rental of this damn tux— and because he'd been confident he could remain in the background. Riane had taken that option away from him. And he wasn't sure if he should be flattered or annoyed that he'd caught her attention.

While she was preoccupied with the attorney general, Joel scanned the room again, searching for the elusive senator. Ellen Rutherford-Quinlan's name had been on the top of the guest list. This charity camp was her daughter's pet project. So where the hell was she?

His head snapped back to the conversation beside him when the attorney general said, "I'm so sorry I missed your mother."

"She didn't want to miss the ball," Riane told her. "But Daddy convinced her that it was more important to celebrate their thirty-fifth wedding anniversary."

Daddy. Joel fought the urge to roll his eyes. How many grown women referred to their fathers as "daddy"? Then the impact of what she was saying registered and he nearly groaned out loud: the senator wasn't going to make an appearance here tonight.

He accepted the fresh glass of beer the waiter brought to him without question and tipped it to his lips, cursing the fact that he'd wasted his time—and his client's money—in attending this gala event. Hell, his whole trip to West Virginia might turn out to have been a waste of time.

Riane said goodbye to the older woman, turned back to him and smiled. Joel felt that quick punch of desire again and had to remind himself of all the reasons that the senator's daughter was off-limits.

She wasn't his type, anyway. She was too sophisticated and high class. Too everything. He preferred a woman with more simple tastes, more basic desires. And blond, he reminded himself, even as his fingers itched to pull the pins out of Riane's dark silky hair to let it tumble freely down her back.

Joel swallowed, hard. Yeah, he definitely preferred blondes.

Like the one beside the window, tall and slender in body-hugging green velvet. Her hand was on the arm of a short, portly man who looked old enough to be her father, but the hefty chunk of diamond on the woman's hand suggested otherwise.

Despite the ring and the presence of her companion, she caught Joel's eye and sent him a blatantly invitational glance from beneath lowered lashes. There was nothing complicated about that one, Joel thought approvingly. Except that he *never* cut in on another man's territory. It was one of few rules he lived by, and one he'd never consider violating. He knew too well how it felt to be on the other side of that equation.

"Meredith Ashcroft," Riane said, close to his ear. "Of the Boston Ashcrofts—by marriage. Now divorced and currently engaged to Justice Cunningham."

"The man in the ill-fitting tux?"

"That's the one," Riane agreed. "He hasn't bought a new suit in the past ten years because he won't admit that he's put on forty pounds. He thinks he has the same physique that impressed his first wife. *She* left him more than a dozen years ago and took half his money. He still possesses a sizable fortune and an impressive position on the bench, which is why Ms. Ashcroft is in line to become wife number three."

"A friend of yours?"

Riane's smile was thin. "An acquaintance," she clarified. "But I could arrange an introduction, if you wanted."

"You said she was engaged."

"Does that matter to you?"

"Yes."

"A cop with morals," she mused.

"I'm not a cop," he said again.

"So you said. But you didn't say what you are."

Not wanting to reveal too much about his reasons for being in West Virginia, he opted to try diversion again. "Do you dance?"

She tilted her head. "Is that a hypothetical question or an invitation?"

"An invitation."

She studied him for another moment, as if considering his motives, then nodded. "All right."

Joel led the way to the dance floor, reassuring himself that he'd issued the invitation solely to prevent her from continuing her inquiry. He wasn't ready for her to find out who he was, his real reason for being there. Not until he knew whether or not she was the answer to his questions.

Then Riane put her hand in his, and desire surged through him. Hot and hard. And he knew that however he chose to rationalize the request in his own mind, the simple fact was that he'd wanted to hold her. She was sexy and beautiful and intriguing, and it had been far too long since he'd been with a woman.

The intensity of his own reaction shook him. He was a man of action, in charge of his life, responsible for his own decisions. Yet the moment she turned into his arms, he felt a spiraling sense of panic, a stunning realization that this was out of his control.

He'd only ever felt this way once before—toward the end of the Conroy investigation. Just as all the pieces seemed to be falling into place, he'd known that it had been a little too easy. He'd ignored the instinct, convinced himself it was paranoia.

He'd been wrong.

There was no way he'd make the same mistake again.

Okay, so maybe he was overreacting a little this time. Riane Quinlan was a woman. She might be beautiful, sexy, intriguing, but she was still just a woman.

Yet his instincts warned him that she was dangerous. Very dangerous. Because the scent of her clouded his mind; the subtle curves of her body made him forget his reason for being there; those full, painted lips tempted him to taste. Riane Quinlan made him not just forget, but *want* to forget, that she was off-limits.

Just a woman?

Like hell. This woman was more dangerous than a roomful

of Zane Conroy's trigger-happy minions with fully automatic Mac 10s.

He misstepped, and her hip brushed against his thigh. The fleeting contact jarred him, and he felt his blood begin to migrate southward. He forced himself to concentrate on moving his feet, determined to avoid any more such accidents so that she wouldn't notice how affected he was by her.

Not that his physical response should surprise her. He was, after all, just a man, and she was as warm and soft as the scent that clung to her. And she fit in his arms as if it was where she was meant to be.

Joel gave himself a mental shake. It was ridiculous to even imagine such things. Riane Quinlan might fit in his arms, but she could never fit into his life. Nor he in hers. He knew that opposites could attract. He also knew, from personal experience, that they couldn't coexist for very long.

"How long are you going to be in West Virginia?" Riane asked, breaking the silence that had stretched between them.

"I'm not sure," he responded, then he made the mistake of looking at her. She'd tilted her head upward to speak to him, and her glossy lips were mere inches from his own. He only needed to lower his head a fraction and he could taste her. It was a tempting proposition. Too tempting. Too dangerous.

He tore his gaze from her mouth, saw that she was watching him. Her own eyes were dark, aware. He'd feel much more confident in his ability to do his job if he could keep his distance from Riane Quinlan. And he wouldn't be able to keep his distance if she kept looking at him like that.

Focus, Logan.

Somewhere in the back recesses of his mind this niggling reminder from his conscience registered. He knew he was dangerously close to losing his focus, and he couldn't afford to make any mistakes. Not this time.

"Riane," he said. "That's a rather unusual name, isn't it?"

"It's a feminine form of Ryan, which is my father's name."

His preliminary investigation had revealed that fact, but he didn't know if the similarity was by design or coincidence. That was what he needed to find out, and that was why he needed to talk to the senator.

"Isn't your mother usually a supporter of the Quinlan Camp Charity Ball?"

So much for being discreet, he thought, as the question blurted out of his mouth. But he was more worried about self-preservation than discretion at this point.

If Riane was startled by the abrupt change of topic, she gave no indication of it. "Yes," she admitted. "And I was a little worried that her absence this year would affect attendance, but thankfully it hasn't been a problem."

"She won't be making an appearance tonight?"

"I doubt it." She smiled at him once more, drawing his gaze back to that luscious mouth, tempting him all over again. "She's in Thailand."

"Thailand?"

Riane nodded. "She and my father went on a cruise to celebrate their anniversary."

Joel expected to be annoyed, even angry, at this revelation. His sole purpose in being here this evening was to contact the senator. But it was difficult to be angry when there was a soft, fragrant woman in his arms. Impossible to be annoyed that his source of information had been wrong.

"How long will they be gone?"

"What is your interest in my mother, Mr. Logan?"

"Joel," he said, and smiled.

But she'd homed in on the direction of his questions and wouldn't be deterred. "What is your interest in my mother, *Joel?*"

"I was just hoping, since I was in town anyway, that I might have an opportunity to meet with the senator."

"Are you a Republican supporter?"

He realized, with reluctant admiration, that she was trying

to trip him up. And had he not done his homework thoroughly, she might have done so with that question. Her mother was a Democrat.

"I'm not a card-carrying member of any party," he told her.

He wasn't sure if his response convinced her, but she let it drop. Joel accepted the reprieve, recognizing that he'd have to be a little more subtle if he didn't want to raise Riane's suspicions any further.

Preoccupied with these thoughts, he failed to spot the photographer until the flash of the camera's bulb blinded him. He instinctively stepped away, crushing Riane's toes in his haste.

"Ouch."

"Sorry." He mumbled the apology automatically, concentrated on breathing to slow the rapid beating of his heart as different reminiscences assailed him. Flash after flash. The incessant glare blinding. Reporters shoving, shouting. Microphones thrust at him. Headline after headline. Day after day. Until he dreaded even leaving his home.

"Are you undercover?" Riane asked.

Joel scowled. "I'm *not* a cop."

"Then why did you jump three feet when that flashbulb went off?"

"I don't like having my picture taken."

"Why not?"

"I'm not very photogenic," he said dryly.

Riane laughed, and the soft, sexy sound was a welcome distraction from the recent direction of his thoughts.

"I doubt that," she said.

"I didn't know the press would be here," Joel admitted. But he should have known, and he should have been prepared.

"I would have been disappointed if they weren't," Riane told him. "The more publicity we can generate for the Quinlan Camp, the better. High-level exposure equates to high-level contributions."

He understood that. Just as he understood that Riane was accustomed to living in the spotlight—the last place Joel wanted to be. He'd had his life scrutinized by the media before, and he never wanted to live like that again.

He could only hope that some enterprising young reporter didn't dig deep enough to discover the identity of Riane Quinlan's dance partner. Then as soon as this case was closed, he'd be out of her life forever.

Still, as the song began to wind down, Joel found himself reluctant to let her go. He knew she was a distraction he could ill afford, a complication he wasn't prepared for, but he couldn't deny his attraction to her.

And when the final notes of the song merged into the first bars of the next, he didn't figure it would hurt to hold her just a little while longer.

Then there was a firm tap on his shoulder and a smooth, masculine voice saying, "If you don't mind, I'd like a dance with my fiancée."

Chapter 2

Riane felt the censure in Joel's gaze as he relinquished her hand to Stuart without comment and walked off the dance floor. She wanted to follow him, to explain, but pride prevented her from doing so. He had no right to make judgments about her, and besides, a well-bred lady didn't chase after any man.

Instead she concentrated her attention on her new dance partner, who had already swept her into his arms and was moving smoothly to the strains of the music. Stuart's movements were effortless, each step and turn flawlessly executed. There wasn't anything that he didn't do well, and he was an incredible dancer. But his touch didn't heat her blood the way Joel's had done. Her body didn't yearn to press close to his as it had when she'd been dancing with the mysterious Mr. Logan.

She pushed the traitorous thoughts impatiently aside. She was a twenty-four-year-old woman, not a hormonal adolescent. It wasn't like her to react to a man on such a primal

level. Human beings were supposed to be civilized, to have
power over their more basic urges.

Still, she couldn't deny that something about Joel Logan
appealed to her on a most fundamental level. Unwillingly,
her gaze strayed to the back of the room where he'd once
again stationed himself.

The formality of his attire failed to disguise the raw power
he exuded. He had to be well over six feet—as she'd had to
tip her head to meet his gaze despite the three inches her
heels added to her five-foot, ten-inch frame—with broad
shoulders tapering to a trim waist and long, lean legs. Just
the memory of those muscles, solid and unyielding, caused
her breath to quicken, her pulse to race.

"You seem lost in thought," Stuart commented lightly.

Riane started, felt her cheeks flush. "Just tired."

"You've had a busy few weeks preparing for tonight."

"Yes," she agreed, grateful for his easy acceptance of her
explanation. Still, she was embarrassed to admit, even to herself, that Stuart's absence had gone unnoticed until he'd interrupted her dance with Joel. She'd been so preoccupied
with the success of the charity ball she hadn't spared him a
single thought.

And then she'd met Joel Logan, and she hadn't thought
about anything else.

She felt a twinge of guilt at the realization, but only a slight
twinge. After all, she wasn't *really* engaged to Stuart Etherington III. Although they'd talked, in abstract terms, about
marriage, she resented his reference to her as his "fiancée,"
as if their engagement was a fact rather than a possibility.
But she wasn't in the mood to take issue with his vocabulary
now. It had been a wonderfully successful evening and she
wouldn't ruin it by bickering with him.

So she ignored the multitude of recriminations running
through her mind and only said, "You were late."

"I'm sorry." His apology was more automatic than sin-
cere. "I got tied up in meetings."

She wasn't surprised. Stuart had a successful corporate law

practice and was often required to work long into the evening and frequently on weekends. She knew his hours would grow longer still when he launched the political career he wanted so much.

"You missed dinner," she told him. "Cream of artichoke soup, warm chicken salad with rosemary dressing, poached salmon with tarragon sauce, champagne sherbet and peppered strawberries."

"That sounds much better than the Italian takeout I had delivered to the office."

"I'm sure it was," she agreed. "But as long as you paid for your ticket, I won't complain about the squandered meal."

"You're a mercenary." There was admiration mingled with amusement in his tone.

"This camp is important to me. And to the kids who visit every summer."

"I know," Stuart placated. "And, yes, I paid for my ticket."

She smiled. "Then I thank you for your support."

"Has it been a successful evening?"

"Very," she told him. "Even more so than last year."

"You have a knack for this sort of thing," Stuart told her. "Organizing, fund-raising, delegating. Valuable qualities in a politician's wife."

Riane's smile was strained. She resented Stuart's implication that tonight's charity ball was an exercise in politics for her; she hated that he couldn't understand how much the camp mattered.

And yet, despite this fundamental difference of opinion, Riane believed that they were well suited for one another. They had similar goals and interests. They'd both been raised in political families, and they both understood the expectations and responsibilities of living in the public eye.

She sometimes wondered if he was more attracted to her political connections than her person, but she could hardly judge him when her own motives were less than ideal. Ultimately she and Stuart wanted the same thing: the White House. He had the ideas and the connections to take him there, and when he did, Riane had no qualms about exploiting her position as his wife and first lady to focus attention on the plight of underprivileged children in this country and around the world.

Yes, her relationship with Stuart was exactly what she wanted. She just sometimes wished he made her feel…

The thought fizzled. She didn't know what was missing; she only knew that she wanted to feel the way she'd felt when Joel had held her in his arms.

She glanced toward the back of the room, searching, seeking.

But he was already gone.

Joel awoke the morning after the charity ball with the mother of all hangovers. He winced against the bright sunlight flooding through the window and cursed himself for not remembering to close the curtains the night before. Slowly he eased his legs over the side of the bed and found the floor. Satisfied that the world was once again solid beneath his feet, he scrubbed a hand over his cheek. It had been a lot of years since he'd drunk himself into a stupor, but he'd done it often enough in the past that he should have known better.

Women, he thought disparagingly. They were all the same. From his mother, who'd abandoned him when he was six, to Jocelyn, who'd dumped him with no hint of remorse when the going got tough, they weren't to be trusted. It was a lesson he should have learned long ago.

Unfortunately, he was a man, and there were times that basic urges couldn't be denied. But sex and love were different things, and he'd managed to avoid emotional entanglements for the most part. Since Jocelyn, anyway. He was smart enough and discerning enough to seek companionship from women who wanted the same thing he did: simple, uncomplicated sex.

Riane Quinlan had almost made him forget that. There was

nothing simple about the way she'd looked at him. Nothing simple about the feelings she'd roused inside him.

He shook his head, then winced at the explosion of pain that resulted from the movement. He'd obviously been too long without a woman if he could be taken in by a pair of dark eyes.

Cursing Shaun McIver for ever asking him to take on this case, everyone with any connection to the name Rutherford, and Riane Quinlan in particular, he stumbled to the bathroom and turned on the faucet. He splashed cold water on his face, then filled a glass and fished a couple of aspirin out of the bottle.

He winced again when the shrill ring of his cell phone echoed in the empty room. He might have been tempted to ignore it, but he knew the only person who would be calling this early on a Sunday morning was his partner. And Mike would only be calling if he had information to share.

"Logan."

"I tracked Felicia Elliott to Flint, Michigan," Mike said without preamble. "She was in a women's shelter there for a few months after she left her husband."

"Have you spoken to her?" Joel was less interested in the trail than he was in the results.

"She moved out several weeks ago."

"Where is she now?"

"The director of the shelter wouldn't give me that information."

Although Joel understood the reasons for such a policy, he was frustrated. Every time he started to make any headway in this case, yet another obstacle was thrown in his path.

"Maybe I should go to Michigan," he suggested. He needed to wrap this case up and move on to something else. Somewhere else. Anywhere but West Virginia.

"I wouldn't bother," Mike told him. "I left our number with the woman at the shelter. She agreed to pass it along to Felicia Elliott if she hears from her again."

Joel knew it was the best they could hope for, which only

frustrated him further. ''Do you have any new leads to follow?''

''I could get in touch with Gavin Elliott again, to see if
he's remembered any other details that might be helpful.''

''Don't bother,'' Joel said, rubbing absently at the throbbing behind his temple. ''It looks like we're just going to
have to cool our heels on this one until we hear from Mrs.
Elliott.''

''You haven't made contact with the senator yet?'' Mike
asked.

''No,'' Joel admitted. ''Apparently she's in Thailand.''

''*Thailand?*''

''Yeah, that was pretty much my reaction,'' Joel agreed.

''Do you know when she'll be back?''

''Her daughter wasn't exactly forthcoming with the details.''

''You've spoken to the daughter?''

Unbidden, a series of images came to mind. Riane moving
toward him. Long legs, short dress, easy smile. Riane in his
arms on the dance floor. Creamy skin, subtle curves, intoxicating scent. Riane with her fiancé.

Fiancé.

None of the information Joel had gathered indicated that
Riane Quinlan was engaged, and he was certain something
like that would have been splashed across all the society
pages. Still, he'd recognized the man who'd intruded on their
dance. Stuart Etherington III, a corporate lawyer at one of
the biggest firms in nearby Huntington and an up-and-comer
on the local political scene with big ambitions. Apparently
Senator Rutherford-Quinlan's daughter was one of his ambitions.

''Joel?'' Mike's voice intruded on his thoughts. ''Did you
meet with the daughter?''

''Yeah,'' he said again.

There was a brief silence on the other end of the line, then,
''What was your impression?''

Long legs, short dress— Joel severed the thought abruptly this time. "I'd say there's more than a passing resemblance between the two women," he said instead. "And too many other coincidences to ignore."

His years on the police force had taught him to be wary of coincidences, and the scandal that ended his career had given him more than enough reason to distrust anyone with the name Rutherford.

When Joel had first started to examine the potential Rutherford connection in this case, Mike had accused him of letting his personal quest for vengeance interfere with his professional judgment. Joel couldn't deny that his impartiality had been compromised, but regardless of his personal feelings, facts were facts. And all the facts in this case had led him to West Virginia.

"I just can't believe that someone trying to pass off someone else's child as their own wouldn't at least change the name," Mike said.

"The spelling is different," Joel pointed out.

"So is the date of birth," Mike reminded him.

"Do you really think I'm looking for something that isn't there?"

"It would take quite a conspiracy to pull it off."

"Or a lot of money," Joel countered.

There was a long pause, then Mike said, "You know I have the greatest respect for your instincts, but I can't help thinking that your interest in this case is more about digging up dirt on the Rutherfords than finding the woman we're looking for."

"I know what my job is," Joel said coolly. But if he happened to find some dirt in the process of doing that job, he sure as hell wasn't going to wipe it off his hands and pretend it didn't exist.

"Okay," Mike relented.

Joel sighed as he disconnected the call. It looked as if he was going to be stuck in West Virginia for a while after all.

* * *

West Virginia.

He'd known that he'd find her. He hadn't expected it to be so easy. And he hadn't expected it to be in West Virginia.

He was a little disappointed. He'd wanted a challenge. A task worthy of his time and attention. She had rarely been either.

He should forget about her. He knew that was the smart thing to do. But he couldn't forget—or forgive—her betrayal.

She would pay for what she'd done.

But that was only the first part of his plan.

Four days after the charity ball, Riane hadn't stopped thinking about Joel Logan. Even sitting across from Stuart at their usual table at the Casa, where they dined every Wednesday night, she couldn't help but think about the other man.

It was because of Joel that she'd decided to shake up her relationship with Stuart a little. Maybe Stuart wasn't passionate with her, she reasoned, because she didn't inspire him to passion. So she'd bypassed the dark blue Chanel suit in favor of a scarlet silk A-line dress she'd bought several months earlier but hadn't yet found the courage to wear. The dress had a plunging neckline and a back slit that cut more than halfway up her thighs. It was bold, vibrant, daring. Everything she wasn't. Everything she wanted to be.

Stuart hadn't even commented on the dress except to say, as he always did, "You look lovely, Riane."

Not stunning.

Not sexy.

Lovely.

Several hours later, as Stuart pulled through the gates of the Quinlan estate, Riane found herself exhausted and frustrated. Dinner had been delicious, the service impeccable, their conversation monotonous.

It was all she could do not to scream.

When they arrived at the house, Stuart parked his Mercedes in front and came around to open her door. Always the gentleman, she thought, with an unfamiliar hint of resentment.

He walked with her up to the front porch, then touched his lips to hers. She willed herself to feel something, anything, in response to his kiss. But there was no tingle, no warmth, no desire. Nothing.

And then it was over.

"Good night, Riane."

"Good night, Stuart." She held back the sigh until he was in his car again and driving away.

Sophie was waiting for Riane when she stepped into the marble-tiled foyer.

"Good evening, Miss Quinlan."

The housekeeper's presence, as much as the formality she'd used, surprised Riane. "I told you not to wait up, Sophie."

"You have company, miss."

"Company?" Riane frowned.

"A gentleman." Sophie's eyes twinkled mischievously.

Riane's frown deepened.

"He's waiting in the den," Sophie told her.

Riane didn't want to deal with anyone else tonight. Her dinner with Stuart had been an exercise in monotony; his good-night kiss at the front door had left her uninspired. And she mentally damned Joel Logan for showing up at her charity ball and making her feel as though she was missing something.

All she wanted now was to slip into her favorite pair of satin pajamas and climb into bed. But she was a Quinlan, and the responsibilities she bore as such were equal to the rights and privileges. She squared her tired shoulders and turned toward the den.

The unnamed visitor was standing in front of the window, his back to the door. He didn't turn around; he didn't need to. Riane recognized him immediately. She wasn't sure if it was the breadth of his shoulders, the tension in his posture, or maybe just his aura. But she knew it was Joel, and her breath caught in her throat, her heart thudded heavily against her ribs.

She chided herself for the instinctive reaction. She was twenty-four years old, not a law school freshman enamored of the editor of the Law Review. But the feelings he stirred in her weren't so different from those she'd felt the first time she'd set eyes on Cameron Davis. And the first time he'd smiled at her, she'd been halfway in love.

The mental comparison terrified Riane. She didn't want to have these feelings again. She didn't want her emotions to be out of control. She didn't want to be vulnerable.

That niggling fear bolstered her lagging resolve. She wasn't twenty years old anymore—she was a woman. A strong, independent woman, and she could handle this man and her unexpected and inexplicable attraction to him.

"Mr. Logan," she said, in what she hoped was a casually disinterested tone.

He turned slowly, and she realized then that he'd been standing at the window watching for her. That he'd seen her arrive. That, in all likelihood, he'd seen Stuart kiss her good-night.

"Good evening, Ms. Quinlan."

She didn't insist that he call her Riane this time. She'd already decided it would be best to keep this man at a distance—as far a distance as possible. He was too potentially dangerous to her peace of mind to allow him to encroach on her carefully ordered life.

"How did you get in here?" she demanded.

"Your housekeeper, Sophie, let me in."

"I didn't mean into the house—I meant through the security gates."

"Sophie again," he told her.

Riane frowned. "She's not in the habit of opening the gates to strangers."

"But I'm not exactly a stranger, am I?"

"You are to Sophie."

"I told her that we'd met at the charity ball, and that I had something that belongs to you."

"And do you?"

He gestured to the wrap draped carelessly over the back of her father's chair. The velvet wrap that she'd belatedly realized she'd left in the ballroom.

"I didn't realize you worked in lost and found."

One side of his mouth kicked up in a half smile. "Apparently I do."

"Well, thank you for returning it."

"You're welcome."

But instead of moving toward the door, as she expected him to do, he leaned back against the corner of a bookcase and folded his arms over his chest. His pose was deliberately casual, his gaze leisurely as it skimmed over her. His self-confidence bordered on arrogance, the boldness of his stare almost insolent. It unnerved her, and aroused her.

"You look…" Joel paused, his deep blue eyes filled with heat as he sought the appropriate word to complete his thought, "…stunning."

Stunning.

Riane felt her cheeks flush with guilty pleasure. Why did it matter what Joel Logan thought? Why did his reluctant compliment mean so much to her when Stuart's words had only annoyed her?

The answer came quickly, unbidden. Because Joel Logan made her feel like a woman—feminine, attractive, desirable. With Stuart she only ever felt like an accessory—a suitable companion for any press conference or primary.

Uncomfortable with the comparison, with the feelings he stirred inside her, Riane refused to acknowledge the comment. "Was there something else you wanted, Mr. Logan?"

"I expected at least a few minutes of small talk, maybe the offer of a drink."

Riane bit back another sigh, resenting that the manners so carefully ingrained since childhood demanded that she participate in such formalities. But she'd managed to convince herself that Joel Logan had gone back to wherever he'd come from, and his unexpected appearance here—in her home—disconcerted her.

"Forgive my lack of manners, Mr. Logan. It's been a very long day and I wasn't expecting company." She didn't care that her apology sounded more like an accusation. She would go through the motions, but that was all. "Would you care for a drink?"

He inclined his head slightly, watching her intently. She stood firm, unflinching beneath his steady gaze.

"I'll have whatever you're having," he said at last.

She crossed over to the sideboard, removed the crystal stopper from the Waterford decanter and poured a generous amount of scotch into two highball glasses.

She passed one to him, careful that their fingers not brush in the transfer. She was determined to avoid any and all physical contact with him. She'd let him have his drink, find out what he wanted and send him on his way.

But Joel obviously had other plans, because he set his glass down on the shelf and brushed his fingers over her bare shoulder, down her arm, linking them loosely around her wrist. She felt the jolt of awareness reverberate through her system, sending tingles from the top of her head to the tips of her toes and all the erogenous zones in between. Still, she refused to let him see how he affected her, refused to let him know that her whole system went into overload when he touched her.

She looked at his hand on hers, raised a brow. Most of the men she knew would have taken the not-so-subtle hint and terminated the unwanted contact, but Joel either didn't understand her signal or simply refused to comply with it. She suspected it was the latter.

"How long have you been engaged?" he asked.

The abruptness of the question, as much as the hint of annoyance in his tone, startled her. "The engagement isn't official yet," she told him, silently wondering if it ever would be.

"No wedding date set?"

"No." She tugged out of his grasp and stepped away. She tipped her own glass to her lips and drank deeply, the scotch burning a fiery path down her throat that didn't compare to the heat on her arm where he'd touched her.

He picked up his glass again and sipped. "Nice scotch."

Riane downed the last of her drink, set the glass down with a snap. "Did you come her to discuss my wedding plans, my father's scotch, or was there something else you wanted?"

"Have I said or done something to upset you, Ms. Quinlan?"

Yes, damn it. She wanted to scream the words at him, to let her anger and frustration spill over. She'd been perfectly happy until Joel Logan had come into her life. Okay, maybe that wasn't entirely true. But she'd been content, for the most part, because she hadn't known what she was missing.

She still didn't know, but every time he looked at her, every time he touched her, he made her wonder.

"You're here," she said simply.

"I was thinking if either one of us had a right to be annoyed," he said casually, "it would be me."

"Why?"

"Because a woman who's engaged to be married shouldn't look at another man the way you were looking at me Saturday night."

She dropped her gaze and moved to refill her glass. "I'll apologize for the fact that you obviously misunderstood my intentions."

"I didn't misunderstand anything," Joel said coolly.

Riane lifted a shoulder in a careless shrug, raised the glass. Joel was at her side before it touched her lips, his fingers wrapped around the wrist that held her drink.

Her first thought was that he moved fast.

Her second, he was dangerous.

Her next, she wanted him.

It was irrational, it was insane, but in that instant, she knew it was true. It wasn't the subtle tug of desire she'd felt when she'd danced with him at the ball. There was nothing subtle about this at all. It hit her with the force of a runaway freight train, uncontrollable, unstoppable, undeniable.

Chapter 3

Joel could read the emotions reflected in her eyes.

Surprise. Awareness. Desire.

She wanted him; he wanted her. The attraction between them was simple. Unfortunately, everything else about the situation was not.

Her lips curved slightly and he tightened his grip. He prided himself on having a great deal of control but right now, he was very close to losing it. That sexy little smile almost put him over the top.

Almost.

He dropped Riane's wrist abruptly, unaccountably angry with her for the desire her mere presence stoked inside him. Angrier with himself for not being strong enough to resist. He knew he should back away. Better yet, he should leave—this house, this state. But he stayed where he was, mesmerized by her presence.

Her lips curved again. They were glossy and red, the same tempting shade as her figure-hugging dress and those killer shoes. At the charity ball she'd looked the part of a senator's daughter. Elegant, sophisticated, untouchable. Tonight she didn't look like anybody's daughter. She was all hot, steamy sex appeal in a beckoning package. And if she'd been *his* unofficial fiancée—not that *that* would ever happen—there was no way in hell he'd have said good-night at the door. But the proper Stuart Etherington III had, and his kiss hadn't even smudged Riane's lipstick.

"It's late, Mr. Logan, and I'm too tired for games. So why don't you cut to the chase and tell me why you're here?"

It was a valid question, but he'd forgotten all the reasons he'd contrived for his visit the minute he'd seen her get out of the car. Something about getting answers, he recalled vaguely. He'd decided that the senator's absence didn't have to be a complete roadblock to his investigation, it only required a slight detour. And spending some time with Riane might prove to be a very pleasurable side trip.

But face-to-face with her now, he felt a little uneasy about his agenda. He didn't want to be with Riane under false pretenses; he genuinely wanted to be with her. He wanted to know the woman behind the facade. He wanted to take his time and explore the attraction between them.

But his wants and desires were irrelevant here. His sole purpose for being in West Virginia was to finish the job he'd been hired to do. It was best to remember that, and to remember that a woman like Riane Quinlan was out of his league.

"It looks like I'm going to be in town a while," he said, "and I thought we could spend some time together while I'm here."

"Why?"

He shrugged. "I don't really know anyone else."

Her soft, smoky laugh went straight to his loins, making him again question the wisdom of the course he'd decided to pursue.

"That's the most unique, if not the most appealing, invitation I've ever received," she told him.

"Is that a yes?"

She shook her head. "I don't think so."

Joel nodded, as if her response was what he'd expected. "Your fiancé probably wouldn't approve."

"Stuart's not my fiancé," Riane said again. "And he doesn't dictate how I spend my time."

"Then there's no reason why you can't show me around."

"Except that I don't want to. I'm a busy woman, Mr. Logan."

"I'm sure you are," Joel agreed easily. "I just thought you might enjoy the opportunity to show an outsider the beauty and bounty of your home state."

"There are all kinds of tours you can take if you want to see the sights. You don't need my help for that."

"I was hoping for a more authentic experience."

She smiled again. "Authentic?"

There was something in the mischievous curve of her lips that set off warning bells, something in the gleam of those dark brown eyes that hinted at a secret agenda. Maybe he should back off, reconsider his plan. But he'd never been one to back down from a challenge.

"I'd like to do whatever native West Virginians would do if they had a few days to play."

She studied him for a long moment, considering. "What is it that you really want from me?"

Was she innately suspicious, or had his powers of persuasion been affected by his frustration with this assignment?

Determined to try harder, he smiled. "Just the pleasure of your company."

She raised an eyebrow.

"You're a beautiful woman, Riane. Intelligent, charming—when you want to be. Why do you find it so hard to believe that I want to spend time with you?"

"Most people who seek out my company are more interested in my political connections than sharing conversation," she said candidly.

"Including your fiancé?"

Her eyes narrowed, and her voice, when she responded,

could have frosted the windows. "My relationship with Stuart is none of your business."

"Did I hit a nerve?"

"Not at all," she denied in the same icy tone.

"I'm sorry," he said. And he was. Although he was curious about her relationship with the other man, he was sorry he'd put that guarded look in her eye.

Riane shrugged stiffly.

"I'd appreciate it if you could find some time to show me the sights."

"I'm going to be at the camp all day tomorrow."

"What about Friday, then?"

She hesitated.

"Please."

Sighed. "All right. Where are you staying?"

"At the Courtland Hotel, downtown."

"I'll pick you up at ten o'clock. Wear something comfortable, casual."

"Are you going to tell me where we're going?"

"I'm going to show you some of West Virginia's most impressive sights," she promised.

But Joel didn't wait until Friday to see her again.

He awoke in the morning determined to move on with his investigation. After all, that was his reason for being in West Virginia, and he was certain there must be other avenues to explore, other possibilities to examine.

According to the travel agent he'd consulted, the only cruise ship currently near Thailand had sailed out of Hong Kong nine days earlier and wouldn't complete its journey until it reached Singapore in another six days. Which meant that he had six more days to wait—seven, if the senator and her husband stayed an extra night in Singapore. Surely, he could occupy himself for that amount of time.

Yet when he left the hotel late that morning, he found himself stopping at the front desk for directions to the Quinlan Camp—just in case. When he found himself following those directions, he told himself it was simple curiosity. When he pulled through the wrought iron gates, he figured she probably wasn't even there.

There were several cars parked outside a long, low building built of hand-hewn logs. Colorful blooms spilled out of the large clay pots that flanked either side of the wooden stairs.

Joel parked his dusty Explorer beside a shiny red pickup truck and got out to stretch his legs. It was still early in the day, and the breeze was cool, the air crisp and clean and scented with the tangy perfume of cedar from the surrounding woods. Having grown up in the city, he wouldn't consider himself a nature lover, but he couldn't deny the appeal of this place.

He followed the flagstone path to the wide porch that spanned the length of the building. There were three doors at evenly spaced intervals, the one on the far end slightly ajar. He made his way in that direction, and his heart did a slow roll in his chest as he heard Riane's voice coming from inside.

He paused with his hand against the heavy wood. The rational part of his brain reminded him that he shouldn't be here. There was nothing to be gained by pursuing the attraction between them.

Okay, maybe he was hoping that she could give him some of the answers he needed. And he hadn't completely disregarded the possibility that she *was* the answer he was seeking. But he wasn't entirely comfortable using her in such a subversive manner. He was even less comfortable with the feelings that were churning inside him. Feelings that had nothing to do with his reasons for coming to West Virginia and everything to do with the woman who was Riane Quinlan.

There was a pause in the conversation, and he realized that she was on the phone. Then she laughed, and he felt that quick punch of arousal in response.

He should get back in his truck and go.

He pushed open the door.

Riane glanced up, her eyes widening. First with surprise, then pleasure—just a quick, almost imperceptible glimpse of it, immediately supplanted by annoyance. She frowned.

"Someone just came in. Can you call me back later, Adam?"

Adam? Just how many men was Riane juggling in her life? And why was he willing to stand in line to be yet one more?

She nodded and doodled on the legal pad on her desk as she finished up her call. He took a moment to scan the room—utilitarian furnishings, unadorned walls, a few potted plants. It was safer than looking at Riane, at the loose-flowing tresses that framed her delicate features, at the soft pink lips that curved slightly in response to something he couldn't hear, at the close-fitting sweater that seemed to mold to her breasts—

He tore his gaze away.

"I'll talk to you later, then," she agreed.

She hung up the phone, then tilted her head to look up at him again.

"Mr. Logan." It was more of a question than a greeting.

Without waiting for an invitation he knew wouldn't be forthcoming, Joel folded his frame into one of the hard plastic chairs facing her. Riane picked up the mug of coffee on her desk, took a sip and grimaced.

"Do you want to take a break?" he asked. "We could go somewhere to get a hot cup of coffee."

She set the mug back down. "Why don't you tell me why you're really here?"

"I wanted to see you."

When she looked at him again, her deep brown eyes were wary.

"I didn't plan on coming here today," he admitted. "But I was lying alone in my bed last night, thinking about you. Then I woke up this morning thinking about you. And here I am."

"I'm not going to be a distraction for you while you're in town," she said.

"I just want to spend some time with you."

"I agreed to show you around tomorrow."

"I was bored today."

Riane sighed, shaking her head as she pushed her chair back from the desk and stood up. "Come on," she said. "I'll give you a tour of the camp."

It wasn't quite what he wanted from her, but he figured it was a start. So he walked around the grounds with her, listening as she explained the function of the camp, the program, her plans for expansion. She had such passion for the project, such focused enthusiasm. It was obvious the camp meant a lot to her, more than he'd realized during their brief discussion at the charity ball.

"This will be our fourth season," Riane said proudly. "And two of the counselors we've hired for this summer were campers here our first year."

"You must be very proud of what you've accomplished."

"For the most part," she agreed. "But there are still too many kids turned away each year simply because of the limited size of our facility."

"And that's why you're expanding?" he guessed.

"We have the space," Riane told him. "And, thanks to increased contributions this year, we have the funds. By the start of next season, we'll have six new cabins, each one designed to sleep five campers and a counselor."

"How many buildings do you have now?"

"Twelve cabins, a mess hall, an arts and crafts center," she gestured as she explained, "and the stables."

"Stables?"

She nodded and set off toward a fenced paddock he'd passed on the drive in. "We have half a dozen horses the children are taught to care for and ride."

"How many people work here?"

"In addition to the counselors, who are mostly volunteers, there's a registered nurse and child psychologist on staff. Plus

Jared, our horse trainer, year-round groundskeeper, camp supervisor and chef.''

"Chef?"

"Someone has to feed the kids."

"How many kids?" Joel wondered aloud.

"We have sixty kids for each of four two-week sessions."

"That's a lot of macaroni and cheese."

"Jared does better than that," Riane assured him.

They stopped at the fence that bordered the paddock, leaning against the rails to watch the horses grazing.

"Have I bored you to death yet with all this stuff?"

Joel shook his head. "I think it's a wonderful thing you're doing."

"Even with the expansion, it won't be enough. We're considering weekend programs in the spring and fall in addition to the summer camp. In the not-too-distant future, I'd like to open another site—maybe in Virginia or Pennsylvania. Somewhere close by, so I can stay involved with both.''

She sighed again, a heartfelt expression of frustration and futility. "Let's talk about something else," she suggested.

"Like what?"

"You."

He studied the pair of sleek, chestnut horses grazing contentedly in the paddock. "I'm not very interesting."

Riane clicked her tongue against the roof of her mouth in a sound of disapproval. "That's hardly the kind of statement to impress a woman," she chided.

Joel couldn't help but laugh. "What should I say?"

She shook her head. "I would have thought a guy like you would have figured that out by now."

"And I would think that a woman like you wouldn't be swayed by mere words."

She smiled now, and the curve of those soft, tempting lips did strange things to his heart again.

"You're right," she admitted.

Unable to resist, he reached out and skimmed the pad of his finger over her bottom lip. He heard her breath catch, watched her lips part slightly in response to his touch. When he looked up at her again, her eyes were wide.

"What would sway you, Riane?"

She swallowed, her scrambled brain desperately searching for coherent words to respond to his question. She had to say something, anything, to get him to back off. Anything but the truth. Because the truth was that all it would take to sway her was his touch. He hadn't even kissed her; he'd just brushed his finger over the curve of her lip and her insides had melted.

She'd experienced attraction before but never like this. The jolt of desire, so quick and unexpected, completely debilitated her.

He skimmed his knuckles over her cheek, threaded his fingers into her hair and tilted her head back. She forced herself to meet his gaze, then wished she hadn't done so. Tightly restrained passion simmered in the depths of his blue eyes. A challenge. A promise.

"What would sway you?" he asked again.

She swept her tongue along her bottom lip, unconsciously following the same path as his fingertip.

"Maybe you wouldn't be swayed at all," he murmured, his gaze fixed on her mouth again. "Maybe it would have to be your decision."

"Yes," she agreed breathlessly. Yes, it would be her decision. And yes, she wanted him.

"You're a strong woman," he continued, the low tone of his voice as hypnotic as the desire in his eyes. "Capable. Confident. Passionate."

Her heart melted just a little. No one had ever called her passionate before. No one had ever made her feel so passionate.

"And complicated," he finished, almost reluctantly, before combing his fingers through the ends of her hair and dropping his hand back to his side. "I don't have time for complications."

The desire he'd so effectively stirred up inside of her gave way to hurt and disappointment. She shoved those unwelcome emotions aside in favor of anger.

"What are you looking for, Logan, a quick tumble to satisfy your basic urges?"

"I wasn't looking for someone like you," he admitted.

"Then what are you doing here?"

He looked around, and seemed almost surprised by the setting. "I don't know," he said at last.

"I didn't ask you to come here."

"I know," he admitted. "And I thought I could stay away. But I can't. You've got me all tied up in knots and I don't know what to do about it."

As far as poetry went, it was somewhat lacking, and yet his words touched something inside her. Or maybe it wasn't the words so much as the frustration evident in his voice. He didn't want to want her, but he did. The realization soothed her bruised pride, empowered her fragile heart.

"I'm sorry," he said abruptly. "Why don't we just forget about that little outburst and start over?"

"Sure," Riane agreed, wishing it would be half as easy to forget the unwelcome feelings he'd stirred inside her. She folded her arms against the wooden fence. "Tell me something about yourself."

"What do you want to know?"

Everything. She wanted to know everything there was to know about Joel Logan, especially what it was about him that had her so enthralled. Through her charity work and her parents' political connections, she'd had occasion to dine with millionaires, dance with movie stars, discuss international relations with heads of state. She'd never been flustered by the mere presence of a man—until Joel had shown up at her ball.

But that was hardly an admission she was willing to make, so she opted to start with something more simple. "Where did you grow up?"

He seemed surprised by her question, almost relieved. "Philadelphia."

"Is that where you live now?"

He shook his head. "No. I moved to Fairweather, Pennsylvania, a few years back."

"Is that where your family is?"

"I don't know that I have any family left."

"What do you mean—you don't know?"

"I haven't seen my mother since I was six years old. She left me with my grandmother and took off for parts unknown. My grandmother died five years later."

"Oh," she said, feeling unaccountably saddened on his behalf. Her mother often teased that the kids who came to her camp were her surrogate siblings—the brothers and sisters she never had. Riane couldn't deny that there was probably some truth to that. But if she felt there was something missing from her life, she also knew how fortunate she was to have always had the unquestioning love and support of her parents. She couldn't imagine what it would be like to be well and truly alone.

"What about your father?" she asked.

"I have no idea who my father is."

"You never knew him?"

"I don't know if my mother knew him," he said dryly.

Her brow furrowed; Joel laughed.

"Not everyone has had the life you've had," he said.

Riane felt her back go up. "What's that supposed to mean?"

"You were raised in a perfect little family, in a cozy mansion on the hill. Between your private school education and ballet lessons and horseback riding, you probably never imagined that there were kids who went to bed hungry at night—or kids who had no bed to go to."

Riane's eyes narrowed on him. "Do you think I don't realize how lucky I've been? I may gave grown up in a home of wealth and privilege, and I'm grateful that I've never had to worry about my next meal, but I'm not oblivious to what goes on in the rest of the world.

"My parents were in the Foreign Service when I was born. We lived in various places in Central America, Eastern Europe, Africa. It was an incredible opportunity, and it was incredibly disheartening at times. I saw things most people don't want to hear about.

"I went to visit orphanages with my mother—dirty, overcrowded, unsanitary buildings where most of the children weren't just orphans but were sick or dying. There was one little girl—" Even after so many years, her throat tightened at the memory. "She was about three years old, but she weighed no more than fifteen pounds. She wasn't just malnourished, she had AIDS. Both of her parents had died of AIDS a few months earlier, her older sister only days before I met her.

"There was something about her, this child more so than any other I'd seen, that tore at my heart. Maybe it was the way she so simply and quietly accepted her fate. Knowing it was only a matter of time before she died.

"For almost three weeks, I went to that orphanage every day—to see her, to read stories to her. She loved fairy tales. As she listened, she'd smile and get this faraway look in her eyes, as if she was imagining herself inside the story—a life so much better than the one she was living.

"So don't you dare compare my life to yours and say I don't understand. Why don't you stop feeling sorry for yourself for five minutes and compare your life to hers?"

Riane was out of breath by the time she finished, and a little ashamed by her impassioned outburst. It wasn't like her to go off so easily. She was used to people making judgments about her, treating her commitment to the underprivileged like a hobby or, worse, a stage she would outgrow.

Even Stuart had once suggested that she was too involved with the kids, that she needed to detach herself from their problems. He'd only said it once.

Still, Joel couldn't have known the depth of her feelings, and she shouldn't have taken her annoyance out on him.

"You're right," he said at last. "I'm sorry."

"Forget it." She was more embarrassed than angry now.

"I guess I've spent so much time being bitter and resentful about my childhood that I never considered the others who were less fortunate. My grandmother might have bitched and grumbled every time she put a plate in front of me, but she never let me starve."

She felt his hand on her arm, his touch gentle but firm, forcing her attention back to him. "The little girl in the orphanage, is she the reason you have the camp?"

Riane nodded. "She died just a few weeks after we got there. That was when I resolved to do something to help children like her."

"How old were you?" he asked.

She looked away again. "Twelve."

"That's a hell of a commitment for a twelve-year-old to make."

"It's a hell of a way for a three-year-old child to die," she replied sadly. Then she shook her head, shook off the melancholy mood that had stolen over the moment.

"We were talking about your childhood," Riane reminded him.

"I think you got the gist of it."

"Do you have any brothers or sisters?"

He shook his head. "I had a sister. She was a few years older than me, took off on her own when she was fifteen and died on the street of a drug overdose less than a year later."

"I'm sorry," she said, meaning it. As an only child, she couldn't imagine what it was like to grow up with someone, to lose that someone, to be left alone to remember. For so many years she'd wished for a sister—would willingly have settled for a brother—but her parents hadn't been able to have any more children. Riane knew it had to be easier to have never had a sibling than to have shared such a connection and have it ripped away.

He shrugged. "It was a long time ago."

"You were close," she guessed.

"At one time." Then, in a not-so-subtle effort to change the topic, "Will you have dinner with me tonight?"

Riane shook her head. She'd agreed to play tour guide for him to prove that she was her own person—and to prove to herself that she was immune to whatever chemistry she thought existed between them. Her reaction to his unexpected appearance at the camp today proved otherwise. She wasn't immune at all.

She'd never believed in chemistry or destiny or any other such nonsense. But the more time she spent with Joel, the more she found herself questioning her beliefs. Rational or not—and she was pretty sure it was *not*—she was attracted to Joel Logan. Which was why she was determined to keep her distance from him as much as possible. She may have already committed herself to showing him around the following day, but that was going to be the extent of her involvement.

"Do you have other plans for dinner?" Joel's question interrupted her meandering thoughts.

"Yes."

"With the fiancé?" Joel prompted.

"No."

Joel didn't take the hint. "What are you doing?"

"Not that it's any of your business," Riane said, "but I told Sophie I'd be home to eat."

"What's she making?"

"Pot roast."

"Sounds better than anything room service has to offer," Joel said hopefully.

"I'm not inviting you to my house for dinner." Although there was a part of her that wanted to do just that. She was intrigued by this man who'd appeared in her life seemingly from nowhere. She wanted to spend time with him, to get to know him. All she really knew was that he was a former cop who lived in Fairweather, Pennsylvania. These sparse details didn't begin to satisfy her curiosity.

Despite her curiosity, though, she was afraid. Not of Joel, but of her own responses to him. And it was this fear that held her back.

"Please."

She sighed again. Although she knew it could be dangerous to spend more time with him, they wouldn't be alone together. Sophie would be there.

So she relented, not entirely unwillingly, to his request. "Dinner will be on the table at seven o'clock."

Chapter 4

At precisely seven o'clock, Riane found herself seated across from Joel at the gleaming mahogany table in the Quinlan dining room. On her way home from the camp, she'd called Sophie to tell her Joel would be coming for dinner, and Sophie had set the table with the best china, sparkling crystal and gleaming silver. As if that wasn't enough, she'd added long, slender candles in antique holders and opened a bottle of Riane's favorite merlot.

It was obvious, at least to Riane, that Sophie was setting the scene for romance. But Riane wasn't looking for romance—not with anyone, and especially not with Joel Logan.

Still, that wasn't the worst of the housekeeper's betrayal. Worse, far worse, in Riane's mind, was that Sophie had set the table for two. Sophie usually took her meals with the family, but tonight she'd begged off, leaving Riane to dine alone with Joel—the exact scenario Riane had been confident she could avoid by inviting him to the house.

"That was the best pot roast I've ever had," Joel told Sophie when she came to take their empty plates away.

Sophie beamed at him as though he was a favorite child. "Are you sure I can't offer you another helping?"

"I'm sure," Joel said. "I've already had seconds."

"Then I'll leave the two of you to finish up your wine before I bring out dessert," Sophie said, slipping out of the room as quickly and quietly as she'd slipped in.

"I'm glad you invited me for dinner," Joel said to Riane.

"You invited yourself," she reminded him.

"And you very graciously didn't withdraw the invitation."

Riane felt a reluctant smile tugging at her lips. They both knew there had been nothing gracious about her response.

"Don't do that," Joel warned.

The blossoming smile faded. "Don't do what?"

"Smile. If you do, you might have to admit that you don't detest my company as much as you want to, sweetheart."

"If I really disliked your company, I wouldn't be in it."

"But you're not entirely comfortable with me," he noted. "Why is that?"

She sighed and pushed away from the table. He stood, too, and followed her to the enormous arched window that overlooked the backyard.

"Because I don't know anything about you. Every time I ask a question about what you do or why you're in town, you evade or mislead or redirect the conversation. For all I know, you could be a tabloid reporter or a con man or—"

"A private investigator," he interjected.

"What?"

"I'm a private investigator."

"Oh." She took a minute to absorb that tidbit of information. "Why are you in Mapleview?"

He hesitated.

"Are you going to evade, mislead or redirect this time?"

He smiled, and Riane felt her heart skip a beat.

"I'm thinking about how to answer without revealing any confidential information."

She took a sip of wine, waiting.

"I'm looking for someone," he said at last. "A potential witness to a case I'm working on."

"Oh," she said again. "Why couldn't you tell me that the other night?"

His lips curved again and his eyes were dark, intense as they pinned her with a look that caused her blood to heat. "I wasn't thinking about business when I was with you."

It was a smooth response, and evasive. Again. She shook her head. It shouldn't matter. It *didn't* matter. Joel Logan was none of her concern. As soon as he finished whatever business had brought him to town, he would be gone, out of her life forever. Except that she couldn't shake the uneasy feeling that his business would somehow affect her.

"Why were you at the charity ball?"

His hesitation seemed answer enough.

"You're looking for someone I know."

"I'm following a lead," he admitted.

"Is it someone who's involved with my camp?" She sent up a silent but fervent prayer that the answer would be no. She couldn't bear to think of anything negative impacting her camp and the children who so desperately needed it.

"It has nothing to do with your camp," Joel assured her.

Riane wanted to believe him, but—

"I promise." He interrupted her thoughts with his softly spoken vow. "I know I should have told you, but my interest in you seems to have taken precedence over the case I'm working on."

"I thought your interest in me was solely as your tour guide."

"I lied," he said easily.

Riane lifted an eyebrow.

"Would you have agreed to spend tomorrow with me if I'd admitted I had designs on your body?"

"I can still change my mind."

"You won't. You're not the type of woman who would consciously break a promise. Now you'll just have to take your chances with me."

"I thought it was a violation of your personal code to move in on a woman who is otherwise involved."

"It is," he agreed. "But you've convinced me that you and Stuart aren't engaged."

"Not officially."

"Make up your mind, Riane." He took a step closer, and she took an instinctive step back. It was only when she felt the heavy velvet curtains behind her that she realized she'd been retreating. She forced herself to stand her ground; she wouldn't let him intimidate her.

"You can't use your relationship as a shield when it suits your purpose," Joel said, the low timbre of his voice sliding over her like a caress. "Are you engaged...or not?"

Her throat was dry, her heart pounding. Unconsciously she swept her tongue along her bottom lip to moisten it. His gaze dropped to her mouth, lingered.

"No," she admitted breathlessly.

He leaned closer, and when he spoke again she could feel the warmth of his breath on her cheek. "Then I don't have to worry about violating my personal code, do I?"

She didn't know what to say, how to extricate herself from the situation. She only knew that it was what she had to do. What she really wanted to do, however, was to breach the few scant inches that separated them and touch her lips to his. She wanted to—

"I have cheesecake," Sophie said, returning with two dessert plates in hand and effectively cutting off Riane's building fantasy in midstride. "And fresh strawberry sauce."

Joel stepped back, and Riane exhaled slowly. She should be relieved by Sophie's interruption, but she was unaccountably disappointed instead.

"Mr. Logan was just saying that he has to get back to his hotel," Riane said.

"I'm sure I have time for cheesecake," Joel countered.

Riane glared at him; Joel grinned.

And in that moment, Riane knew that he knew exactly how

his almost-kiss had affected her, how much she'd wanted to experience the touch of his mouth against hers.

"Good," Sophie said, apparently oblivious to the undercurrents passing between Riane and Joel. "I'll bring in coffee for you to have with your dessert."

Riane couldn't sleep, and she knew without a doubt that Joel Logan was responsible for her sudden bout of insomnia. Just as she knew it had been a mistake to invite him to come for dinner—even if it had been his suggestion rather than her own. It had been an even bigger mistake to agree to see him tomorrow.

She had so many other things she should be doing—obligations and responsibilities. She didn't have time to play tour guide for some bored, out-of-town P.I. And she wasn't sure she had the willpower to continue to resist the desire inside her.

With a groan of frustration, Riane pushed back the covers and commenced pacing the length of her bedroom. Pacing helped her to think, to get her thoughts in line and clear out her brain. But she knew, on some basic level, that it wasn't her brain that was the problem. It was her heart.

She groaned again, annoyed with herself for such fanciful notions. Whatever was wrong with her had more to do with her hormones than her heart. Hormones that had been stirred by Joel Logan's mere proximity and that continued to churn restlessly.

She sank down on the edge of her four-poster bed. Why was she so attracted to a man who was so obviously wrong for her? Was there something innately masochistic about her that she was destined to fall for men who could only break her heart?

She pushed herself to her feet again and resumed pacing. She didn't believe in destiny, and she was *not* going to fall for Joel Logan. She couldn't deny that she was attracted to him—what living, breathing, heterosexual woman wouldn't be? But feeling an attraction and acting upon it were completely different things. And Riane had no intention of acting upon this insane attraction.

Besides, she was involved with Stuart. Stuart was a good man—solid, stable, dependable. After her disastrous relationship with Cameron Davis, that was all she wanted.

Then why, a nagging voice from deep in her subconscious wondered, was she feeling so unsettled? And why was she pacing the floor of her bedroom at 3:00 a.m.?

Unable to answer either of these questions, Riane found herself reaching above her dressing table and plucking a toy from the shelf. Her action may have seemed random, but the doll she instinctively sought out was the one she'd called Eden for as long as she could remember. The one she'd always found gave her a measure of peace and comfort when nothing else could.

She couldn't recall when she'd started her collection, and she had dolls from various countries around the world, but Eden had always been her favorite. She smiled wryly in the darkness, embarrassed to admit—even to herself—that she still found solace in the tattered old doll.

She turned back toward the bed as a soft knock sounded at the door, immediately contrite that her nocturnal wandering had awakened the housekeeper. "Come in, Sophie."

The door pushed open, light spilling into Riane's bedroom from the hallway. The housekeeper followed, an elegant gold-rimmed cup in her hand.

"You're restless tonight," Sophie commented, offering the drink.

Riane set Eden down on her pillow and cradled the delicate china between her palms. She raised the cup and inhaled the sweet scent of chocolate. Sophie had played a key role in Riane's upbringing. She understood Riane's moods and needs, and she knew there was nothing that worked better than chocolate when she was feeling unsettled.

"I didn't mean to wake you," Riane said. "Please, go back to bed."

"You didn't wake me," Sophie told her, picking up the

doll Riane had set aside. She smoothed back the tangled hair, straightened the faded skirt of her dress. Riane hid a smile behind the cup as she sipped. It was Sophie's nature to want to fix and soothe, even when it wasn't always possible.

"Do you want to talk about it?" Sophie asked.

Riane wasn't sure she could talk about feelings she didn't understand. She was an intelligent, educated woman, yet the intensity of her reaction to Joel Logan continued to baffle her. "I don't know."

"It's Mr. Logan," Sophie guessed.

"It isn't always about a man," Riane chided, trying to deflect Sophie's focus.

"It is when you're pacing in your bedroom at 3:00 a.m."

Riane frowned. Being up in the middle of the night wasn't usual for her. "I've *never* been up pacing at this hour."

Sophie's smile was smug. "Exactly."

"Sophie, you know that I'm going to marry Stuart."

"I know that you *think* you're going to marry Stuart."

Riane took another sip of hot chocolate. "I thought you liked Stuart."

"I like him well enough for a politician."

"Sophie." Such a statement was almost sacrilege in the Quinlan household, but Riane grinned.

"He's not right for you," Sophie insisted.

"He'd make a good husband," Riane said loyally, wondering why she sounded unconvincing even to her own ears.

"You need someone who can put a sparkle in your eye, a flush in your cheek."

"This is reality," Riane said dryly. "Not a fairy tale."

"The flush in your cheeks was real enough when Mr. Logan was here."

And just the memory of the almost-kiss Sophie had interrupted caused Riane's cheeks to flush with color again. She hid behind the heirloom cup, sipped the hot drink.

"I've seen the way he looks at you and the way you look at him," Sophie told her. "There's chemistry there."

"I never was any good at science," Riane said lightly.

"You can joke about it, but you can't deny it."

Riane sighed. "Okay—I'm attracted to him."

"And that scares you," Sophie guessed.

"I haven't felt this way since I met Cameron Davis in my first year of law school." It was the only time she'd allowed her hormones to overrule her head, and the results had very nearly been disastrous. She refused to make the same mistake again.

"You won't ever be happy if you don't follow your heart."

"I'm happy with Stuart," Riane told her, but even to her own ears she didn't sound very convincing.

Sophie snorted. "Then why haven't you told Mr. Logan to stop coming around?"

"I did."

"And then you invited him for dinner."

"He invited himself," Riane felt compelled to point out.

"He wouldn't have been here if you didn't want him to be."

"He's very persistent."

Sophie chuckled.

"All right," Riane admitted. "And maybe I enjoy his company."

"Maybe?"

Riane shrugged, unwilling to make any further admission. Unable to express feelings she didn't understand. The initial attraction had been purely physical. She'd spotted Joel Logan from across the room at the charity ball and had immediately been intrigued. But it was more than that. There was something about him that tugged at her—something even stronger than the self-protective instinct that warned her away.

She finished the creamy chocolate drink in one long swallow, then feigned a yawn. "I can probably sleep now."

"All right, then," Sophie relented, taking the cup from Riane and exchanging it for the doll she still held in her arms.

"Thank you, Sophie." Riane's comment referred to both the hot chocolate and the understanding.

Sophie nodded and kissed her cheek. "Sweet dreams."

But when Riane finally fell asleep with her doll in her arms, she dreamed of a little girl crying.

Joel was waiting in front of the Courtland Hotel at precisely ten o'clock Friday morning when Riane pulled up in her snazzy little BMW coupe. It was a gorgeous car, and as he slid into the passenger seat of the vehicle, he noticed the driver was gorgeous, too.

She was wearing a red scoop-necked T-shirt and softly faded jeans. Her hair was tied away from her face today, and he itched to loosen the band around the end of the braid and sift his fingers through the silky tresses.

He heard her speak but had been too preoccupied with his little fantasy to decipher the words.

"Did you say something?" he asked, buckling his seat belt.

She gave him a strange look, then glanced down at his feet. "I asked if those were sturdy shoes?"

Joel looked down at the loafers he'd donned with khakis and a golf shirt. "As long as you don't intend to take me rock climbing, I think they're adequate."

"All right." She pulled away from the curb, merging smoothly into the flow of traffic.

"We're not going rock climbing, are we?" he prompted.

"No, we're not going rock climbing."

He waited a beat, but she offered no additional information. "Where are we going?"

"Caving."

"Oh." It seemed harmless enough, if he could forget that he hated close, dark spaces. If he could forget about the day he'd been lured into Conroy's deserted warehouse and trapped for hours with the dank smell and fetid rats.

He rubbed a hand over the scar on his abdomen and tried to relegate the memories and frustrations to a back corner of his mind. There was no point in thinking about any of that now, nothing to be gained by recalling the sense of futility that had plagued him for so long.

Instead, he concentrated on the scenery as Riane drove toward Charlotte's Corridor.

"So named," she explained, "because the man who discovered the underground caverns, David Charlotte, couldn't believe that such an elaborate system of interconnecting tunnels was a naturally occurring phenomenon. He believed they had to be a corridor to some kind of underground civilization."

Riane pulled into a gravel parking lot. "He passed away before anyone could disprove his theory, and the caves have been known as Charlotte's Corridor ever since."

There were several other vehicles already in the lot, a few people wandering around. There were picnic tables in a shaded area at the far end of the parking lot along with a simple square building that advertised tourist information and public rest rooms. What he didn't see was a ticket booth or concession stand or any other inherent signs of what a city dweller would consider civilization. His sense of apprehension magnified.

"These caves have almost twenty-five miles of mapped passages," Riane told him, pulling a canvas backpack out of the trunk. "It's one of the more elaborate systems in this part of West Virginia."

He had no idea whether he should be impressed or not. He couldn't imagine that they'd be expected to walk twenty-five miles—that would take days.

Riane took a long-handled flashlight out of the bag, flicked the switch, then tucked a spare package of batteries into the back pocket of her jeans.

"Where's the rest of the group?" he asked, following her to the mouth of the cave.

She glanced at him over her shoulder, frowned. "What group?"

Uh-oh. "Isn't this a tour?"

She shook her head. "I thought you wanted to experience West Virginia like a native."

He wasn't entirely comfortable with the note of challenge in her voice. Less so facing the huge, black hole in the wall of rock in front of him. "I've reconsidered," he muttered.

She laughed, and his irrational fear receded. He would walk naked through all twenty-five miles of cave to hear that sound again. She had such an incredible laugh. Low and smoky, unconsciously seductive.

"Don't be such a wimp, Logan. The only way to see the caves properly is to explore them on your own."

Joel plunged into the mouth of the cave behind her. There was no way he was going to let her call him a wimp.

Still, he was unprepared for the sudden and complete darkness. It descended thick and fast, obliterating everything else. Riane had a flashlight but he didn't, and the fragile beam from her light dispersed quickly in the large passageway. He could see nothing but dark, feel nothing but damp, and his breath started to come in short, shallow bursts as the horror of that day in the warehouse ambushed him again.

Focus, Logan. He closed his eyes, inhaled a deep breath. The air was cool and moist, but not foul. He opened his eyes again, took a tentative step forward.

"I think I'd like to try a museum tomorrow," he said.

Riane laughed again. He let the sound envelop him, blocking out the awful memories. There was no one here but Riane and him. The reminder was not only reassuring, it was inspiring. He was alone in the dark with a beautiful woman. Maybe this outing had some potential after all.

It only took a couple of twists and turns for him to realize that Riane was a veteran of caving. She moved easily through the winding chambers while he stumbled along, trying not to think about the fact that he had absolutely no idea of where he was going—or where the men with the guns were hiding.

"Maybe we should have taken one of the guided tours," Joel commented from somewhere behind her, cursing under his breath as he tripped over yet another unseen obstacle protruding from the ground.

She reached behind her to take his hand, and he happily linked his fingers through hers.

Riane continued to move ahead, unhampered by the close confines, navigating the narrow corridors and tight corners without difficulty. Of course, *she* was the one with the flashlight.

He had no idea how long they'd been inside the maze of tunnels when she stopped abruptly. Joel bumped into the back of her, mumbling a quick apology as he stepped back again.

"What's the matter?" he asked.

"Dead end," she said, turning to face him.

"We're lost?" He hated the note of panic in his voice, hoped she didn't recognize it as such.

"No, we're not lost," she chided. "We just have to follow this corridor back the way we came and turn around. All the tunnels are interconnected, like a maze. They twist and turn in all directions. A few are dead ends, but eventually they all lead back to the amphitheater."

"Amphitheater?"

"The big chamber that we started out from."

"Oh." It seemed simple, and she sounded confident enough that his uneasiness abated.

Then she moved forward, as if to step past him, and the side of her breast brushed against his arm. The current of awareness jolted him, and he heard her sharp intake of breath. Obviously, he hadn't been the only one affected.

"We have to follow this, um, corridor back," she said again.

"I heard you the first time. I was just thinking that, since we're not lost, there's really no hurry."

"Yeah." She cleared her throat. "There is."

"Why?"

"It's getting hot in here."

"Yeah," he agreed. "It is." He reached out, his hand

coming into contact with her bare arm. Her skin was soft, but he could feel the tension in her muscles. He trailed his fingers down her arm, felt the goose bumps rise on her flesh. He caught her hand, slid his palm against hers, linked their fingers together.

He knew she had the flashlight in her other hand, but the beam of light was directed at the ground, unseen, forgotten. The darkness didn't seem so ominous now, and in the pitch-blackness of the cave, his other senses were heightened.

He could smell the scent of her perfume. Light and spicy. He could feel the heat from her body and the tension in it. He heard her exhale, slowly, deliberately. And he could hear the beating of her heart, loud and fast. Or maybe it was his own.

"We agreed we weren't going to do this," she said, her voice slightly breathless, unsteady.

"Yeah," he confirmed, before his mouth touched hers. Softly. Gently. A fleeting caress.

He felt her stiffen, but she didn't pull away.

He brushed his lips against hers again, lingered this time. A low hum sounded deep in her throat, then her lips softened beneath his and she was kissing him back.

Her response was hesitant at first, almost uncertain. He wanted to take it slow, to savor the moment. But when her lips parted willingly beneath the pressure of his, the tenuous thread of his control snapped. His tongue dipped into her mouth, tasting, testing. She met his searching thrusts with her own, and he was lost.

He groaned, helpless to do anything but surrender to the desire. The depth of her passion stunned him. This was a woman who would hold nothing back, who would demand as much as she gave. And right here, right now, he could refuse her nothing.

It was a terrifying realization for a man who not only prided himself on his independence but guarded it fiercely. He had no time for distractions, no interest in complications. Riane Quinlan was both.

She was also soft and warm and she tasted like heaven.

He had decided there was no harm in savoring the kiss a little longer when he was blinded by a sudden flash of light. Riane pulled away abruptly as a voice came through the darkness.

"Sorry, man. We didn't know this one was taken."

The young, masculine voice was followed immediately by a younger, girlish giggle.

The beam of light that had flashed in his face dropped to the ground, illuminating a couple of cigarette butts, a crushed pop can, a discarded condom package.

Then the light was gone, the voices of the lustful teenagers drifted down the corridor, and he and Riane were alone again.

Or rather he was alone.

He'd felt her push past him, but he hadn't realized she'd moved away until he reached for her and she wasn't there.

"Riane?"

There was no response.

Joel felt a first bead of sweat trickle between his shoulder blades. He closed his eyes and took a deep breath, tried to remain calm despite the fact that he couldn't see four inches in front of his face.

"Riane?" he said again.

Chapter 5

Riane leaned back against the hard rock of the cavern wall, taking slow, deep breaths and willing her knees to stop trembling. Her entire body felt flushed, hot, despite the cool air inside the cave.

She started when she heard Joel calling to her, but she couldn't respond. Not yet. She needed a minute to regain her composure. She was still too shaky to face him.

It had been a mistake to bring him here. She knew that now. She should have taken him to the art gallery or the museum of technology or a minor league baseball game. Somewhere bright and noisy and filled with other people. Somewhere he wouldn't have been able to get close enough to kiss her.

But no, she'd had to bring him to Charlotte's Corridor—dark and quiet and isolated. What had she been thinking?

Obviously, she hadn't been. She'd been annoyed by some of the statements he'd made the previous afternoon at the camp—assumptions he'd made about who she was and what she did. He would have expected an art gallery or a museum, and she'd been determined to shatter his expectations.

Now, after the way she'd responded to his kiss, he probably thought she'd led him into that dead-end tunnel on purpose. And maybe subconsciously she had. Ever since that first night, when he'd held her on the dance floor, Riane had been fighting against the attraction growing inside her.

She leaned her head back against the rock and closed her eyes, fighting against the urge to scream out her frustrations. She could just imagine the headlines in tomorrow's paper if she gave in to the impulse: Senator's Daughter Has Episode in Charlotte's Corridor. People would think she was as crazy as David Charlotte himself.

She heard Joel call to her again, a hint of fear evident in his tone. She shouldn't have left him alone, or she should have left him the light. Her decision to bring one flashlight had been deliberate and, yes, petty. But she'd needed to assert herself as the one in control of the situation, because every time she was near Joel Logan she felt completely out of control. Today had been no different despite the instrument in her hand.

She directed the light at the cavern floor and pushed away from the wall. The meager beam helped her navigate her way through the maze of tunnels, but it gave no answers on how she was supposed to deal with Joel.

"I'm here," she called out, hating that her voice didn't sound entirely steady.

"I thought you'd left me."

She stepped closer to the direction from which his voice was emanating. "Sorry. I forgot I had the light."

She wished she had a second flashlight to give him, but because she didn't, she was forced to reach out and take his hand again. His fingers, warm and strong, wrapped around hers. It should have been no more personal than holding the hand of a child, but there was something incredibly sensual about the way his much larger hand engulfed hers, something undeniably seductive about the touch of his palm against hers.

She cleared her throat. "Follow me."

"I'm as anxious to get out of here as you are, sweetheart," Joel said. "But I think we should talk about what happened."

"Not necessary," Riane told him, tugging on his hand.

But he was bigger and stronger and he wouldn't be budged. "Do you want me to apologize for kissing you?"

His voice had dropped to little more than a whisper, the husky cadence doing strange things to her insides. "No," she said simply, hoping he would let the matter drop.

He didn't.

"Good. Because I'm not going to." He traced circles over the inside of her wrist with the pad of his thumb, and she knew he would feel her pulse jolt in response to the lazy caress. "I've been thinking about kissing you for a long time. Probably since that very first night, the first time I held you in my arms."

She'd thought about it, too. Far more than she should have. She'd wondered how it would feel, the pressure of his mouth on hers, the touch of his hands on her. Now she knew, and the reality had far exceeded any of her fantasies.

But she couldn't admit that to him. So she just shrugged, as if the earth-shattering kiss hadn't affected her at all. "It wasn't a big deal."

She repeated those words again and again to herself as she led the way out of the caves. Maybe if she said them often enough, she might actually believe them. Because despite her verbal dismissal, Riane was afraid that it had been a very big deal.

They left the caves and headed to Memorial Park for lunch. Joel made no further mention of the kiss they'd shared, for which Riane was grateful. She was confused enough without trying to put her feelings into words. The only thing she knew for certain was that no one had ever made her feel the way he did.

Not that she had any visions of a future with Joel. They lived in completely different worlds; they had different wants and expectations. Besides, Joel was only going to be in town for a short while. As soon as he finished whatever business he'd come here to do, he'd be gone. And her life would go back to normal again.

The thought wasn't nearly as reassuring as it should have been. Nor was the realization that she knew very little about his business in West Virginia. He'd told her only that he was looking for a witness, and she hadn't even given that fact as much consideration as she should have done. She'd been distracted by his presence and her growing attraction to him. But after he'd gone last night, she'd wondered. And worried. Was it merely a coincidence that he'd hoped to meet with his witness at her charity ball? Or was his witness someone she knew?

The possibility had kept her awake long into the night, and it niggled at her subconscious again. He'd promised that his investigation had nothing to do with her camp, and she believed him. But how was he supposed to track down his witness when he was spending so much time with her?

It was a question she should ask him, but she wasn't entirely sure she wanted the answer. She didn't want to know that Joel's interest in her was motivated by something other than the attraction between them.

She bit back a sigh as she unfolded the thick Mexican blanket. Joel took it from her hands, his fingers brushing hers—deliberately?—in the transfer. Deliberate or not, the casual contact sent that heated awareness zinging through her body again. This time she wasn't quite able to bite back the sigh, and it carried more than a hint of frustration.

Joel sent her a quizzical look, then busied himself spreading the blanket on the grass beneath the widespread branches of an old red maple tree. Riane set the picnic basket on the woven fabric and began unloading the array of food Sophie had packed.

"Why did you become a cop?" Riane asked, determined to channel their conversation toward impersonal matters.

Joel was, understandably, startled by the question. He bit into a fresh buttermilk biscuit and swallowed before responding. "Maxwell Archer."

"Who?"

"He was a cop with the Philadelphia PD."

"How did you meet him?" Riane asked, toying with the potato salad on her plate.

"He arrested me." Joel grinned at the memory and helped himself to a piece of fried chicken. "Caught me with a pocketful of stuff outside a convenience store, took me down to the station. We went through the motions—mug shots, fingerprints, et cetera. The routine wasn't new to either of us.

"At the end of the whole process, he sat me down and talked to me. He didn't lecture, he didn't preach. He looked me in the eye and talked to me. It was weird," he said, shaking his head a little at the memory. "It was the first time in my life I could remember someone talking *to* me instead of at me, and listening to what I had to say.

"Not that I had much to say," he admitted. "I was too tough, too cool, to make any excuses for my behavior. Especially to a cop."

He shook his head. "And then he did something I'll never understand."

"What was that?" Riane uncapped the thermos and poured lemonade into two plastic cups. She passed one to Joel, took a sip of her own.

"He took me home with him. I was a juvenile delinquent on the fast track to a life of crime, and he opened up his home to me like some kind of invited guest. Hell, I could have cleaned the place out while he was sleeping."

"But you didn't."

Joel shook his head again. "No. And I guess he knew I wouldn't. In any event, I only wanted someplace to spend the night. Just until I figured out where I was going the next day."

"How long did you stay?"

He grinned. "Four years."

"And that's why you became a cop."

"He was a great cop. It was never just a job to him. He believed in truth. He fought for justice. He made me believe."

Riane smiled. The way he'd talked about Max, with genuine admiration and reluctant affection, made her realize how important this man had been to him. He'd become, whether Joel realized it or not, the father he'd never known.

"Max was there when I got my badge. It was the happiest day of my life."

Riane smiled. "He must have been very proud of you."

"He was," Joel agreed. He picked up his cup, drank deeply.

She saw the cloud come over his eyes, knew the joyful memory had been supplanted by one less pleasant. She waited silently for him to continue, not willing to pry into his painful memories but wanting him to share the rest of the story with her.

"He was there the day they took away my badge, too," he said at last.

"What happened?"

"I was working undercover in a drug importation and distribution center, compiling the evidence we needed to shut it down. I had the names of suppliers and local dealers, shipment dates. Everything was carefully logged and checked and double-checked. I was careful."

He shook his head. "Not careful enough. We thought we'd zeroed in on all the key players, but we'd missed one. We'd never considered that the game couldn't have gone on as long as it had without somebody on the inside."

"A cop?" The words were blurted out before she could stop them.

"There was a cop," he agreed. "But she'd been under suspicion for a while. My investigation confirmed her involvement. It was the judge we didn't know about.

"I still don't know what they had over him," Joel mused. "He was independently wealthy, from a prominent family in the community. But for some reason, he was in their pocket."

"What happened?" she prompted.

"We went to him for a warrant, after a big heroin shipment had come in from Colombia. I knew exactly what was there; I'd helped unload it. But the judge wasn't convinced of the veracity of the affidavits I'd sworn. He asked to see me personally, to verify the information.

"Of course, he'd already notified Zane Conroy. Conroy was—is—the head honcho of the syndicate. And although the judge eventually signed the warrants, by the time they were executed, everything was gone. Every single shred of evidence was gone. We didn't find so much as an empty baggie."

Riane flinched at the barely suppressed anger in his tone.

"And that wasn't the worst of it," Joel told her. "Somehow the media got wind of the investigation, the screwups, and focused on my role in it. Undercover Cop Turncoat the headlines claimed. It was all crap, of course, but it created enough of a ruckus that I was suspended pending investigation into the matter."

"Is that when you quit?"

"No. I waited until the investigation was complete, until internal affairs had concluded that I'd been a victim as much as anyone, and then I quit.

"Through all of it, Max stood by me. He never believed any of the accusations made against me. He was the only one. His confidence meant a lot to me, and I needed to prove that it wasn't misplaced." He dropped his gaze, set aside his empty plate. "Max died a few weeks before the investigation was complete."

"I'm sorry," Riane said gently.

Joel just shrugged.

"What happened to the judge who compromised your case?"

His eyes darkened, his mouth thinned. "Nothing."

"He's still on the bench?"

"No. He retired shortly after the investigation fell apart."

"And that one case destroyed your confidence in the system," she guessed.

"It made me realize that there isn't one system," he told her. "We pretend there is. We promote the ideal of 'justice for all.' But the truth is that the laws are applied and interpreted differently for different members of society."

Riane frowned, but didn't dispute his statement.

Joel finished his glass of lemonade in one long swallow. "Now it's your turn," he said.

"My turn for what?"

"To share the events that decided you upon your course in life."

"I'm not sure I know what that course is," Riane admitted. "I'm supposed to start work at my father's law firm in September, but I can't seem to envision myself drafting partnership agreements and corporate memos for the rest of my life."

"What do you want to do?" he prompted.

She sighed and began packaging up the leftovers. "I want to concentrate on the camp. Increasing our funding, expanding our capacity, improving our programs."

"Then why are you considering anything else?"

"I don't know. Maybe I feel I owe it to my parents to use the education they gave me. Which is ironic, when I think about it, because they've never pressured me to do anything I didn't want to do."

"No suggestion to follow your mother's footsteps into politics?"

Riane shook her head.

"I imagine you'd be well suited for the role, though," Joel said. "After all, you grew up in the public eye."

"Mostly I grew up in unknown countries. I was thirteen when my parents left the Foreign Service to come back to the States. That's when my dad opened his law practice and my mother ran for office. It was hard at first," she admitted.

"I was used to being with her almost all the time, and suddenly there were all these other demands on her. But it got easier as I got older, when I started to understand the importance of what she does."

"What about your father? Does he ever feel like he's in her shadow?"

Riane was genuinely surprised by the question. "Of course not. He's always been supportive of her career."

"It sounds like they have a good relationship."

"The best," Riane agreed. "She wouldn't be half as successful as she is without his support."

"Is that what you're looking for with Stuart—a husband who will support your career ambitions?"

"It's a valid consideration," she said, hating that she sounded so defensive. She snapped the lid back on a salad container, set it inside the basket. She reached for the plate of cookies, but Joel's hand on hers halted the motion, forced her attention back to the intensity of his deep blue gaze.

"What about passion?" The heat in his eyes, the low timbre of his voice, were enough to heat her blood without any discussion of passion.

She tugged her hand away, covered the plate of cookies. "What about it?"

"Was it a consideration?"

"I don't see how that's any business of yours."

His lips curved in a slow smile. "I've seen you together," he reminded her. "You generate about as much heat between you as a subzero freezer."

"It's difficult to be demonstrative when your every move might be recorded by the media," she responded coolly.

Joel seemed to consider her statement for a moment, then he shook his head. "I might buy that explanation...except that I've kissed you."

Damn it, she did *not* want to be reminded of that kiss. "What is *that* supposed to mean?"

His eyes glinted with challenge. "You're a passionate

woman, Riane. You need a man who can elicit your passion, share your desire."

Until she'd met Joel, she'd always believed herself to be rather dispassionate. Even with Cameron, she'd wanted to want him more than she really did want him. Frowning at the memory, she put the plate of cookies in the basket, picked up the bowl of strawberries. Joel deftly plucked a ripe berry from the top, popped it in his mouth.

"Mmm. These are fabulous," he said.

Riane tried to focus her attention on gathering up the remnants of their lunch, but the unadulterated pleasure in his voice stirred something inside her. Passion? she wondered, feeling a little bewildered and a lot intimidated by the depth of her reactions to this man.

"I used to want to fall in love," she told him, surprising herself with the admission. "I wanted to know the deep, abiding, forever kind of love my parents share."

"Why are you using the past tense? You can't have given up already."

She shrugged. "Love isn't always what it's cracked up to be."

"That's a rather cynical statement for a woman of twenty-five years."

"Twenty-four," she corrected stiffly.

Joel grinned, and Riane's pulse leaped.

"Respect and affection are more important, more enduring, than some elusive emotion glorified through Saint Valentine." She had respect and affection with Stuart, and if their relationship lacked the passion she'd sampled with Joel—well, there were more important things than passion.

"I can't disagree with you," Joel said. He reached for another berry, but this time, instead of biting into the juicy fruit himself, he offered it to her.

Riane shook her head.

He skimmed the deep red berry over the curve of her bottom lip. It was cool and fragrant and she had to clamp her lips together to prevent herself from accepting his offering.

She refused to be drawn into whatever seductive game he was playing.

"But don't you think it's possible to have it all?" he asked, the warmth of his breath caressing her cheek. "Respect, affection and passion?"

She averted her gaze, unable to respond. Unwilling to say anything that might betray the longing in her heart.

"Does your passion scare you, Riane?"

She cleared her throat. "I'm not…"

Whatever words she'd intended to utter in protest strangled in her throat when his lips touched the pulse beating erratically at the base of her jaw. It was a feather-soft caress, not even a kiss, but the brief contact jolted her heart as effectively as a fully charged defibrillator.

"You're not what?" he prompted, his breath warm on her cheek. "Were you going to deny your passion—or your fear?"

She swallowed, struggled to find the words she'd lost, but he nipped at her earlobe. She couldn't deny that she was afraid. In fact, she was terrified. Not of Joel, but of the feelings he evoked. Feelings she didn't know how to respond to, didn't dare even acknowledge. It was the acknowledgment of this fear, however, that mobilized her. She pulled away abruptly, away from the tempting lure of his lips, away from her own desires.

"You need an outlet for all the passion churning inside you," Joel said. "And Stuart isn't it."

"And I suppose you are?" she asked coolly.

"We connect on a very basic level, sweetheart. You can't deny that."

"Maybe not," she admitted. "But I'm not going to throw away my future for a few nights in your bed."

"It would be a mistake to marry Stuart."

"Why do you care?" she demanded.

"Because I care about you."

"I'm not naive enough to believe I'm anything more than a diversion for you while you're in West Virginia."

He was silent for a long minute, then he said, "That might have been true at first. It isn't true anymore. I do care about you, Riane."

His words, as much as the emotion evident in his tone when he spoke them, unnerved her. She'd deflected a lot of masculine overtures in the past several years, although substantially fewer since her involvement with Stuart had become public knowledge. But one thing she'd learned in averting such advances was that it was easier to do when there weren't emotions involved. And in that moment she knew that her emotions were already involved. To what extent she wasn't certain, but she wasn't about to risk having her heart broken.

"I'm not going to sleep with you, Joel."

That slow, sexy smile spread over his face again, and her heart practically melted into a puddle at his feet. "If I had you in my bed, I wouldn't waste a single minute of the time sleeping," he promised her.

"Well then…" She felt her cheeks flush as her mind immediately conjured all-too-vivid images of what they might be doing rather than sleeping. And the warmth in her face quickly spread to other parts of her body. "You should know that I have no intention of ending up in your bed, either."

"It's going to happen, Riane."

The unwavering confidence in his voice annoyed her. Taunted her. Terrified her.

"That kiss we shared was—"

"It was a mistake," she interjected quickly. Frantically.

"Maybe it was," he agreed. "It was also like dropping a match in a pool of gasoline—fiery, explosive, irreversible."

"My mother always warned me not to play with matches," she said lightly as she resumed packing up the rest of their dishes.

"Do you think she'd warn you about me?"

She managed a smile. "Aren't you the kind of guy *all* mothers warn their daughters about?"

Joel grinned. "Do you always listen to your mother?"

"Always."

"And yet, you were just as much a part of that kiss as I was."

"It won't happen again," she assured him.

He linked his fingers with hers, tugged her a little closer. "It would be easy enough to prove you wrong," he taunted softly, his mouth hovering mere inches above hers.

Riane was mesmerized by the intensity in his eyes. She blinked, forced herself to look away. "I should be getting home."

He smiled, as if her response was exactly what he'd expected.

"Soon," he agreed. Then he pulled her braid over her shoulder and started to unfasten the elastic at its end.

"What are you doing?"

"I like your hair loose."

"I like it tied back," she countered.

"Too bad," he said, already unwinding the interwoven strands.

There was something strangely intimate about his fingers sifting through her hair, something incredibly erotic about the touch of his fingertips against her scalp. Then he slid his hand to her nape and clutched a handful of hair in his fist, tilting her head back. "Yeah," he said softly. "This is just how I pictured it."

"Wh-what?"

"How you'd look when I kissed you." Then his mouth came down and took possession of hers.

His kiss stole what little breath she had left, silenced her soft sigh of pleasure. Her eyelids fluttered, closed; her hands moved instinctively to his shoulders, held on. His tongue touched her lips, and they parted willingly, eagerly. The heat that he'd stoked with that first kiss continued to build inside her, filling her with a sense of warmth and anticipation she'd never felt before.

Then he stroked her tongue with his, and the fire flamed hotter. She tried to breathe, but his scent filled the air, intoxicating her. His fingers untangled from her hair, traced slowly down her spine to the bottom of her T-shirt. When his hand dipped beneath the fabric and his palm splayed against her bare flesh, her skin felt seared by the touch.

She gasped, shocked by the flood of sensations coursing through her. She leaned into him, needing his strength to keep her upright as the world tilted. She arched as his fingers skimmed over her rib cage, the curve of her breast. She felt her nipple pebble, straining against the lacy fabric of her bra. Tremors coursed through her, hot, pulsing. When his thumb brushed over the aching peak, she gasped with shock, with pleasure.

She made no protest as he laid her back on the blanket, covering the length of her body with his own. She could feel the throbbing of his arousal between her thighs and the answering, aching heat that pooled inside her.

Joel had said she needed a man who could elicit her passion. What he didn't know was that he was the only man who ever had. And whatever resolutions she'd made earlier about not becoming involved with him scattered like so many remnants of last year's dried leaves in the brisk spring breeze.

Then the snap of a branch echoed in the stillness like a gunshot, shattering their idyllic paradise. Riane pushed him away, gasped for breath.

"I seem to have a knack for choosing all the wrong places," Joel commented wryly as he dragged a hand through his own hair.

"Maybe it's a sign."

"Of what?"

"A reminder that we shouldn't be doing this."

"Are you still going to deny that you want this?"

She shook her head. "No. But wanting something and getting it are two separate issues."

He grinned. "I won't put up much of a fight."

"If it was just sex, it would be easy," she said. "But as much as I'd like to, I can't fall into bed with a man I barely know."

"So get to know me."

She laughed softly. "I'm not your type of woman, Logan. I'm looking for more than a night or a week."

"I won't make you any promises I can't keep, sweetheart."

She knew that, and maybe that's why she wanted so desperately just to be with him. Just for now. "We should head back."

Joel sighed, then nodded. "Let's go."

Joel made his way through the lobby of the hotel toward the elevator. *Alone.* He'd considered inviting Riane up to his room, was confident that if he got her there he could have her naked and horizontal in short order. But he hadn't issued the invitation because he hadn't wanted to pressure her.

She wanted him, but she didn't want to want him, and he'd sensed that confusion within her. He wanted her—period. His own doubts about the wisdom of becoming involved with Riane had been supplanted by the fierce desire that swept through him whenever he was near her. But his conscience wouldn't let him take advantage of her uncertainty. It wasn't often difficult to silence his morals, but two factors held him back: Riane's unspecified relationship with Stuart and the fact that Joel really did care about her.

It had been a long time since he'd cared about anyone, and he wasn't entirely comfortable with the feelings he had for Riane. He couldn't have found a woman who was more wrong for him if he tried. And yet, knowing they were so completely ill suited did nothing to tame his libido.

Maybe the promise of forbidden fruit had made him want her more. That was exactly what had happened with Jocelyn. He'd known her father disapproved of their relationship from the outset. He hadn't known that his disapproval was the greatest part of the attraction for Jocelyn.

This bitter reminder should have been more than enough to make him rethink the insane attraction he felt for Riane, but hadn't she already proven she was different from Jocelyn? At the charity ball Riane had even referred to the waiter by name. Jocelyn hadn't seen the servants who hovered around except to scream at them when something wasn't exactly as she'd thought it should be. Then again, just because their methods differed didn't mean their attitudes did. After all, Riane was the daughter of a politician—and even a servant had a vote.

He scrubbed his hand over his jaw. He'd tried to keep things in perspective, to remain objective, but it was already too late for that. He wanted to believe Riane was different; he wanted her to be different. Because he wanted her.

The shrill ring of his cell phone was a welcome intrusion. He didn't want to think about Riane Quinlan anymore. He didn't want to remember how close he'd come to laying her down on the grass and—

"Logan," he barked into the phone.

"You okay?" Mike asked. "You sound like you're having trouble breathing."

"Bad connection," Joel grumbled, in no way prepared to admit to his friend that he'd become aroused by his own prurient fantasies. "You better share whatever you've got before we get cut off."

"I spoke with the director of social services in Tucson," Mike said. "And I'm beginning to think I was wrong to ever doubt your instincts."

The infamous instincts went on high alert. "What did you find out?"

"She remembered the child's name."

"Are you sure?"

"She was adamant. She said she remembered because the name was uncommon. I gave her the approximate time frame we were looking at, and she dug out her old telephone logs. Sure enough, she found a notation about a call regarding Rheanne Elliott."

"Did she follow up?"

"She referred the matter to another worker," Mike said.

"A Camille Michaud. Ms. Michaud, however, denied any involvement with the child."

"Yet another futile lead," Joel surmised, not entirely dissatisfied. Despite his earlier conviction that Riane was the woman he was looking for, he was now willing to be convinced otherwise. He wanted to be free to pursue a relationship with her without the threat of secret agendas or hidden pasts to come between them.

Mike's next words annihilated that possibility.

"I think she was lying."

Joel frowned. "Why would she lie?"

"That's what I was wondering," Mike admitted. "But I found it strange that a woman who never met the child remembered the name after so many years while another, who apparently was sent to investigate the complaint, claimed never to have heard the name."

"Is that what she said?"

"Not in those words," Mike told him. "In fact, she seemed very careful about the information she disclosed. What she said was that the name didn't sound familiar and that if she'd had any contact with the family she would have made a note of it. If there's no file, obviously there was no reason for social services to get involved."

"How does this help us?"

"After I spoke with Ms. Michaud, I did some digging— to see if there was any connection between her and Samuel Rutherford, the attorney who handled the adoption. I didn't find anything. But I did find a connection between Camille Michaud and Ellen Rutherford."

"Now Ellen Rutherford-Quinlan, the Democratic senate representative from West Virginia?" Joel guessed.

"Bingo."

Joel shook his head, impressed by the information his partner had managed to uncover, perplexed by the increasing facets and layers of the case, and disturbed by what this meant for his developing relationship with Riane.

"There's more," Mike told him.

Joel waited.

"According to the baptismal records of St. Jacob's Church, Camille Michaud is Riane Quinlan's godmother."

Chapter 6

He adjusted the knot of the tie at his throat. The silk was smooth beneath his fingers. He brushed his hands over his trousers. The pleats fell in perfect alignment to the tops of his polished loafers. He'd always taken pride in his appearance. It was important to make a good first impression.

It had never been more important than today.

He didn't have a mirror. He wouldn't have believed the reflection in the glass, anyway. He'd lost weight over the past few months, added some lines to his face. But he was still handsome. Still charismatic. And he still knew how to play the game.

He would be earnest, contrite, acquiescent.

Then he would be free.

Free to implement his plan. Free to seek his revenge.

Riane convinced herself that she'd done the right thing by ending her day with Joel early. She needed some time to think and she couldn't do that while he was around. But even now, she was having a difficult time concentrating on anything but the kisses they'd shared that afternoon. Hardly the most appropriate thing to think about as she was getting ready for dinner with the man she planned to marry.

She wished her mother was home. There was nothing she couldn't talk to her about. Ellen Rutherford-Quinlan might be in her second term in the Senate, but first and foremost, she was Riane's mother. No matter how pressing her schedule, she always found time for her daughter.

Riane missed her terribly. She knew that she could contact the ship, but she didn't think her personal crisis was an emergency that warranted interrupting her parents' second honeymoon. They deserved this time away together, and Riane was thrilled that they'd finally decided to take the trip they'd put off for so long. Still, she missed both of them.

When the phone rang, she pounced on it, appreciative of any reprieve from her confused hormones.

"Mom." Grateful desperation gave way to genuine delight as she heard Ellen Rutherford-Quinlan's voice on the other end of the line. "Where are you?"

"We've just docked at Brunei and are getting ready to venture into the city."

There was something in her mother's voice, even over the long-distance connection, that concerned Riane. "What's the matter?"

"What do you mean?"

Riane could almost see the false smile plastered on her mother's face. The smile that never failed to fool political allies and adversaries but had never worked on Riane or Ryan. They knew her too well.

"You're tense, Mom. Is everything all right? Is Daddy okay?"

"We're both fine, honey. I guess I was just missing you. We both miss you."

"You're on a second honeymoon. Neither of you should be thinking about anything but each other," Riane admonished.

Her mother laughed, as Riane had hoped she would. "How is everything with you?"

"Good."

"Have you met any interesting people lately?"

Riane frowned, wondered—briefly—where that question had come from. "What has Sophie been telling you about Joel Logan?"

"Logan?" Ellen sounded genuinely surprised. "I haven't heard anything. Is there something I should know?"

"No," Riane denied quickly. Then she added, "I don't know."

"Oh, baby." Ellen managed a laugh. "It's not like you to sound confused about anything, much less a man."

"I've never met anyone like him," Riane admitted.

"Where did you meet him?"

"At the charity ball last weekend."

"He can't be all bad if he supported your camp," Ellen teased.

Riane smiled. She was so glad her mom had called, but somehow hearing her voice and knowing she was so far away only made her miss her more. "I wish you were here," she said softly.

"We can fly out of Muara if you want."

Riane laughed. "No. You can't cut short your vacation to try and sort out my messed-up life."

"We'd do anything for you, Riane."

"I know, Mom. But you'll be home soon enough."

There was a pause. "Will you do me a favor?"

"Anything," Riane promised.

"Give me a call—day or night—if you're contacted by a Michael Courtland."

"Who?"

"Michael Courtland," Ellen repeated.

"Who is he? And why will he be contacting me?"

"I'm not sure that he will," Ellen answered, ignoring her daughter's first question. "But call me if he does."

Riane frowned, wanting to press for further details, but the chime of the doorbell from downstairs alerted her to Stuart's arrival. "Okay."

"Thanks, honey. I've got to go now. Your father's looking at his watch."

"Give him my love."

"I will. And ours to you."

Riane hung up the phone, her conversation with her mother only adding to her confusion. She couldn't make any sense of her mother's request—or her own feelings about anything right now. She wished, for once, she could just crawl into bed and shut out the world. Instead she put a smile on her face and went downstairs to greet her future husband.

When Stuart drove Riane home after their habitual Saturday meal at LeJardin, he asked if he could come in to talk to her. His request was unexpected, a break in their pattern, and it concerned Riane. Stuart didn't like anything to upset his carefully structured routine.

He turned off the ignition and climbed out of the car, then he came around to open her door. It was an action performed more out of convention than consideration, but she respected the habitual gestures that were such an integral part of their relationship. They gave her a sense of security and stability she'd only started to appreciate after spending time with Joel. She didn't want her world shaken—not when it left her heart pounding and her knees trembling. Not when it made her feel so completely out of control.

So resolved, she pushed the lingering thoughts of Joel from her mind and focused on Stuart. She led him into the den, feeling unaccountably apprehensive about this unexpected turn of events.

"Can I get you a drink?" she offered.

"Please."

She uncapped the decanter and splashed a generous amount of scotch in a glass for him, then poured another drink for herself.

"What did you want to talk about?" Riane asked.

"A couple of things." Stuart set his glass down and reached for the Louis Vuitton briefcase on the floor by his feet. She was so accustomed to seeing Stuart with it in hand that it hadn't struck her as odd when he'd brought it into the house with him.

He set the case on the table and flipped open the locks, then withdrew his date book. "I have a meeting with the arts committee next Saturday afternoon, but my morning is open. If your schedule is clear, I thought we could go to the jewelers."

"Jewelers?" she echoed blankly.

"To get your engagement ring."

"Engagement ring," she echoed again, wondering where was the burst of joy, the rising anticipation she'd always thought she'd feel at this moment.

"Is your schedule clear?" he asked, his voice tinged with impatience.

"Um…yes…I think so," Riane admitted. "But, Stuart, you haven't actually asked me to marry you."

"I didn't think I needed to get down on one knee," he said, making the idea sound ridiculous.

Riane washed down the lump of disappointment with a mouthful of scotch. Maybe she was old-fashioned, maybe she had high expectations, but she'd heard the story of her parents' engagement a hundred times—a tale of candlelight and wine and soft music, culminating with her father on bended knee offering more than a ring—offering his heart and his love and his devotion. Was it so unreasonable to want more than an appointment to pick out a piece of jewelry?

"You don't have to do anything," she said softly. "I just…never mind."

Stuart gave her a strange look, then penciled "jeweler" into his agenda for the following weekend. He snapped the book shut, smiled. "Good. That's settled then."

Riane forced her lips to curve, wondering why she suddenly felt so *un*settled.

"The other matter I wanted to discuss," Stuart said, forging ahead with absolutely no clue as to his "fiancée's" feelings, "is your inappropriate association with this Mr. Logan."

Inappropriate association? It was all Riane could do not to roll her eyes.

"There is nothing inappropriate about my association with Joel Logan." Okay, maybe those kisses hadn't been entirely appropriate, but she wasn't going to think about those now. She wasn't going to think about those ever again.

Stuart looked decidedly annoyed by her contradiction. "I know you've been spending time with him."

"How?"

He smiled thinly. "It's a small town, Riane. Surely you didn't think I wouldn't find out."

"I wasn't hiding anything," she said, feeling guilty nonetheless. "He's in town for a short while and wanted someone to show him around."

"Why is he in town?"

She sipped at her scotch again, uncomfortable with his scrutiny. "I don't know."

"Riane," he chided gently, shaking his head. "What do you know about the man?"

"I know he's a private investigator," she said, uncertain why she felt compelled to justify her association with Joel.

"Who used to be a cop," Stuart said.

Riane frowned. "How do you know that?"

"I did a background check on him."

"What? Why?"

"Because I thought it was important for at least one of us to know something about the man you've…befriended. And because he seemed a little too focused on you the night of the charity ball."

"Is it so hard to imagine that another man might be interested in me?"

"Of course not," Stuart denied.

"But you immediately assumed he had ulterior motives."

"He does."

Riane set her glass carefully down on the desktop, hating that his statement came so close to her own suppositions about Joel that first night and determined not to exhibit any of the frustration churning inside her.

"I've dealt with this my whole life," she said softly. "People either seek out my company or turn away from it depending on their ambitions and their politics, and we both know that you're not any different."

"I care about you, Riane."

She sighed, because she knew he did. Still, she didn't understand why he was making an issue of her spending time with Joel. She wanted to believe his reaction was emotional—that he was concerned he might lose her affection to the other man. Unfortunately, she knew his actions were fueled by an interest in self-preservation. Investigators and reporters were often useful tools in furthering political aspirations; they could also be dangerous enemies.

"Don't you want to know what my investigation revealed?"

"No. You had no reason to dig into his life."

Stuart smiled thinly. "His life is digging into other people's," he reminded her. "And if you weren't so blinded by your attraction to him, you'd agree that my actions were completely reasonable."

She decided it was best not to respond to that comment, because she couldn't deny that she was attracted to Joel, not after the way she'd responded to his kiss. Not after the way her body had heated and quivered in response to his touch. Just the memory of that stolen interlude brought a warm flush to her cheeks and made her wish, even if just for a minute, that she could know what it was like to make love with Joel Logan.

No other man, Stuart included, had ever made her feel the way she'd felt when she was in Joel's arms. No other man had inspired the kind of erotic fantasies she'd succumbed to since she'd met him. Would his lovemaking be as awesome and passionate as his kiss had been? Would the aching emptiness inside her be filled by the physical union of their bodies? Would the overwhelming desire she could scarcely even comprehend be satisfied by this man?

Stuart was right. It was entirely possible that her attraction to Joel Logan was clouding her judgment.

"Have you slept with him?" Stuart asked.

"No!" Riane was indignant. She couldn't believe he would even ask such a question. Whatever erotic fantasies she might have were just that—fantasies. She would never become physically intimate with one man while involved with another.

"Why not?"

"Why not?" she echoed, stunned.

He shrugged. "If you're attracted to him, why not just sleep with him and get it over with?"

Disbelief turned to shock. "You *want* me to sleep with this man?"

"I'm merely suggesting that sex with him might help purge the attraction from your system. As long as you're discreet about it, of course."

Riane folded her arms across her chest as she stared at the man she'd been involved with for the past three years. "I can't believe we're having this conversation."

"I'm only being practical, Riane. I don't expect you to take a vow of chastity when we're not sleeping together."

"Obviously, *you* haven't," she said, feeling unaccountably bitter.

Stuart sighed. "Why are you making an issue out of this?"

"Because it should be an issue. Damn it, Stuart, not five minutes ago we were talking about getting engaged. I thought that meant, on some basic level, you cared about and respected me."

"I do," he said solemnly.

"But you're sleeping with other women."

"I'm hardly being promiscuous."

"One other woman is too many," Riane said.

He sighed again. "I want to marry *you*."

She shook her head sadly as all her hopes and dreams for the future tumbled like a house of cards around her. "I want to be with someone who wants to be with me. Not because I fit his image of the woman he wants as his wife, but because of the person I am."

"Is that why you think Logan is with you?"

"This doesn't have anything to do with Joel."

Stuart slipped a manila folder out of his briefcase and offered it to her.

Riane eyed it suspiciously. "What's that?"

"It's the information my sources uncovered about Logan," he said. "Take a look at this, and then tell me he doesn't have an ulterior motive for wanting to be with you."

She took the folder and tossed it onto the desk. "Why are you so preoccupied with Joel?"

Stuart nodded toward the discarded folder. "Read it," he said again. "After you've checked it out, you'll reevaluate your position."

She tucked the file into the desk drawer without opening the cover. She couldn't deny a certain amount of curiosity, especially since Stuart seemed convinced that the information he'd obtained would alter her feelings for Joel. She wouldn't play those games. If there was something she needed to know, she'd wait for Joel to tell her.

Joel had never before suffered pangs of conscience. Then again, he'd never before made the mistake of mixing business with pleasure. And he was starting to feel uneasy about his deception; starting to acknowledge that his feelings for Riane were growing.

It would be smart, he knew, to call in his partner—to have Mike take over this part of the investigation. But he didn't want to be smart, he wanted to be with Riane. Which meant that he needed to tell her the truth about his trip to West Virginia.

And he couldn't put it off any longer.

When he'd returned to his room after his picnic with Riane, he'd found a complimentary copy of the local weekly paper, the *Mapleview Mirror,* on the table in his room. It had given a fair amount of coverage to last weekend's charity ball, including several photos. Joel cringed when he saw the picture of him and Riane, although the caption beneath the photo referred to him only as an "unknown guest."

Still, the picture was clear and it reminded him that spending time with Riane was detrimental to his anonymity. He didn't want to live in a media circus again, but he also didn't want Riane finding out about his investigation from anyone else.

So it was that he found himself standing back on her doorstep several hours after he'd left her there. He'd passed Stuart's car on its way out, so it was safe to assume that Riane was still up. And alone.

"It's after eleven o'clock," Riane said when she opened the door. "What are you doing here?"

"I wanted to see you."

"Can't it wait until tomorrow? I was on my way to bed."

"Don't let me stop you."

"Funny, Logan."

He grinned. "Can't blame a guy for trying."

"Right now you're trying my patience."

"Give me ten minutes, sweetheart," he cajoled.

She sighed. "Ten minutes," she agreed, stepping away from the door so he could enter. "As long as you promise to leave when your time's up."

"Scout's honor."

She lifted an eyebrow. "You were a Scout?"

"No." He followed her into the den, enjoying the gentle sway of her hips in the clingy yellow dress she was wearing. "But I do keep my promises."

She turned to face him, folding her arms across her chest. She probably didn't realize how the movement thrust her breasts together, providing a delectable view of cleavage above the low V-neckline of her dress. "The clock's ticking," she said.

He'd been rehearsing the words throughout the ride across town. But now he was nervous. He knew she would be angry, she might even hate him, but he couldn't continue to deceive her.

Before he could tell her what had driven him to her door, however, the ring of a cell phone intruded. Hers this time.

Frowning, Riane dug the device out of her purse.

"Is this going to cut into my ten minutes?" Joel asked.

Riane ignored him and connected the call. "Hello?"

He turned away to give her some privacy for her conversation. He moved over to the bookcase, studying the photos aligned on the top shelf. Riane as a child in her school uniform, her lips curved in a mischievous smile, her deep brown eyes sparkling at the camera. Riane in a prom dress, several years later, absolutely stunning in the shimmering gold gown that only hinted at curves she now possessed. Riane graduating from Harvard, proud and happy and breathtaking. Riane and her parents, all formally attired, a beautiful and cohesive family unit.

Or were they?

Uneasiness stirred as he reviewed his conversation with Mike. He had so many questions, too few answers.

"Okay. Wait right there, Adam, I'm on my way."

She disconnected the call, already moving toward the door, as if she'd forgotten Joel was even in the room. Her easy dismissal annoyed him, probably more so because he now knew she'd been summoned away by another man.

He stepped into her path. "Who's Adam?"

"I don't have time for this, Joel. I have to go."

"It's after eleven o'clock," he reminded her. "I'm not letting you run off in the middle of the night with no idea where you're going."

"Then you can come with me," she offered.

Riane was grateful for Joel's company on what she knew could only be an ill-fated mission. She'd been to Adam's neighborhood once before, in the middle of the day, and that had been a scary enough experience. She'd have to be insane to venture there alone in the darkness of night.

She was also grateful for Joel's silence. He said little as they made their way across the city to the impoverished east end, and most of the questions he asked were in the nature of directions. While Joel was driving, Riane made a few phone calls.

"Turn right at the next light."

"Are you going to tell me what's going on?" Joel asked.

"As soon as I know," she told him. "There." She gestured to a run-down apartment building in front of which a crowd of spectators had gathered along with three police cruisers, a paramedics truck and an ambulance.

Joel's car wasn't completely stopped at the curb when Riane unfastened her seat belt and pushed open the door. She plunged into the crowd and up the broken sidewalk that led to the entranceway of the building. She didn't see the faded and chipped brick, the boarded-up windows, the peeling paint on the trim. She was only thinking about Adam.

The exterior door was propped open by a rock, the narrow hallway inside dimly lit and thick with the scents of old garbage and—she felt her stomach lurch—something even less pleasant that she was probably better off not trying to identify.

Her heels clicked loudly on the metal stairs as she made her way up to the third floor. With each step, the air grew thicker, the nauseating scent stronger. She heard Joel's footsteps behind her, but didn't wait.

The door to apartment 3A was open and—she exhaled a shaky sigh of relief—Adam was still there. Staring at her mutinously through the tears in his eyes, but there. Handcuffed, she noted with shocked disbelief, to the leg of a scarred coffee table.

She turned to the uniformed officer seated on the battered sofa, idly thumbing through an outdated fashion magazine. "You cuffed him?"

He glanced up, shrugged unapologetically. "It was the only way I could be sure to hold on to him."

"He's a *child*." Joel's voice came from directly behind her now, and he sounded equally stunned.

"He's slippery and he's fast and he's got a helluva kick," the officer said defensively, rubbing a hand over his shin.

Riane turned her attention to the child. "You kicked him?"

Adam didn't give any indication that he'd even heard her. She knew that he viewed her phone call to the police as a betrayal. He didn't trust anyone in uniform, and although she knew he had valid reasons for this distrust, she thought he at least trusted *her* enough to know that she'd never put him in any danger.

"Ever heard of assaulting an officer?" she tried again.

Adam continued to ignore her.

"You Quinlan?" the cop asked Riane.

She nodded, her attention still focused on Adam, and dug into her purse for identification. She passed him her driver's license.

"The lady from social services is on her way with some papers," he said, returning her ID. "Do you think you can handle him until she gets here?"

Riane nodded again.

The cop bent over to unlock the cuffs. As soon as he was freed, Adam backed away, into the corner of the room, rubbing the red mark around one slender wrist where he'd strained against the metal enclosure. His gaze darted from Riane to Joel and back again.

"You called the cops," the child said accusingly.

Riane knelt down in front of him, mindless of the skirt of her Carolina Herrera dress. "I had to, Adam."

"Why?"

"Because if there was any chance that your mom was still alive—" she'd seen the body bag they'd loaded into the back of the ambulance, so she knew she wasn't "—I had to get someone here fast to help her."

"But you said *you* were coming."

"And I did."

"Who's that?" he demanded, glancing warily at Joel again.

"He's a—" Riane hesitated, not sure how to answer the question "—a friend," she said at last.

"Another cop," Adam said derisively.

Riane had to hold back a smile. She should have guessed that Adam would peg Joel so quickly, probably even more quickly than she herself had done. "He says he's not," she confided.

Adam snorted.

"I'm a private investigator," Joel said, stepping farther into the room.

Adam instinctively moved closer to Riane. "What's he doing here?"

"He's not here to take you away," Riane promised the child.

She could tell he wanted to stay angry with her, but there were too many emotions competing inside him. Too much horror and heartbreak for a six-year-old to handle. He blinked, fighting for control, but the first tear spilled over, tracked its way slowly down his cheek.

Riane held her arms open, and after a brief hesitation Adam launched himself at her, desperate for contact, for comfort. She folded her arms around him, her own eyes filling with moisture as his rail-thin shoulders trembled against her. She lifted him off the ground effortlessly—he didn't weigh half as much as a six-year-old should—and moved to the dirty sofa the cop had abandoned, cradling the child in her lap.

Joel felt his heart lodge somewhere in the vicinity of his throat as he watched Riane settle back into the old sofa with Adam, oblivious to the fact that his tears and snot were staining the front of her designer dress. And in that moment he finally understood how dedicated she was. Not to the ideology of her camp, but to the children who needed it—and her—so desperately. And he realized how truly incredible she was.

He took an instinctive step back, as if to protect himself from the unwanted feelings that stirred to life inside him.

"What's going to happen to me?"

The child's tentative question reminded Joel that there were more immediate problems than his conflicting emotions about Riane.

"Don't worry about that right now," Riane said gently.

"Are they going to take me away again?" He looked at her, eyes wide, terrified.

Again? Joel wondered.

"They won't take you away," she said firmly.

"But now that my mom's—"

"They won't take you away," she said again. "I promise."

And that promise was enough for the child, apparently, because he nodded his head, snuggled against Riane's shoulder, and promptly fell asleep.

"You have no business making promises you can't keep," Joel told her, careful to keep his voice low enough so as not to disturb the sleeping child.

"I don't."

"The cop said social services has already been contacted."

"I know. *I* contacted them."

"There's a procedure they have to follow in these situations," Joel told her. He'd thought, because of her work through the camp, that she'd have some kind of understanding of the system. Apparently not. "The procedure generally involves placement in a group or foster home pending review—"

"I'm aware of the procedure," Riane interrupted. "I also know that Adam's mother has a sister. He'll stay with me until she can be found."

"You're going to take the kid home with you?" He couldn't keep the skepticism from his voice.

''I'm going to take him home,'' Riane confirmed.

Joel just shook his head, certain she was in for a wake-up call when the authorities got there.

He was wrong.

Chapter 7

As Joel watched Riane tuck the child into bed in one of the numerous spare rooms of the Quinlan mansion, he knew he should have expected that she would somehow manage to skirt the rules that applied to the rest of the world. She was, after all, a Rutherford.

Strangely, though, the thought didn't bother him as much as it might have a week earlier. Oh, there was no doubt that Riane had used her political connections to get her own way in this case, but how could he resent that when she'd obviously done so to help this child?

He glanced at his watch as he followed Riane down the stairs. It was nearly 4:00 a.m. "I need to get some sleep."

"I can make up another one of the guest rooms," Riane offered.

Tempted as he was to stay close at hand—to ensure she didn't run off on any other crazy missions—her proximity wreaked havoc on his hormones. He was exhausted, both mentally and physically, and still he wanted nothing more than to take her in his arms and spend hours making slow, sweet love with her. Which, considering the frightened child sleeping upstairs, wasn't likely to happen anytime soon.

So he shook his head in response to her invitation. They'd both be better off if he went back to his hotel, far out of reach of temptation.

Yet he was reluctant to go. "How long have you known Adam?"

"Long enough to know that he's better off here than in an emergency intake shelter."

He didn't blame her for sounding defensive. He'd made it clear that he doubted the wisdom of her actions tonight, but he was curious about her relationship with this child. "I wasn't questioning your motives..."

Her raised eyebrow effectively communicated her disbelief. Joel managed a wry grin.

"I'm just trying to understand your connection to him."

"He's been coming to my camp for the past three years," she told him. "That makes him my responsibility."

"Three years? But he's only six."

Riane nodded. "We usually don't take children younger than five, but we make exceptions when circumstances warrant it."

"What were his circumstances?"

"Adam's social worker contacted me after reading an article about the camp," she explained. "She was desperate for anything to get him out of his home for a few weeks. A lot of children who go there are abused—physically, emotionally, sexually. Adam wasn't abused in any traditional sense, but he was horribly neglected.

"At three years of age he was still confined to a playpen for most of the day. He didn't walk, he could barely speak. He was undernourished, understimulated, barely functioning."

"Why the hell didn't the social worker put him in a foster home?"

"She wanted to. But it's hard to prove neglect, harder still when the parent knows her social assistance will be cut off if she loses the child. Every time the worker visited the home, the mother was there. She might not have been feeding Adam three meals a day, but there was food in the refrigerator. He was clothed, if not always adequately.''

''Why did the mother let him come to the camp?''

''Because it was only supposed to be for two weeks, and it wouldn't affect her assistance. But when the two week period was over, his mother couldn't be found.''

''So he stayed,'' Joel guessed.

Riane nodded. ''For almost two months.''

''Is that when she finally came for him?''

''She didn't come for him. Near the end of Adam's third week there, the police picked her up on Queen Street, already higher than a kite, trying to score more drugs.''

''What happened?''

''We got her into rehab.''

''There's usually an extensive waiting list for beds in the publicly funded facilities,'' Joel commented. ''You were lucky to find one available.''

Riane glanced away. ''I sent her to Newhaven,'' she admitted, naming an exclusive private clinic.

''And you paid for it.''

''I did it for Adam. To give him a chance.''

And Joel would bet he wasn't the first child she'd done something like that for. The realization caused something inside his heart to shift, settle. ''Is Adam the youngest child you've had at the camp?''

Riane shook her head. ''He was the first, but not the youngest. We had two-year-old twin girls last summer.''

''And your heart breaks for every one of them,'' he guessed. ''Not just the little ones, but every single kid who walks through the gates of that camp.''

''Am I that transparent?''

''You're that devoted,'' he said. ''I've never known anyone who gives so much for so little in return.''

She shook her head again. ''I get so much more than I give. Every day I spend with those kids is a gift.''

"Ah. The lonely, only child syndrome."

"Maybe." She shrugged. "I've always wanted a sibling, or a dozen siblings. A sister was my first choice, but I would gladly have settled for a brother."

Her admission, and the undisguised yearning in her voice, tugged at something inside Joel. It might very well be within his power to give her what she'd always wanted, but at what cost? If Riane really was Arden Doherty's sister, that revelation would tear the rest of her family apart.

Would she thank him—or hate him—for the part he would play in bringing that fact to light? He couldn't know. He only knew that he didn't have the energy to tackle any more truths with her tonight.

"I really should be on my way," he said. "So you can get some sleep."

If she thought the change of topic abrupt, she didn't comment on it. She just walked him to the front door. "Thank you for coming with me tonight. I'm glad you were there."

Unable to resist, he cupped her cheek in his hand, rubbed his thumb gently over the fullness of her bottom lip. How was it, he wondered, that this woman who was so obviously unsuited for him could nevertheless have come to mean so much so soon?

"Me, too."

She smiled, a slow curving of the lips that did strange things to his insides.

And before he knew what he was doing, before he could remember any one of the dozen reasons that it was a bad idea to get more involved with her, he lowered his head and touched his mouth to hers.

Her lips were soft and warm, and he sank into the kiss. He tried to keep it simple, to maintain some distance. But then her tongue slipped inside his mouth, searching, tasting, teasing, and he was lost. With a groan Joel slid his hands down her slender torso to her hips, pulling her more fully against him. Soft curves molded to hard angles, joining them together as completely as two pieces of a puzzle.

Oh, man, he was obviously in big trouble if he was starting to think in terms of romantic clichés. He wasn't ready for this, he didn't want this, but he was damned if he could do anything about it. His attraction to Riane was one thing—he could dismiss that as purely instinctive, nothing more than a natural physical reaction. But the sweetness of her kiss, the yielding of her body, were doing strange things to his heart. He didn't want to get emotionally involved. He couldn't.

His mind screamed at him to retreat; his body urged him to advance. Since he feared his body might collapse from sheer exhaustion, and since he knew he couldn't take their relationship to the next level until he'd clarified the reasons for his presence in West Virginia, he opted for retreat.

Slowly, regretfully, he eased his lips from hers.

Riane opened her eyes. Then she ran her tongue over her bottom lip, as if to savor the taste of him there. The unconsciously seductive gesture only aroused him further. He forced himself to take a step back.

"I'll call you tomorrow. Later," he amended.

And he made a hasty retreat.

He didn't call, Riane thought with more than a little annoyance when she walked into the kitchen later that morning. If he'd called, she could have prepared herself. Instead he'd just shown up, and she was helpless to prevent the silly flip-flops her heart was doing in her chest when she found him at the table enjoying a breakfast of pancakes and bacon.

"You said you would call," she said by way of greeting.

Joel's head swiveled toward her, his eyes skimming over her short, silky robe with obvious approval.

"Good morning," he said. "And I did call. Sophie said you were sleeping and invited me to come for breakfast."

"I didn't think you'd mind," Sophie said, flipping more pancakes on the griddle. "Especially considering how helpful Mr. Logan was last night."

Riane took a mug from the cupboard. "I thanked Mr. Logan for his assistance. I'm sure breakfast wasn't necessary."

"Not necessary," Joel agreed. "But appreciated. These are great pancakes, Sophie."

Sophie beamed and refilled his plate, then set another plate at the table for Riane.

"Sit," Sophie directed.

"I'm not hungry," Riane said.

"Eat."

Riane sighed and sat. Sophie continued to watch until Riane picked up the fork.

"Where's Adam?" Joel asked, not bothering to hide his smirk.

"Still sleeping." He'd been restless and whimpering, so Riane had sat beside his bed throughout the night, his hand secure in hers. She didn't mind—she hadn't been able to sleep anyway as the memory of that bone-melting, skin-tingling kiss she'd shared with Joel had kept her body stimulated long past the hour when her brain was more than ready to shut down.

"You should be sleeping, too," Sophie told her.

"I'm okay," Riane said, stifling a yawn.

Sophie's look was one of patent disbelief but she made no further argument. "I'll go see if he's ready for breakfast," she said, dropping a fresh stack of pancakes on the platter before ducking out of the room.

"Actually, I'm glad you're here," Riane said to Joel.

"Why's that?"

"Because I want to hire you."

"Sorry?"

"You are a private investigator, aren't you?"

"Yes," he agreed slowly.

She nodded. "I've been thinking about this all night. As much as I want Adam to stay here, I know his aunt needs to be found."

"Social services will track her down," Joel said.

"I know. Eventually. But you could do it faster."

"I could," he agreed. "Why are you so anxious to find her?"

"Because Adam has a right to know what's going to happen to him. He's had enough upheaval in his life lately, and I don't want him to get settled here only to be torn away again."

"What if the aunt can't take him?"

"Then at least we'll know, and we'll deal with it."

He hesitated. "I'm not sure I should get involved in this."

Riane shrugged. "If you can't do it, I'll find someone else. I just thought, since you were here, with so much time on your hands…"

"Ahh. You're trying to keep me occupied—away from you."

"I'm offering you a legitimate job. Take it or leave it."

And that was how Joel found himself driving through the streets of Woodburn, Pennsylvania, on Monday morning. It had been remarkably easy to find Lois Ryder. A phone call to a friend at the Department of Motor Vehicles and he had her address—1314 Paradise Avenue.

If it wasn't really paradise, it was a hell of a lot closer to it than the run-down apartment complex where Adam had lived with his mother. The neighborhood was postcard pretty, with well-kept houses and neatly manicured lawns littered with bicycles and toys. Number 1314 was a large two-story with blue siding and white gingerbread trim.

Joel parked his vehicle across the street and picked up his digital camera, snapping a few quick shots.

If only his search for Rheanne Elliott had been half as successful.

Rheanne. Riane.

He knew it wasn't just a coincidence. His gut didn't believe in coincidences.

Unfortunately, his gut was a little short on facts.

He tossed the camera back onto the empty passenger seat and pulled away from the curb, unable to shake the feeling that the woman he'd been hired to find was right in front of him.

* * *

After his trip to Woodburn, Joel decided to return to Fairweather to check in with his client, and they agreed to meet for coffee at the courthouse café.

"I'm glad you could meet me on such short notice," Joel said, as Shaun McIver pulled out the empty chair across from him.

"I'm anxious for an update," Shaun told him.

"I don't have much to tell you," Joel warned. "It's almost as if the child ceased to exist when she was taken out of her parents' home."

"Gavin Elliott wasn't any help?" Shaun prompted.

"Not much." In his brief meeting with Rheanne's biological father, Joel had got the impression the man was holding something back, but he didn't share that feeling. "He did lead me to a Samuel J. Rutherford, the attorney who handled the adoption."

"Well, that's something," Shaun said.

"It's a dead end," Joel said dryly. He waited for the waitress who'd refilled their coffee cups to move out of earshot before continuing. "Sam Rutherford passed away three years ago.

"His secretary still works at the firm and she found an old file labeled Elliott-Adoption. But the only documentation in it was a copy of Rheanne Elliott's birth certificate, which we already had from the registrar's office.

"We really don't have anything else," Joel admitted. "By all accounts, Rheanne seemed to drop off the face of the earth before her second birthday. But in August of that year, another child's birth was registered through the American Consulate in Tavaria. Her name is also Riane, spelled *R-I-A-N-E.*"

"But she would be two years younger than the woman we're looking for," Shaun pointed out.

Joel shook his head. "The child's birth wasn't registered until she was two years old."

"You think the people who adopted Arden's sister took her out of the country and registered her as their own child?"

"I think that's a possibility," Joel agreed.

"Do you have any other evidence?"

"It's all circumstantial," Joel warned.

"I'm not worried about it holding up in court," Shaun said dryly. "I just want to find my fiancée's sister."

"Okay." Joel summarized the few facts he and Mike had managed to compile: "The lawyer who handled the adoption of Rheanne Elliott is a distant relative of the other Riane's mother, and the caseworker assigned to investigate the complaint is her godmother."

Shaun considered this information. "Don't you think they would have changed her name, not just the spelling?"

"That bothered me at first," Joel admitted. "But the child was almost two years old. It would have been traumatic enough for her to be removed from her home and sent to a new family in a new country without changing her identity as well."

"Where is this Riane now?" Shaun asked.

"Mapleview, West Virginia."

"You've seen her? Met with her?"

"Yes, on both counts."

"When can I meet her?" Shaun said.

Joel hesitated. "If this woman is Arden's sister, she has no idea she was adopted."

"I hadn't considered that possibility," Shaun admitted.

"There's something else you need to consider."

"What's that?"

"If I'm right—and I still can't be one hundred percent certain—the adoptive mother is Ellen Rutherford-Quinlan."

Shaun frowned. "Rutherford-Quinlan? As in *Senator* Rutherford-Quinlan?"

"Yeah."

"Christ."

Joel just nodded.

"I know it would mean the world to Arden to find her

sister," Shaun said. "But I'm not sure she'd want to turn Rheanne's whole world upside down in the process."

"Arden still doesn't know you're looking for her?"

Shaun shook his head. "I wanted to wait until we knew something definite."

"The senator and her husband have been out of town," Joel told him. "They should be back on Friday."

"Do you think you'll get anything out of her?"

"I can only hope." Without any concrete evidence that the senator and her husband had adopted a child, there was little else he could do.

"If she won't cooperate, what about DNA testing?"

"It's something we could consider," Joel agreed. "As a last resort. There are a few problems with that approach, however."

"Such as?"

"Primarily the fact that Arden and Rheanne are only half sisters. Without a comparative sample from the mother, the results wouldn't be one hundred percent conclusive. Plus, the labs are so backed up with DNA testing for criminal trials and paternity cases, it could be months before we got any results."

"I can't wait months."

"Are we working on a deadline?"

"Not really." Shaun raked a hand through his hair. "I just want this to be over for Arden. She hasn't seen her sister in more than twenty-two years, but I know not a day has gone by in all that time that she hasn't felt the void in her life.

"I see her looking at that picture sometimes—the same picture you have a copy of—and I know she's wondering, worrying. She needs to know. She wants to move on with her life, to put the past behind her, but I don't think she'll ever be able to do that until she knows what happened to her sister."

"Then you want me to follow up on this?"

Shaun nodded, giving him the green light to go back to West Virginia.

Joel wished he could be making the trip for any reason other than to destroy Riane's beliefs about her perfect family.

On Tuesday, Riane received Joel's report on Lois and David Ryder. By courier. She sat at her father's desk in the den and thumbed through the pages, wondering what it meant that Joel had chosen to send the file rather than deliver it himself.

Maybe he'd found the witness he'd come to Mapleview in search of. Maybe he'd finished his business in West Virginia and had gone back to Pennsylvania. Maybe he'd found someone else to show him around—a woman who might be willing to play tour guide in the bedroom.

Riane groaned and shook her head. She'd hired Joel to find Adam's aunt, and he'd done that. Anything else he did or didn't do wasn't any of her business.

So, resolved, she focused her attention on the information in front of her. Lois Ryder, thirty-seven years of age, high school physics teacher. Married twelve years to David Ryder, an electrical engineer and Little League coach. Lois and David were the proud parents of two boys, Matthew and Michael, ages ten and eight. Photos of their home, a four-bedroom in Woodburn, Pennsylvania, were in the file, as was a telephone number.

Tuesday night Riane called Lois Ryder. Wednesday Lois came to pick up her nephew. Her easy and immediate acceptance of the child she'd never known reassured Riane. He was going to a good home, a good family. And he'd been so thrilled to meet his cousins he didn't even look back as they drove away.

It was a positive resolution, and Riane was confident that the security of a new family would help Adam adjust—as much as possible—to the loss of his mother. She was thrilled that he would finally have a future to look forward to.

Why then, she wondered as she watched the van disappear, was she crying?

* * *

Twenty-four hours.

In twenty-four hours Ellen and Ryan Quinlan would be home and he could get answers to the questions that had plagued him for the past several weeks. That was the first thought on Joel's mind when he awoke two days later.

Two excruciatingly long days in which he'd focused his attention on one goal: staying away from Riane. The realization that his feelings had grown so quickly out of control scared the hell out of him, and he knew his only hope was to keep his distance and forget about Riane in any context except how she might be the answer to his investigation.

He grabbed his keys and headed for the door. He needed to get out of this room, to stop thinking about Riane. He told himself he was going out for a bite to eat. Yet somehow he found himself pulling into the long winding drive that led to the Quinlan mansion.

"I thought you'd skipped town," Riane said, when she came downstairs and found him waiting in the den.

He managed a smile, wondering if he'd ever get used to her stunning beauty, wondering if he'd ever see her again after he finished the job he'd come here to do. "I wouldn't go without saying goodbye."

"Is that why you're here?"

"No. I was just thinking about you and somehow this is where I ended up." He glanced around the room. "Is Adam gone?"

She nodded, blinked away a hint of moisture in her eyes. "Yesterday."

He knew there was nothing he could say to make her feel better, so he just put his arms around her. After a brief hesitation, she leaned into him, accepting his comfort.

"Have dinner with me tonight," he said, his earlier resolution to avoid spending time with her pushed aside by a more basic need just to be with her.

Time was running out. He knew the end of the charade was inevitable, but he wasn't yet ready to let her go. He didn't know if he ever would be. There could be no future for them—the senator's daughter and the reclusive P.I. But the logic of the mind couldn't suppress the yearnings of his heart.

"I can't." Riane pulled out of his arms with obvious reluctance. "There's a charity auction at the country club that I promised to attend."

"With Stuart?" he guessed, feeling oddly annoyed.

She nodded.

"Tomorrow, then?" He was begging for scraps of her time, and he didn't care.

But she shook her head. "My parents are coming home tomorrow."

Somehow, the return of the senator and her husband lost all significance when he was with their daughter.

"Maybe I'll stop by to meet them." He was only half teasing. After all, making contact with the senator was his reason for coming to West Virginia in the first place.

"You could," Riane said. "I'm sure they'd like that."

Her confidence only made him feel more guilty. "They wouldn't worry that I was trying to corrupt their daughter?"

"They trust my judgment," she told him.

"Only because they haven't met me."

Riane smiled. "You think your tough-guy persona will intimidate them? We've known people—some were friends, some not so friendly—who make you look like the Boy Scout you never were."

"Did they even have Boy Scouts in Tavaria?" he asked.

As soon as the words were out of his mouth, he recognized his mistake. He'd been drawn into the easy banter, had forgotten to be cautious, but the silence that greeted his question let him know how thoroughly he'd blown it. Just as he knew he'd never have made such a stupid mistake if he hadn't let himself become personally involved with the subject of an investigation.

"How did you know I was in Tavaria?" she asked.

He hoped it wasn't too late for damage control. "You must have mentioned it," he said lamely, unable to meet her gaze.

"I didn't."

"Then I must have, uh, read it somewhere."

"You've investigated me," she said, hurt and anger mingled in her tone.

He wanted to deny it, but he couldn't. He felt guilty enough about his deceptions without adding to his list of sins.

"I should have expected this. I'm used to people prying into my past—it's part and parcel of who I am. But I thought you were different. I *wanted* you to be different."

She laughed, but it was without humor. "The most ironic part of all of this is that I would have told you whatever you wanted to know."

He didn't know what to say. He wasn't sure there was anything he could say that wouldn't make the situation worse.

"Why?" she demanded. "Why were you digging into my past? What did you expect to find?"

"You weren't the focus of my investigation," Joel said. That, at least, was the truth. Initially, anyway.

"The fact that I spent the first six years of my life in Tavaria isn't common knowledge. The only way you could have found that out was if you were researching me…" Her voice trailed off as another thought occurred to her. Her eyes widened in shock, disbelief, anguish. "Or my parents."

He should never have left his hotel room.

"Why? What's going on, Joel? What haven't you told me?"

"I can't talk about this. I'm sorry, but I can't."

"You can and you will," she insisted. "I'm not going to let you use me to hurt my family."

"I'm not trying to hurt anyone," Joel told her.

She laughed, bitterly. "It's an election year—I should have expected this."

"Expected what?"

"Someone trying to sabotage my mother's career. What was the plan? Were you supposed to seduce me and get compromising pictures to discredit her stance on family values?"

Joel was stunned, not just by the accusation but by the hostility in her tone. "You can't really believe I'd do something like that."

"What am I supposed to believe?" she challenged. "You pretended to be interested in me, all the while digging into my life without my knowledge or consent."

"I didn't have to pretend to be interested in you," Joel told her.

"Then why have you been with me?"

"Because I *want* to be with you." He turned away, raked his hands through his hair. "Damn it, I knew this was a bad idea."

"What was a bad idea—investigating me, using me, or lying about everything?"

"You were never part of my plan."

"Oh, that's reassuring," she said sarcastically. "So nice to know you just used me because it was convenient."

"I never used you."

"What am I supposed to think? What am I supposed to believe?"

"Just trust me, Riane. Please."

She laughed. "You want me to trust you? You've lied to me since the day we met."

"I've never lied to you."

"A lie of omission is still a lie."

Client privilege be damned, Joel decided. He couldn't let Riane continue to believe the worst. "I came to West Virginia to see your mother."

"Why?"

"Because I thought she might be able to help with a case I'm working on."

"What kind of case?"

"I have a client who's trying to find someone."

Some of Riane's anger seemed to dissipate, her brow furrowed. "A missing person?"

"Not missing, exactly," Joel hedged.

"Then what—exactly?"

"The woman I'm looking for was adopted twenty-two years ago."

"Why do you think my mother can help?"

"The child was adopted privately. The lawyer who handled it was Samuel Rutherford, your mother's second cousin. He died a few years ago, and the file pertaining to the adoption has either disappeared or been destroyed. In any event, I haven't been able to access the relevant information. I can't find the child's biological mother, and the father hasn't exactly been forthcoming with any details."

"What does any of this have to do with my mother?" she asked again, clearly starting to lose patience with him.

He hesitated, reluctant to state the conclusion that would crumble all of Riane's conceptions about her life. But the fierce determination in her eyes forced his hand. She wouldn't let him continue to evade. More compelling than that, however, was the realization he owed her the truth.

"I think you're the woman I'm looking for."

She took an instinctive step back. "I'm not adopted."

"I think you might have been."

"Th-that's ridiculous." Her words were disdainful, but he heard the tremor in her voice, the uncertainty. He saw the questions, the confusion, the panic that swirled in the depths of her eyes.

He stepped toward her, softened his tone, as if it might somehow soften the impact of what he was saying. "Your birth wasn't registered until almost two years after you were born."

"I was born in T-Tavaria," she reminded him. "When the country was on the verge of civil war." She wrapped her arms around herself. "I'm sure my parents had more important things to worry about than registering my birth with the appropriate authorities."

"Or maybe they didn't adopt you until you were two years old."

She shook her head.

"Why won't you even consider the possibility?"

"Because it's ludicrous."

"Just listen to me. Please."

"No. I refuse to waste any more—"

"Your name is the same," he interrupted.

She shook her head. "Is that the basis for your claim? The fact that I have the same name as someone who was adopted more than two decades ago?"

"It's an unusual name," Joel pointed out.

"Unusual, not unique."

"Your birth dates are close—"

"Close?" Riane cut off his explanation. "This is unbelievable. You expect me to accept your asinine theory on the basis of a name and a birth date that isn't even the same?"

"And the fact that the case worker assigned to the missing child was Camille Michaud."

"My—" she swallowed "—my aunt Camille?"

He nodded. He could tell this piece of information surprised her, but she recovered quickly.

"Are you suggesting that Camille just took this baby from its home and gave it to my parents?"

He had to admit it sounded a little far-fetched when she put it in those terms. "I have some questions about her involvement in this situation, and some questions for your parents."

"Maybe Camille knows something about this person you're looking for," she allowed. "But I know my parents aren't involved. They wouldn't lie to me about something like this."

"Are you absolutely certain?" he asked gently.

She stared at him, stunned, hurt, bewildered. And he wished—for the hundredth time—that he'd never accepted this assignment.

"I have pictures," she said at last, seeming to seize that thought with both hands.

"Pictures?"

"Baby pictures."

He frowned. "Baby pictures?"

She crossed to the bookcase and pulled down an old, worn-leather photo album and opened the cover. She pointed to the first page, to the picture of a sleeping infant.

Joel took the book from her. He was hardly an expert on children, but he knew the baby in the picture wasn't more than a few weeks old. Definitely not two years old. He flipped through several pages, his frown deepening as he viewed photographs depicting stages of the baby's growth. First smile, first tooth, first steps.

He'd been so sure his instincts were right this time. He'd been wrong. He closed the cover of the album and met Riane's gaze.

"This might be where you apologize for being a complete ass." Her tone was stiff with anger, her eyes filled with pain.

His heart felt as if it was overflowing with grief and regret. The last thing he'd wanted was to cause her any pain. "I'm sorry, Riane."

"You should be. And maybe this whole incident could have been avoided if you'd been honest about why you wanted to see my mother in the first place."

"Maybe it could have," he admitted.

She snatched the book from his hands, her eyes bright with unshed tears. She turned away and stuffed it back onto the shelf. "I think you should go now."

"Riane, please—"

"No. I want you to leave. *Now.*"

"It was a possibility I couldn't ignore," he told her.

"A possibility," she scoffed. She faced him again, almost defiantly. "If you were as lousy a cop as you are a private investigator, it's no wonder you had to find another job."

Chapter 8

She hated to do it. She hated to admit that it even mattered to her. But after the accusations Joel had made that afternoon, Riane still had too many questions unanswered. So she dug out the file Stuart had given to her—the information *his* investigator had compiled on Joel Logan.

There were newspaper clippings regarding the case he'd told her about—the investigation that had gone bad, ending his career as a cop. Reading through the reports, she could understand why he hadn't wanted to go back to working for the system that had turned on him.

She also got details he hadn't shared with her. The fact that the judge who'd blown the case was named Marcus Rutherford. Seeing the name in black-and-white had given her pause, made her wonder if that was the real reason for Joel's visit to West Virginia. Was there a missing person, or was that another story he'd made up? Was it possible he was pursuing some personal vendetta against her family for the actions of a distant relative she'd never even met?

She read further into the article, learned about the injury

he'd sustained. A near-fatal gunshot wound that had required emergency surgery to remove the bullet lodged in his abdomen. Just the thought made her skin go cold. He could have been killed. She told herself it didn't matter, she didn't care. But she did.

Then she saw the picture. The clipping was dated several years earlier than the rest, but there was no mistaking the nature of the photo or the man in it. It was a wedding picture—Joel's wedding picture.

The pain sliced into her, so sharp and deep it took her breath away. Still she couldn't tear her eyes from the image, painfully clear even through the sheen of her tears. After the initial shock passed, she forced herself to close the cover of the folder. She didn't read any more. She didn't want any more details about his betrayal. She didn't need any more proof to know what an idiot she'd been.

It was time to get ready for her dinner with Stuart, anyway.

In a cheap motel room outside Wheeling, West Virginia, he was also getting ready.

He sat alone in the darkness. Oblivious to the bright sun beyond the drawn curtains. Oblivious to everything but his own agenda.

It was almost time. His plans had been made, each and every detail carefully plotted and scrutinized. The scenario had played out in his mind so many times he didn't doubt that everything would go exactly as he'd envisioned. He closed his eyes, let himself watch the events unfold once more.

She was surprised to see him. That was her first mistake.

She should never have underestimated him, never challenged his domination. He had the power. He was in control. She was helpless. Crying. Begging for mercy.

She didn't deserve mercy. Not after the way she'd betrayed him. But he let her plead. He listened as she cried. Her tears and pleas were proof of his power. He became aroused by the imaginary cries and whimpers.

He wouldn't need to imagine them very much longer.

She thought she'd gotten away. That she was safe. It was just one more illusion to be shattered.

Soon. Very soon.

"What's the matter, honey?"

Riane lowered herself onto the edge of her parents' bed and forced a smile in response to her mother's question. "Nothing."

"Riane," Ellen said patiently.

She sighed, thinking it both a curse and a blessing to have a mother who knew her so well. They'd been home from the airport less than an hour. Her father had already been called into the office to deal with some kind of crisis, signaling that his vacation was well and truly over, which left her mother to zero in on Riane's discontent. "I don't want to talk about it."

"Problems with Stuart?"

"Yes," she admitted, although she'd relegated those problems to the furthest recesses of her mind in response to more immediate concerns.

"Do you want to tell me about it?"

"There's not much to say," Riane said. "I'm not—I can't marry him." She'd always known Stuart didn't love her, but his lack of genuine affection didn't bother her half as much as his admitted unfaithfulness. And after the charity auction they'd attended together the previous evening, she'd told him in no uncertain terms that their relationship was over.

The senator sat on the edge of the bed beside her and put an arm across her shoulders. "Are you okay?"

"It was my decision."

"That doesn't mean you can't be hurting."

"I'm okay," Riane assured her. At least she was confident that the decision she'd made regarding her relationship with Stuart had been the right one. Her feelings for Joel were a lot less clear, the pain of his betrayal more intense.

"I must admit, I'm a little relieved."

Riane turned to her mother, startled. "You are?"

"I like Stuart," Ellen said. "I just never felt that he was the right man for you."

"You never said anything."

"I wasn't dating him," her mother said simply.

"You've always let me make my own decisions—and my own mistakes." Riane sighed, rubbed a hand over the ache in her chest. "I made a big one."

"So this isn't about Stuart?"

"No," Riane admitted.

"Is it Joel?"

Riane wasn't surprised that her mother remembered the name. She nodded.

"What happened?"

Riane just shook her head. She couldn't bear to give her mother all the details, to admit what a fool she'd been. Again. After her disastrous relationship with Cameron Davis, she'd been understandably cautious. Her decision to get involved with Stuart had been a practical one, based on logical reasoning. With Joel she'd followed her heart. And had it broken all over again.

"I'm so sorry, honey."

Riane forced a smile. "Me, too."

"And I'm sorry I wasn't here for you."

"You're here now." Riane's smile came more easily this time. "And I want to hear all the details of your trip. Right now, though, I have to get over to the campground."

"But we just got home," Ellen protested.

"And Daddy's already dealing with yet another crisis at the office," Riane pointed out.

"All the more reason for you not to abandon me, too."

"I won't be long," Riane promised. "I just want to go over the changes the architect has suggested before the construction crew comes back in the morning."

It could have waited until the next day, but she was still feeling a little raw about the whole situation with Joel and she needed some time alone.

"Riane?"

She turned back to her mother.

"I love you, baby."

Riane's eyes filled with tears as she went into her mother's arms. The rest of her life might be a mess, but she knew she could always count on her parents. Her family was everything to her—her safe harbor through any storm—and she would never forgive Joel for trying to take that way from her. "I love you, too."

Joel could hardly believe that his whole theory had been blown to pieces by baby pictures.

But the photos Riane had pulled out were tangible and undeniable proof of his mistake. If the senator and her husband had adopted Rheanne Elliot when she was almost two years old, they wouldn't have pictures of her as an infant.

So now that Joel knew Riane Quinlan wasn't Rheanne Elliott, there was just one reason for him to stay in Mapleview: Ellen Rutherford-Quinlan. She was still his only connection between the parties involved, so he reverted to Strategy B— hanging around West Virginia to speak with the senator.

Still, having a contingency plan didn't make him feel like any less an idiot. His instincts had let him down again. The first time they'd failed, he'd lost his job—and nearly his life. This time, he'd followed his gut and he'd lost the woman he...

Joel wasn't sure how to complete the thought.

How did he feel about Riane?

He cared about her, more than he'd expected to in such a short period of time. And he hated that his deception and speculation had hurt her. Which was the main reason he wished he could just skip town—as if distance might somehow assuage his guilt.

Besides, Riane had made it clear that she didn't want to have anything more to do with him. It was his own fault, he knew. He should have been honest with her from the outset.

All he could do now was track down the real missing child

and put this whole situation behind him. And the only hope he had of doing that was to talk to Senator Rutherford-Quinlan. So instead of heading back to Pennsylvania the next morning, as he wanted to do, Joel found himself driving toward the Quinlan mansion.

He'd followed the same route so many times in the past few days that his car could probably negotiate the course on its own. As he pulled up in front of the house he was grateful that Riane's car was absent from its usual parking space. Not only did he want to spare her the discomfort of another confrontation, he was certain she would do everything she could to prevent him from talking to her mother.

Yes, Riane's absence was a good thing.

Why, then, did he feel so empty inside?

He pressed the doorbell, expecting it would be Sophie who responded to the summons. Expecting to have a few more minutes to prepare his speech before he had to see the senator.

But the woman who opened the door could be none other than Ellen Rutherford-Quinlan herself. He'd seen pictures of her, of course, and clips on the news. She wasn't a blend-into-the-background politician. She had strong views and never missed an opportunity to express them. But nothing he'd read or heard had prepared him for this face-to-face meeting.

She was attractive, tall, although not as tall as Riane, and quite slender. Almost delicate. He reminded himself that there was a sharp mind and steely determination behind the delicate facade. And if he misstepped on this assignment again, she could—and very likely would—squash him like a bug.

"Senator Rutherford-Quinlan."

Ellen smiled, and in the half second it took her lips to curve, his assessment changed from "attractive" to "stunning." She extended a hand. "Can I help you?"

"Joel Logan." He accepted the proffered hand. "I'm a

private investigator. If you have a few moments, I'd like to speak with you regarding a case I've been working on.''

Her smile dimmed, her gaze sharpened. ''What kind of case?''

''Could I come inside to discuss this?''

She hesitated a second, then nodded and stepped back. She gestured to the French doors that led into the den, the room he'd waited in the first night he'd come here to see Riane. It seemed like a lifetime ago rather than the ten days he knew it to be.

''I'll have Sophie bring in coffee,'' she said, continuing down the hall toward the kitchen.

She returned a few minutes later, Sophie behind her with a gleaming silver coffee service on some kind of antique cart. Sophie acknowledged his presence with a brief nod of greeting and none of her usual warmth. Was her reserved demeanor a result of the senator's presence or a reflection of Riane's animosity?

''Tell me about this case you're working on,'' the senator said when Sophie had left the cart and exited the room.

Joel forced his thoughts away from Riane. ''I'm trying to find a child who was adopted twenty-two years ago.''

If she was surprised, she didn't show it. Which made Joel consider that his visit might not have been completely unexpected. Had Riane warned her mother about the nature of his investigation—or had Mike's discussion with Camille Michaud somehow come to the attention of the senator?

''How do you think I can help you do that, Mr. Logan?''

''I believe the adoption of this child was handled by Samuel Rutherford.''

There wasn't the slightest flicker of recognition. Of course, she was a politician—she was accustomed to public scrutiny, to hiding her personal feelings behind the party line.

''He was your cousin?'' Joel prompted.

''Second cousin, actually.'' She moved to the cart Sophie had left, filled two cups with the fragrant hot brew. She passed one to him. "I believe Sam's specialty was criminal law."

"It was," Joel agreed. "Which is probably why his secretary remembered this particular case."

Her hand trembled, very slightly, as she added a splash of cream to her cup. She seemed to pull herself together again, faced him. "Why do you think any of this concerns me?"

"Camille Michaud," Joel said simply.

The senator met his gaze levelly, unflinching.

"She was your roommate at Vassar."

"She was," Ellen agreed.

"Are you still in contact with her?"

She hesitated briefly, then nodded. She obviously knew he could check her phone records if he wanted to.

"She was the social worker assigned to the case. My partner has been in contact with Ms. Michaud, but she claims not to remember the child."

The senator finished stirring her coffee, took a sip.

Stalling for time, Joel guessed. Considering her strategy.

"Who's paying you to find this child?" she asked at last.

"Why does that matter? Are you going to offer a larger fee not to find her?"

"If you want my cooperation, Mr. Logan, it would be wise not to insult me."

She was right, of course, and he had no reason to make such an accusation. Except that the senator was a Rutherford, and Rutherfords were notorious for bending the rules to suit their own purposes. But he forced down his irritation, unwilling to let his quick temper blow his only lead. "Are you going to cooperate?"

"I want to know who's looking for this child."

"Her sister."

Her cup clattered in her saucer. She set both onto the glossy tabletop and lowered herself to the edge of the sofa, smoothing her hands over her skirt. "Sister?"

He nodded, intrigued by this hint of nerves, the first genuine evidence of any emotion. "The child who was adopted had a half sister, older by about eight years."

"Why would only one child have been taken away?" she wondered aloud.

"The older sister was taken out of the home by a relative. An aunt on her father's side," he explained. "The biological mother of the girls wouldn't consent to this aunt taking the younger child, since there was no blood between them."

"But she let her children be separated?" The senator seemed genuinely shocked, distressed even, by this possibility.

"Apparently."

Before either of them could say anything else, the front door slammed shut and Riane stormed into the room, eyes flashing with venom and fury.

"What the hell are you doing here?"

The senator rose to her feet, obviously shocked by her daughter's outburst.

At that moment the resemblance between the two women struck Joel. It wasn't so much their looks, although they were both tall and both had dark hair. It was the way they carried themselves. With confidence and grace. Although right now every inch of Riane's graceful form was practically vibrating with tightly suppressed anger.

"Riane, honey—"

Riane paid no attention to the warning note of her mother's voice or the restraining hand the older woman laid on her arm. She didn't so much as spare a glance in her direction, but aimed all of her fury at Joel. "Get out!"

"I need to talk to—"

"Haven't you done enough damage without insulting my parents with your neophyte theories?"

"Your mother might be the only person who can help me find the child."

"That isn't her problem, it's yours."

"Riane—"

She shook her head, tears glistening in her eyes. "Get out."

He couldn't give up when he was so close to getting through to the senator. He also knew he couldn't stay now, not when he could see how much Riane was hurting. Not when he was the one responsible for her pain.

He took a business card out of his pocket, passed it to the senator. "If you think of anything at all that might help me, I'd appreciate hearing from you."

The senator took the card from his hand but didn't glance at it. Her gaze seemed to dart from her daughter to him and back again, concerned, wary and all too understanding.

Joel decided to make an exit while he still could.

It was a long moment after she'd watched Joel's truck disappear before Riane felt composed enough to face her mother again. She was embarrassed by her outburst. It wasn't like her to give free rein to her emotions, but when she'd pulled into the driveway and seen his vehicle parked in front of the house, something inside her had snapped. And all the hurt and anger and frustration she'd kept bottled up inside had burst forth.

"I'm sorry," she said at last, turning to her mother. "I didn't really believe he had the nerve to come back here or I would have warned you."

Ellen glanced down at the business card in her hand, brushed her thumb over the simple black lettering. "Court-land & Logan Investigations," she murmured. "I should have guessed."

"Courtland," Riane repeated, feeling an unaccountable chill despite the sunny warmth of the room. "Is that the same Courtland you asked me about?"

"I would guess so."

"Then you knew…about Joel's investigation?"

Ellen shook her head. "Not enough, apparently."

Riane felt the pressure building at her temples. "How could you know?"

"Camille contacted us on the ship."

"Then she is…involved in this?"

When Ellen looked at her, Riane noticed that her mother's face had gone white beneath her tan, and her eyes were wide, wary. "I didn't want it to come out like this."

"What? You didn't want *what* to come out like this?" Riane asked, a heavy emptiness settling in the pit of her stomach.

"Ryan and I have talked about almost nothing else since Camille's phone call," Ellen admitted. "And we still hadn't come to any decisions about what to do. But now, after what Mr. Logan said…"

"Now *what?*" Riane demanded impatiently. "What is Camille involved in?"

"It isn't just Camille," Ellen admitted, a single tear sliding slowly down one pale cheek.

Riane had never seen her mother like this—so flustered and obviously upset. She didn't know how to respond. Nor was she certain she wanted any of the answers she'd demanded.

"Camille arranged a private adoption without the knowledge or consent of social services. She could have lost her job, she might have faced criminal charges, but she did it because she knew the child needed a good home and she knew a family who desperately wanted a child."

"Is this the child Joel is looking for?"

Ellen nodded, heedless of the tears that now streamed down her face. "We did what we thought was best. We never knew…"

The "we" scared Riane even more than her mother's tears. It confirmed what she'd suspected, even though she'd refused to admit it: somehow her parents were involved. The throbbing at her temples escalated. She ignored the pounding and put an arm across her mother's shoulders, wanting to comfort her and yet feeling hopelessly inadequate at the task.

"Forget about it, Mom. No one needs to know what happened. Joel doesn't have any evidence. If he did, he wouldn't have come here on a fishing expedition."

But Ellen shook her head sadly. "I can't keep this secret anymore."

The sick feeling inside Riane intensified along with an almost desperate need to halt her mother's next words. She shook her head. "Forget it. Forget he was ever here."

"I'm sorry, Riane."

"Sorry? Why?" Riane didn't realize her own cheeks were wet.

Ellen looked at her, her soft green eyes filled with regret and sadness. "The child he's looking for is you."

Chapter 9

Riane stepped away, stunned. Even though she'd somehow known, in her heart, that it was true, hearing the words hit her with the force of a physical blow. She leaned against the edge of the desk, gulping in lungfuls of air, desperately trying to stop the room from spinning.

Slowly she turned back and faced the woman she'd always believed was her mother. "I was adopted?"

Ellen nodded.

"Why?"

"Because we were desperate to have a child, and the doctors said I wouldn't ever be able to have one of my own."

It was a valid explanation, but it wasn't what Riane wanted to know. "Why did you hide the truth? Why didn't you tell me?"

Ellen dropped her gaze, folded her hands together in front of her. "We couldn't."

"What do you mean—you couldn't? Why couldn't you?"

"Do the details really matter?"

Riane was stunned, infuriated. "Of course they matter. This is my *life* we're talking about."

"We gave you a good life," Ellen reminded her. "We gave you everything."

"Except the truth."

"We did what we thought was best at the time."

"Best for who?"

"For all of us, I like to think." Ellen sighed. "But mostly for me. It was so hard for me to admit that I'd failed."

"Failed how?"

"By not being able to have a child of my own."

"There are lots of women who can't have children."

"I'm not saying my situation was unique, I'm only trying to make you understand how *I* felt."

"Try harder," Riane said bluntly. "Because so far I'm not understanding any of this."

"I was an only child, and my father had been making noises for years about wanting to be a grandfather. I'd always felt that he was disappointed in me, because I hadn't been the son he wanted. I couldn't bear to let him down again."

"So you secretly adopted a child and passed it off as your own to placate your father?" Whatever explanation Riane had expected, this was not it. "Did you even *want* a child? Or was having a baby a calculated maneuver to ensure your inheritance?"

Blinded by tears, she didn't see Ellen's hand swing toward her. But she felt the sting of the palm against her cheek, heard the slap resound in the tense silence of the room. Never, in her entire life had her mother—*Ellen,* she mentally amended—hit her.

Riane gingerly touched her fingertips to her hot cheek. "Was I hitting a little too close to the truth?"

"No!" Ellen's eyes were wide, horrified. "Oh, God, Riane. I'm sorry. So sorry."

She reached out a hand, as if to comfort, but Riane recoiled from the gesture. "Are you sorry for hitting me? Or because it's true?"

"It's not true." Ellen shook her head from side to side vehemently. "Of course I wanted a child. For years Ryan and I tried desperately to have one of our own."

"And when you couldn't, it was easy enough to take someone else's." She didn't try to keep the bitterness from her tone; she couldn't stop the anger and resentment building inside her.

"None of this was easy."

"For twenty-two years you raised me as your own and never gave any indication otherwise." Everything she'd ever believed about herself and her family had been a lie. A whole series of lies, one piled on top of another, until the truth had been buried so deep it should never have been discovered. And it wouldn't have been, if Joel Logan hadn't started digging.

"As far as we were concerned, you were our child." Ellen wiped at the tears sliding down her cheeks. "You *are* our child."

Riane had basked in that knowledge over the years. Now, faced with the realization that Ellen and Ryan weren't really her mother and father, that none of the past twenty-two years had been real, she didn't know how to feel. She was hurt and angry, but overriding all else was an aching emptiness deep inside. A void that obliterated any sense of self she'd ever possessed.

"From the moment you came to us, I believed you were meant to be ours. That God sent you to us—"

"God?" Riane interrupted, her tone derisive. "Are you suggesting that Camille was on His payroll?"

"The Lord works in mysterious ways," Ellen said evenly.

Riane shook her head. "How dare you claim divine intervention as justification for your actions?"

"Whether you believe it or not, *I* believed it. I believed you were given to us because you needed a family to love you as much as we needed a child to love."

"I hope that helps you sleep at night."

"And when *you* go to sleep at night, it's in the home we provided for you," Ellen reminded her tersely.

Riane fell silent.

"You have a right to be angry," Ellen continued, "but I am still your mother and I deserve your respect."

Riane bit back the sharp retort that sprang to her lips, because despite the fact that Ellen hadn't given birth to her, she had been her mother in every way that mattered. And that was why her betrayal struck so deeply. "Did you—" She swallowed around the lump in her throat. "Did you ever really love me?"

The tight lines around Ellen's mouth relaxed a little. "Always. And so much more than I ever would have thought possible."

The unwavering certainty in Ellen's voice sliced through Riane's anger, tore at her heart. She swallowed. "Then why did you have to ruin everything by telling me the truth now?"

It was a ridiculous question, of course. But as furious as Riane was that the truth about her parentage had been hidden for the past twenty-two years, she couldn't deny there was a part of her that wished the lie had continued. So long as she'd been Ellen and Ryan Quinlan's daughter, she'd been someone. Now she didn't know who she was, what was expected of her.

"Do you remember the Christmas when you were four years old?"

Riane frowned. "No."

"I do." Ellen smiled, almost wistfully. "You asked for only two things from Santa that year: a ballerina doll and a sister."

"What does that have to do with anything?" Riane demanded impatiently.

"Have you ever wondered why you wanted a sister so desperately?"

"Only-child syndrome," she guessed, unconsciously echoing the label Joel had used a few days earlier.

"Maybe. Or maybe it went deeper than that."

The throbbing in Riane's head grew faster, stronger.

"Maybe you didn't want *a* sister," Ellen continued, "you wanted *your* sister."

"What—" she swallowed "—what are you getting at?"

"According to Mr. Logan, you have a sister. She's the one who hired him to find you."

"No." She shook her head furiously, refusing to believe it. "You're lying."

"Do you really think I'd lie about something like that?"

"You've lied about everything else!"

Ellen blanched. "You're right. I'm not going to make excuses, because a lie of omission is still a lie." She stepped toward her daughter; Riane stepped back. "I'm not lying about this."

"I would remember if I had a sister," Riane insisted, desperately needing to believe it.

But what if she was wrong?

"You weren't even two years old when you came to us," Ellen reminded her gently.

"If I have a sister, then you took me away from her."

"No! We didn't know. Camille never mentioned another child."

"Would it have made a difference?"

Ellen was silent for a long moment. "I like to think so, but I'm not sure. I'd had four miscarriages in the three years before we went to Tavaria, and each one was more devastating than the last."

Riane didn't want to feel any sympathy. Her emotions were chaotic enough without the tug of empathy that responded to this admission.

"It was one of the reasons we decided to go overseas," Ellen continued. "But I still couldn't escape the sense of failure I felt. And when Camille called and said she'd found a child we could adopt—well, I probably didn't ask as many questions as I should have."

"Then you believe it's true—I have a sister?"

"I don't think Mr. Logan would have made such an allegation if he didn't have the evidence to back it up."

"Evidence," Riane scoffed. "He didn't even have my correct date of birth."

"October second," Ellen said softly.

"October second?" Riane echoed. "But my birthday is August twenty-fourth."

"We changed your birth date to coincide with the date we adopted you," Ellen admitted. "To celebrate the day you came to us."

Riane shook her head. She couldn't believe this was happening, that her whole life was unraveling before her very eyes. Not even her birthday was really hers, but an arbitrary date her parents had chosen.

How many more secrets would be uncovered before this nightmare was over? How many lies had been manufactured to cover the truth? How many deceptions had she unquestioningly accepted?

The questions swirled through her mind now. She wanted to demand answers, but she was afraid to know. She wanted to demand the truth, but she wasn't prepared to accept what it might be.

Instead, blinded by a haze of confusion and tears, she simply walked away.

Not long after he'd left the Quinlan mansion, Joel received the call that he'd started to think would never come. From Felicia Elliott—or Reynolds, as she now called herself—the biological mother of Rheanne Elliott.

After he spent no less than ten minutes assuring the woman he hadn't been hired by her ex-husband to track her down, she finally agreed to meet him.

It was ironic, he thought, that he'd chased this woman from Arizona to California to Michigan, only to find that she was now in Wheeling, West Virginia. Another bizarre coincidence in a case that seemed to be full of them.

He checked out of the hotel and met her at a public coffee

shop. Despite the assurances about his reasons for tracking her down, the former Felicia Elliott was obviously still wary. It was apparent in the way she jumped every time the bell above the door rang, the way her eyes darted around the room, and in the way she was dressed.

There was no doubt that Felicia had once been a beautiful woman, but her thick dark hair was threaded with gray and chopped short, her deep brown eyes were shadowed and bare of makeup, her slender figure hidden beneath baggy pants and an unfashionable sweater. Considering the abuse she'd suffered for so many years at the hands of her second husband, none of this surprised Joel. What surprised—and disturbed—him was her careless habit of referring to the child she'd given birth to and given away as "the kid."

And although he didn't think she was deliberately withholding any information, her recollection about the events of twenty-two years ago was unclear. Joel took a sip of the bitter coffee and reworded his question. "Did you want to give up your baby, Ms. Reynolds?"

She shrugged her thin shoulders. "The kid was difficult. Cried all the time. Always hungry, fussing. I couldn't handle her. My husband couldn't handle her. We did what was best."

"But you hadn't considered adoption until you were approached by this woman?"

"Never thought about it," she admitted. "What are you looking for, Mr. Logan? Do you want me to say that we felt pressured by this woman? That she forced us to give up the kid?" She shrugged again. "Maybe we did feel pressured, but we also felt relieved. Once she was gone, I didn't regret my decision. I don't regret it now."

"Do you remember the name of the people who adopted your child?"

"I don't recall that we were ever told."

He pushed his cup aside, not sure if it was the caffeine eating a hole in his stomach lining or this woman's blatant disregard for the child she'd borne. "It didn't bother you, not knowing who would raise your child?"

"I had other things to worry about. And Gavin never really wanted the kid, anyway."

No matter how many questions he asked, no matter how many times they went over the facts that she did remember, nothing changed. Desperate to jog her memory, Joel pulled a picture out of his wallet. "Do you remember when this was taken?"

A trembling finger traced the faces of the two young girls in the photo. "It was Arden's ninth birthday. Rheanne was about eighteen months old."

It was the first time she'd mentioned either of the girls by name, and the wistfulness in her voice made Joel realize that she had, at least at one time, loved her children. And if she had cared about them, she might have kept some mementos.

"Would you happen to have any other pictures of Rheanne?" Joel asked. He knew he was grasping at straws, but if he could get a better photo, he might be able to have it enhanced and computer aged. He needed something more than what he had in order to continue his search for Arden's sister.

But Felicia shook her head. "We gave away the pictures with the kid."

Riane kicked the tire of her BMW coupe, as if it was somehow the fault of the vehicle that she'd run out of gas. She knew it was her own stupidity. She'd been driving for hours since she'd left home, following the same path in and around Mapleview, never once looking at the gas gauge. But she wasn't feeling very rational or logical at the moment. She didn't know how or what to feel. Hell, she didn't even know who she was anymore.

Except that she was alone. Completely and utterly alone, and stranded on the side of a road going to God only knew where.

She reached into her purse for her cell phone, resigned to

calling the automobile club and admitting that she'd been a scatterbrain. It would probably make the papers: Senator's Daughter Runs Out of Gas on Roadside. She gave a half laugh. Except that she wasn't the senator's daughter, not really.

Well, running out of gas wasn't so bad. It could be worse—such as her cell phone battery being dead.

Riane threw the phone onto the passenger seat in disgust.

Damn Joel Logan, anyway. If he hadn't started digging around, prying into her past, she'd be at home right now in her nice warm bed.

She glanced around, could see nothing but thick trees lining either side of the gravel road. The sun was starting to go down, which meant it would be dark in about an hour. Riane sighed and looked down at her attire. She was still wearing the silk dress and high-heeled pumps she'd put on to pick her parents up from the airport. Now she was going to have to trudge down this dusty road in search of a phone.

But who was she going to call when she found one? The auto club was the obvious choice. They could tow the car or take her to a gas station. Then what was she going to do? She wasn't ready to go home, but she had nowhere else to go.

She closed her eyes, irritated when her thoughts strayed to Joel once again. No. There was no way she'd turn to him for help. Not when he was the one responsible for this whole mess.

Joel was on his way back to Mapleview when he found Riane's car, apparently abandoned, on the side of the road.

Riane, however, was nowhere in sight, and the night was dark and heavy. He drove along a little farther, but the street was deserted. He called the house, even though he knew she wouldn't be there if her car was here. The senator reluctantly confirmed that Riane had left a few hours earlier, upset after a discussion they'd had.

He didn't need to be told that Riane Quinlan was Rheanne

Elliott, nor did he get any satisfaction from the fact. The only thing that mattered now was finding Riane.

He couldn't begin to imagine how she'd felt when she'd realized that everything she'd believed in had been a lie. She was probably still angry with him, too, and he knew she had reason to be. It didn't make him feel any better to know that he'd finally succeeded in doing the job he'd been hired to do. Which reminded him that he should contact his client to share the news, but not yet. Not until he found Riane and knew she was okay.

After several more miles had passed with no sign of Riane or any kind of dwelling, he turned around and went back in the other direction. He slowed his vehicle as Rusty's Tavern came into sight. He couldn't imagine that Riane would ever set foot in such an establishment, but he couldn't disregard the possibility. She wasn't the kind of woman who was easily overlooked, and maybe someone inside would remember seeing her.

He felt responsible, at least in part, for Riane's disappearance. He wanted to blame her parents—the senator and her husband. After all, they were the ones who had lied to Riane for twenty-two years. But he knew it wasn't that simple. And it had been his investigation that had precipitated the crumbling of the foundation of her whole world.

Was it some kind of white knight syndrome that made him want to lift her up from that crumbling foundation? Or had he really fallen for the senator's daughter?

The strains of a mellow country-western tune drifted out the open windows of the tavern. He pushed open the door of the bar and stepped into the dimly lit interior.

A quick scan revealed most of the tables around the perimeter of the dance floor were occupied, as well as a majority of the stools that lined the scarred expanse of bar. And that was where he found her.

She was sandwiched between two men, her long dark hair falling straight down the back of the same peach-colored dress she'd been wearing earlier. She turned her head to respond to something the man beside her said, and her eyes locked with his.

He didn't believe in déjà vu, but the sensation that curled in the pit of his stomach when she saw him was reminiscent of the night they'd first met at the charity ball. Unlike that first night, however, she didn't smile. She didn't make a move toward him. She just turned her head away, tossing her hair over her shoulder, dismissing him.

Joel moved purposefully across the room, leaning down to brush a quick kiss on her lips before she could avert her face. It was a tactical move, yet it gave him enough of a taste of her that he craved more. He knew that if he tried to take it, though, she'd probably deck him. So he smiled. "Sorry I'm late, sweetheart."

When she turned to glare at him, he sent a meaningful look at the cowboy seated beside her. The other man took the nonverbal hint and pushed back his stool, moving on to search for other company.

"Clint and I were in the middle of a conversation," Riane said coolly, picking up the glass of beer in front of her.

"Your parents are worried about you," he said.

"Is that why you're here?"

"Partly." He straddled the now-vacant stool beside her, ordered a draft beer. "I was worried about you, too."

"Well, as you can see, I'm fine."

"You're drinking watered-down beer in a country-western bar," Joel said mildly. "I don't think you're fine."

"I like this place," Riane told him. "The people are friendly, the mood is mellow, the beer is cold."

"How much of that beer have you had?" he asked, passing a few bills to the bartender for the glass set in front of him.

"Not enough," she said.

"Drinking yourself into oblivion isn't the answer, Riane."

"It's a start."

"Why don't we go somewhere to talk about this?"

"I don't want to talk about it. And I *definitely* don't want to talk to you."

"You can't blame me for something that happened more than twenty years ago."

"Maybe not," she acknowledged. "But I can, and I do, blame you for what's happening now."

"I was only doing my job, Riane."

"I hope that helps you sleep at night." Then she slid off her stool, not looking entirely steady on her feet, and moved to the other end of the bar where the cowboy she'd been speaking to earlier had relocated.

Joel sipped his own beer. He'd be damned if he'd chase after her. He *had* only been doing his job. This wasn't his fault; she wasn't his responsibility. And yet he knew he couldn't leave her here. It had taken only one glimpse into those dark eyes of hers to see that she was feeling alone and vulnerable. And the cowboy was looking decidedly encouraged that Riane had sought out his company again.

Resigned to settling in for the night, Joel finished his beer and went outside to make a phone call.

Riane wasn't sure whether she was relieved or disappointed that she'd managed to brush Joel off so easily. She didn't want him here; she didn't need him. And yet, even in the crowded room, she felt alone.

And she felt like a coward. It wasn't in her nature to run away from something just because it was unpleasant. Her parents had taught her to take a stance, adhere to her principles. People had often commented that she was a lot like her mother—strong and determined—and she'd always been proud of that fact. But Ellen Rutherford-Quinlan wasn't really her mother.

She sighed and finished the last few drops of beer in her glass, still stunned by the realization that the truth about her parentage had been hidden from her for so many years.

The song on the jukebox changed to something softer, slower.

''Dance with me,'' Clint said, rising to his feet.

It wasn't really an invitation, but Riane didn't care. Maybe dancing would help get her mind off other things. That's really all she wanted right now—to forget. Forget that everything she'd thought and believed about herself and her life had been a lie.

The cowboy pulled her into his arms, a little too close for comfort, but she didn't protest. She laid her cheek against his shoulder, closed her eyes. It was nice to feel his arms around her, to lean on his strength. He wasn't Joel, but—

She pushed aside the thought. She didn't want to be with Joel. If she should be thinking about anyone right now, it was the man who was holding her. The man whose hand was inching lower, from her waist to her hip, from her hip to the curve of her behind, lower still, until he was cupping her buttock. He pulled her closer, tighter against him, until she could feel the evidence of his arousal. Panic began to rise inside her, slowly, steadily, as he ground his pelvis against her.

He dipped his head to skim his lips over her ear. His breath was hot against her neck. He was an attractive man; she should be attracted to him. But she wasn't. Because he wasn't Joel. And she mentally cursed Joel Logan again for being the first thought on her mind. It wasn't fair that he'd gotten to her so effortlessly, turned her entire life upside down and walked out again.

She forced her attention back to the cowboy. Clint, that was his name. He was sweet and attentive. Okay, he was a little too free with his hands, but maybe what she really needed to forget this whole mess that was her life, was a night of mindless sex. It always seemed to work in the movies, anyway. And cowboys always had starring roles in romance novels. She wondered if they made love with their boots on, and giggled at the thought.

Giggled?

Riane *didn't* giggle. Ever.

She giggled again.

Maybe she'd had more to drink than she'd thought. She couldn't really remember how many times the bartender had set a new glass in front of her.

The hand that was on her butt squeezed lightly again, the other moved along her side, skimmed the side of her breast. Riane felt her stomach lurch, and she pushed away from him.

"Hey," Clint protested, grabbing for her again. "What's the matter?"

Riane shook her head. "I'm sorry. I can't— I…I have to go."

He didn't let go of her. "You're not going anywhere, honey. Your car's broken down on the side of the road, remember?"

She closed her eyes, groaning softly. She had forgotten. She was well and truly stranded.

"Why don't you come home with me, honey? We'll come back out here in the morning and take a look at your car."

She knew it was a bad idea, although her brain seemed pretty foggy right now and she wasn't sure exactly *why* it was a bad idea. "Can't you look at my car now?" she asked.

"It's too dark out there to see what's wrong," he told her.

"I think I just ran out of gas." Yes, she was sure she remembered now. She'd been driving a long time and had forgotten to monitor the gas gauge.

"Then we'll come back in the morning with a can of gas," he said. "You're in no shape to drive home tonight, anyway."

She nodded, then wished she hadn't when the room started to spin. He was right, of course. It would be better to find someplace to sleep, then reevaluate the situation in the morning.

"Are you ready to go?"

She started to nod again, thought better of it. "Yes," she said instead.

Chapter 10

Joel had been in his share of scrapes in his life, and he'd always held his own well enough. But he'd never been in a bar fight, he'd never fought over a woman, and he didn't intend to start now. He also didn't intend to let Riane leave with the cowboy who was currently directing her toward the door.

Joel stepped into their path, pasted what he hoped was a friendly smile on his face. "Thanks, pal," he said to the man at Riane's side. "But I can take it from here."

The man might have backed off easily enough before, but he wasn't inclined to do so now. Of course, Riane had given him additional encouragement on the dance floor, allowing him to grope her in public. Which was when Joel realized, without a doubt, that she was drunk. Not tipsy, not happy, not just a little uninhibited. She was completely, stinking drunk, and she probably had no idea that the man beside her was mentally ticking off the minutes until he could have her out of the sexy little dress and on her back.

"I don't think so," the cowboy drawled, tightening his

arm around Riane's shoulders. "The lady's coming home with me tonight."

"The lady's not going anywhere with you," Joel denied.

"Take it outside, boys," the bartender called over, obviously anxious to avoid any brawling in his establishment.

Joel looked at Riane, concerned, as her face seemed to go from flushed to pale in half a second. "Are you okay, Riane?"

"She's fine," the cowboy responded for her.

"Riane," Joel said again, trying to appeal to reason.

"I think I'm going to be sick," she said, pulling away from the cowboy and pushing through the front door.

The cowboy backed away so fast he almost created a draft. He didn't seem to mind taking advantage of an intoxicated woman, but he didn't want to have to clean up after her.

Joel shook his head and followed Riane out the door.

She was leaning against the side of the building, her cheeks still pale, her lips trembling, a fine sheen of perspiration on her forehead.

"Are you okay?" he asked gently.

She started to shake her head, then apparently thought better of it. "I think I'm drunk," she told him.

His lips twitched. "You're wasted, sweetheart."

"I can't be. I don't get drunk. Ever."

"There's a first time for everything," he said.

She started to shake her head again, then bent at the waist and threw up.

Joel caught her hair and pulled it back, holding it behind her head and out of the line of fire as she continued to retch. Apparently, she'd consumed quite a bit of alcohol, more than he'd have thought she'd be able to hold inside and still stand up. It almost made him admire her tenacity, even though he had no idea what he was going to do with her now.

"Do you feel better?" he asked, after the bout of vomiting had finally stopped.

"No." She straightened and shook off his hand. "But I don't think I have anything left inside me."

She didn't protest when he led her over to his truck. Or when he opened the passenger side and helped her inside. "I'll be right back," he told her.

"Wait." She put her hand on the door and looked up at him with watery eyes. "Don't leave me here."

"I'm just going inside to get you some paper towels."

Still she hesitated.

"I'll be gone half a minute," he told her. "I promise."

"Okay," she relented.

He was gone only as long as promised, returning with a handful of paper towels he'd moistened in the bathroom. He opened the passenger door again and gently wiped her face. The cool water must have helped revive her, because she took the towels from him and finished the task herself.

"Why are you here, Joel? Why did you come back?"

"I needed to see you again. I want to try and explain."

She closed her eyes, leaned her head back against the seat. "Do you think anything you have to say will make a difference at this point?" Her voice was sad, resigned, and he hated that he'd had any part in bringing this misery upon her.

"Probably not," he admitted. "But I didn't want you to think that you didn't matter to me, because you do."

She opened her eyes, looking at him with a combination of wariness and sadness.

"Are you ready to go home now?"

"No." Her response was immediate and vehement.

"You can't run away from this forever," he said.

"I know. I just can't face them tonight." She closed her eyes again. "Not like this."

"Okay," he relented, already knowing he would regret it.

Riane was mortified. Completely and utterly mortified. She wasn't sure if she'd really puked all of the alcohol out of her system, but she'd sobered up enough to be thoroughly embarrassed by her own behavior. She'd *never* done anything like this; she never would have dared. But the Riane Quinlan who'd been raised to always be on her best behavior, who was conscious that any wrong step could be exploited by the scandal-hungry media, hadn't been inside Rusty's Tavern. The woman at the bar, desperately and ineffectually trying to drown her misery in watered-down beer, had little in common with the senator's daughter. She didn't even know who she was.

Now, she was at some two-bit motel off the side of the highway with a man she barely knew. Well, at least she knew Joel better than she knew Clint, and she'd almost been ready to go home with him. *That* would have been a mistake of monumental proportions.

Maybe she should have allowed Joel to take her home. It probably would have been the smartest thing to do. But she just wasn't ready to deal with any of this right now. She wasn't ready to face her own feelings about everything.

Did that make her a coward?

Maybe.

She was leaning against the hood of his truck, taking deep breaths of the cool night air. Her head was still spinning, and her stomach was a little unsettled, but she thought the worst of it had passed. Now she was just waiting for Joel to come back with their room keys, then she could drown herself in the shower.

"They only had one vacancy," Joel told her, holding up the single key on a square plastic holder.

Riane scanned the sad exterior of the building. The faded orange brick, the peeling paint around the dingy windows, the rusted numbers nailed into scarred doors. But sure enough, there were vehicles parked outside of almost every unit. Except for the second one from the end.

"Number 9," Joel said. "It has two beds."

"That's fine." Riane knew she was in no position to object.

"There was a little general store attached to the office," he told her, passing her a small brown paper bag. "So I picked up a few things I thought you might want."

Riane opened the bag as he went around to the trunk to

get his suitcase. He was obviously a little more prepared than she for this roadside adventure. She knew it was silly to be annoyed by the fact that he would have a change of under-wear and she wouldn't, and any hint of resentment was for-gotten when she dipped into the bag and found a toothbrush and toothpaste, a travel-size bottle of shampoo, and a bag of corn chips. She almost wept with gratitude. "Thanks."

He shrugged, as if it was no big deal, but it was. At least to her. She was hot and sweaty and embarrassed, but maybe she wouldn't need to drown herself in the shower, after all. If she could just wash her hair and brush her teeth, she might actually feel human again.

"I thought you might be hungry," he said, then grinned as her stomach growled in response to his statement.

"Starved," she admitted, only now realizing she hadn't eaten since breakfast. She hadn't even given a thought to food. But she did so now, taking out the bag of corn chips and tearing it open.

"Well, you can start with those," he said, gesturing to the bag. "And we can always order a pizza if you're still hun-gry."

"Pizza?" She perked up immediately. Joel laughed.

Riane followed him into the room. It wasn't much more than he'd said—two twin beds, each with horrid orange floral covers. She wondered if the decorator had consciously tried to match the interior decor with the exterior facade. What other reason could there be for such a particularly putrid shade?

She continued her cursory survey of the room. A single table with a lamp sat between them. On the other wall was a long dresser with a television on top of it and a paper card advertising several triple-X movie options. Past the dresser was a closed door. Riane pushed it open and flipped on the light. The bathroom was as sparse as the bedroom—a shower stall, toilet and pedestal sink. But it looked relatively clean, and the towels were neatly folded.

"I'm going to take a shower," Riane told him.

"I'll order pizza," Joel said.

She offered him a tired smile. "Thanks. Sun-dried tomatoes, artichoke hearts and hot peppers." .

She didn't see the face Joel made as she closed the door.

The pizza delivery boy had just left when Riane stepped out of the bathroom.

Joel did a double take. She stepped out of the bathroom wearing only a silky camisole with tiny straps and a matching pair of high-cut underwear. Her skin glowed, her hair was damp, and her nipples pushed against the fabric of her top. What was she trying to do to him?

He snapped his jaw shut, unstuck his tongue from the roof of his mouth, and somehow managed to speak. "Where's your dress?"

"I hung it up in the bathroom."

"I think you should put it back on."

She frowned. "I can't sleep in it."

"You're going to sleep in *that?*"

"I left my pajamas in the bar," she said dryly.

He'd never even thought about what she was going to sleep in. He had his suitcase because he'd checked out of the hotel after his meeting with the senator, but Riane had been stranded on the side of the road with nothing but whatever she carried in that little purse. Obviously, a pair of pajamas wasn't an option.

"I have a T-shirt you could put on," he offered.

"This is fine," she said.

"No, it's not," he grumbled, wondering how the hell he was supposed to get any sleep knowing that she was in the bed beside him in a couple of scraps of tantalizing silk, thinking about how easy it would be to strip them from her body and get his hands on her naked flesh. He lowered the pizza box to hide the evidence of his wayward thoughts, and only then remembered it was there.

"Pizza's here," he said.

"Great. I'm starving."

So was he. But he had no interest in the pizza anymore.

He passed the box to Riane and picked up the remote for the television. He needed a distraction, any kind of distraction, to get his mind off all that tempting skin Riane was displaying. He pressed the power button.

Panting and moaning filled the room as a tangle of naked limbs appeared on the screen. It took Joel less than three seconds to realize that it was a pornographic movie—two seconds longer than it would have if all the blood hadn't already drained from his head into his lap when Riane came out of the bathroom practically naked. He hit the power button again to shut off the television and dropped the remote onto the table with a clatter.

Riane glanced at him strangely. "What was that?"

He shook his head. "Nothing you'd want to watch."

"What was it?" she asked again.

"It wasn't the Disney channel," he said dryly.

"Porn?" She sounded more curious than offended. "I've never seen a pornographic movie before."

"And you're not going to see one now."

"Why not?"

"Give me a break, Riane."

"What's wrong with wanting to expand my horizons?" she demanded.

He tapped the pizza box. "Eat."

She frowned as she flipped open the lid on the box. Her frown deepened as she inspected the contents. "This doesn't look like sun-dried tomatoes and artichoke hearts."

"Expand your horizons."

"You expect me to eat this?" she asked, looking at the pepperoni and sausage with distaste.

"You will if you're hungry," he said easily.

"I'm not sure I'm *that* hungry."

He reached across for a slice. "It has hot peppers."

She still looked skeptical.

Joel bit into his slice, unconcerned. He was hungry, and there was no way he was going to order—much less eat—

something that had no meat on it. He was reaching for his second slice when he heard Riane's stomach growl.

She was eyeing the pizza more wistfully than skeptically now. He offered the slice to her. After a brief hesitation, she took it from his hands.

Joel indicated the two cans of ginger ale on the table. "I found a vending machine outside," he said. "You're probably thirsty."

She nodded, her mouth full of pizza. "Thanks," she said, after she'd swallowed.

He concentrated on his own slice, determined to look anywhere but at her, at all that tempting flesh exposed by her skimpy attire.

"I owe you an apology," Riane said softy.

"For criticizing my pizza?"

She managed a smile. "For calling you a lousy investigator. I guess you were closer to the truth than I wanted to admit."

Joel shrugged. "Forget it."

"I wish I could." She took another bite of pizza, then, "Why didn't you tell me you were married?"

He stiffened instinctively. "I'm not."

"Stuart did some investigating of his own," she admitted. "Trying to find out who you were and why you were interested in me—"

"If Stuart couldn't figure out why I was interested in you," Joel interrupted, "then he's a bigger idiot than I thought."

"He was right to be suspicious, though, wasn't he?"

Joel didn't respond.

"Anyway," Riane continued. "He gave me the file he'd compiled, including a copy of your wedding photo."

"Apparently the file wasn't up-to-date."

"What do you mean?"

"I'm divorced."

"Oh," she said again, a slight furrow marring her brow as she reached for another slice of pizza. "What happened?"

"My wife didn't like my being a cop," he told her. "She kept trying to convince me to go to work for her uncle, who had a security consulting business."

"I can understand why she wouldn't be thrilled by your choice of career," Riane told him. "But I'd have thought, if she loved you, she would have supported you in whatever you wanted to do."

"Obviously she didn't love me." He'd realized that fact soon after they were married. Too late to undo the damage that had already been done, and too soon to understand that they would hurt each other a lot more before they were through.

She'd married him, she admitted later, because her father had forbidden her to do so. It shouldn't have hurt him. It shouldn't have surprised him. It did both.

He wasn't sure he'd loved her, either, but he'd been awed that a woman of such class and sophistication would want him. And he'd cared for her, believing that their marriage would last, that their vows were forever.

"The irony of the whole situation," Joel admitted, "is that we split up when my career with the police department fell apart. We've been divorced for several years now."

Afterward, after the divorce was final and he was alone again, he'd realized he preferred it that way. None of the women who'd moved through his life had brought him anything but heartache and grief.

"Oh," was all Riane said.

"I should have realized it was doomed from the start."

"Why?"

He shrugged. "I was a cop—a bad boy in uniform. She was a college professor's daughter—wealthy, privileged, sheltered."

"You don't think class differences can be overcome?" she asked.

"I don't think we even tried," he admitted. "She wanted the grisly details of my cases to shock her high-society friends, but she never considered how my job affected me."

"I'm sorry," Riane said softly.

He shrugged again, wondering why he was even talking to her about his ex-wife. He'd never shared the details of his ill-fated marriage with anyone, and Riane hardly seemed a logical choice of confidante. Especially since she came from the same kind of wealthy, privileged background as his ex-wife.

On the other hand, maybe Riane was exactly the right person with whom to unburden his soul. After all, he knew everything there was to know about her, it only seemed fair that she be given some inside information about the man who'd destroyed her fairy-tale existence.

He gave himself a mental shake, as if to shake off the guilt that weighed heavily on his shoulders. He shouldn't feel guilty—he wasn't the one who'd lied to her for twenty-two years. But he hadn't been completely honest with her, either, and he refused to hide behind any more half truths. He needed her to know that she was more than a case to him.

"Despite the problems in my marriage—" and there were more than a few "—I never cheated on my wife. And I wouldn't have kissed you if I'd been involved with someone else."

She dropped her eyes, a faint blush staining her cheeks. He would like to think just the memory of those kisses caused her body to heat, but he couldn't rule out the residual effects of alcohol.

"Did you have any children?" she asked, reaching for her can of ginger ale.

"Thankfully, no."

"You don't like kids?"

"I don't have enough experience with them to really say one way or the other. I only meant that I'm glad we never had any. I hate to see what happens to them when a marriage falls apart."

She nodded and took another slice of pizza from the box. It was her third, and she'd devoured the previous two without a single additional complaint about the lack of artichoke hearts.

"Why didn't you leave me at the bar with Clint?" Riane asked, after the last of the pizza had been consumed and the empty box tossed aside.

"Because I didn't want to be responsible for you doing something I knew you'd regret."

"No one's responsible for me but me," she told him.

"You weren't yourself, sweetheart."

"You don't know me."

"Yes," he insisted. "I do. I know the kind of person you are, and I know it's not a habit of yours to go home with men you meet at bars."

"Is this something your investigation revealed?"

"No." He might have dug deeper into her background, he realized, except that he'd felt guilty for intruding as much as he already had. He wanted to know so much about her, but he wanted her to share the information. "I just know it's not you."

She laughed, bitterly. "How can you know the kind of person I am? I don't even know *who* I am."

"Finding out that your mother didn't give birth to you doesn't change the basic facts of who you are."

"It changes everything," she insisted. "Everything I've believed for more than twenty years has been a lie. I'm a fiction—a child they created. They even changed my date of birth."

"Why?" Joel was still puzzled by that bit of information.

"My mother said it was because they wanted to celebrate the day I came to them." Riane didn't sound convinced.

"You don't believe her?"

Riane shrugged. "She seems to have a ready answer for everything. How am I supposed to know what's fact and what's fantasy?"

"I'm not going to pretend I agree with, or even understand, what your parents did," Joel said. "But after talking to your mother today, the one thing I am sure of is that she loves you.''

Riane shrugged again, but he noticed the sheen of tears in her eyes. ''We've always been close. We never went through the usual mother-daughter difficulties. She's always been unquestioningly supportive, unfailingly understanding.''

''Because she loves you,'' Joel said again.

''If she really loved me, how could she lie to me?''

''She told you the truth now,'' Joel pointed out. ''Doesn't that count for something?''

''Maybe she just knew she couldn't keep it a secret much longer.''

''Do you really think that's what prompted her confession?''

Riane sighed. ''No,'' she admitted. ''I think she's genuinely sorry about what happened. The way it happened. But I don't know. I'm not sure I can trust my own feelings about any of this.''

''It's going to take some time to get used to,'' Joel agreed.

''I have a sister I know nothing about,'' she said, speaking almost to herself. ''Someone who apparently cared enough about me to want to find me all these years later, and I don't even remember her. What does that say about me?''

''It doesn't say anything about you. You weren't even two years old when you were adopted.''

''But shouldn't I have known? Shouldn't I have remembered something about the family I'd left behind?''

''You were a child,'' Joel said again. ''You can't take responsibility for everything upon yourself.''

Riane wanted to believe what Joel said was true. Logically, she knew that most people didn't have memories of anything prior to the age of five. But in her heart she felt as if she'd let her sister down by forgetting her. Especially when her sister obviously hadn't forgotten Riane.

She rubbed her fingers against her temple, trying to assuage the throbbing ache as she contemplated the complete upheaval of the past several hours. It was hard to believe that she'd only picked her parents up from the airport that morning. She felt as if she'd lived a lifetime in the interim.

Her parents. Ryan and Ellen. She knew they were probably worried about her, but she couldn't deal with them just yet. She didn't know what to say to them; she didn't know how any of them would handle the disclosures that had been made today. But she did know that if the truth about her parentage ever came to light, if the public ever found out that her mother had sworn false affidavits regarding Riane's birth, Ellen's political career would be over.

Somehow, thinking of her mother's political career brought to mind her own ambitions. And reminded her that the fairy-tale life she'd once envisioned with Stuart was no longer an option. It didn't matter that she'd already decided she couldn't marry him. Her concerns about their partnership were irrelevant now. There was no way Stuart would marry her with the lies of her past ticking like a time bomb, liable to blow up in all their faces at any moment. The truth hit her with the force of a prizefighter's blow. *She was alone.*

"Riane?"

She started when Joel's hand came down on her shoulder. She'd been so preoccupied with her thoughts, her own misery, that she'd forgotten for a moment that he was there. And she needed him now, she needed the comfort of his presence more than she'd needed anything else in her life.

"Are you okay?" he asked, his hand dropping off her shoulder to gently stroke her bare arm. The physical contact banished all other thoughts from her mind, and she turned her head to look at him. She could see the concern in his eyes. Concern…and something else she wasn't sure she recognized. Awareness, maybe. Desire.

Acting purely on instinct, she breached the scant distance that separated them and touched her lips to his. She couldn't have said which of them was more surprised by the boldness of her action. She'd never initiated a kiss with Joel before—

she'd always let him take the lead, as if doing so absolved her of responsibility. Because she'd been afraid.

The realization almost made her pull away. She was afraid of so many things: the emptiness inside her, the uncertainty of her future, the desires she'd never felt before she met Joel. And she was especially afraid that he'd walk out of her life tomorrow and she'd never know what it was like to make love with him.

It was that fear which bolstered her courage. She stroked her tongue over the seam of his lips, slipped inside the warmth of his mouth. He tasted spicy and hot, dangerously tempting.

She heard a low groan rumble in his throat, then she was on her back on the bed, Joel sprawled on top of her. He took control now, his kiss neither coaxing nor gentle this time. Instead he was insistent, demanding. Riane wrapped her arms around him and responded with a passion she hadn't known she possessed.

His hand inched upward along her thigh, his fingers burning a path against her skin.

She felt his hand slip under the edge of her camisole, glide over the skin of her abdomen. Then his hand was on her breast, his thumb teasing the nipple. She arched toward him, her hips rising off the mattress, her pelvis moving against his.

She heard him groan, felt the insistent thrust of his erection against the soft cleft between her thighs, and heat flooded her body. His mouth trailed hot, hungry kisses down her throat. She had never been kissed like this before. She'd never felt so desperately wanted, so desperately needed. She'd never wanted so much that she actually ached inside.

Then his mouth was on her breast, through the silky fabric of her top. His teeth grazed the nipple, sending sharp, hot currents to the very center of her being.

"Oh, Joel, please."

He pushed up her top, eliminating the barrier, and covered her breast with his mouth again. Riane couldn't think, she couldn't breathe. She was assaulted by sensations. Overwhelmed. Out of control. And yet, she wasn't afraid, because it was Joel.

She tugged his shirt out of his pants, wanting to touch him, taste him, explore. She ran her hands eagerly over the taut muscles of his abdomen, the wide, hard planes of his chest, the strong breadth of his shoulders. His skin was hot and damp. She pressed her lips to his shoulder, let her tongue savor the salty warmth of his skin. His low groan of pleasure encouraged her, and she skimmed her lips along the curve of his collarbone, nibbled at the base of his throat.

She let her hands skim down his torso, over the bulge at the front of his jeans. He groaned again. She stroked him through the denim, felt the pulsing response of his erection even through the fabric. She fumbled with the button of his jeans, slid her hand beneath the waistband of his briefs and wrapped her fingers around the hard length of him.

Joel groaned and removed her hand. He rolled onto his back, away from her, his breathing shallow and labored.

It wasn't quite the reaction Riane had hoped for.

She sat up, stunned and aching from his sudden withdrawal. "What's wrong?"

"We can't do this."

"Why not?"

"Why not?" he echoed, scrubbing his hands over his face. "I can think of a hundred reasons."

She straightened the front of her camisole, stung by his rejection, then pushed herself off the bed and walked over to the window. Tears burned her eyes, but she held them back. She wouldn't let him see her cry.

She jolted when his hands settled on her shoulders, hated that she had to fight the urge to lean into him as he stroked down her arms. How could she want him still? Was she so pathetically needy that she would turn to this man again, after he'd already turned her away?

"Your whole life has been turned upside down today," he said gently. "This isn't a good idea."

"Thanks for your input," she said shortly. "But I've been making my own decisions for a while now."

"I don't want to be something you'll regret."

She laughed, but there was no humor in it. "Don't worry about it, Logan."

"I care about you, Riane."

"Is that supposed to let me down easily?"

"You're completely misreading this situation."

"I don't think so."

He turned her to face him, his expression guarded and somehow dangerous. "Do you think I don't want you?"

"I'd think that's pretty obvious."

He hauled her into his arms again, banded his arms around her and covered her lips in a kiss that screamed of anger and frustration. This time she didn't question the desire. She couldn't. It was strong and fierce and all consuming.

But as quickly as he'd pulled her into his arms, he pushed her away. "I want you, Riane, but I don't want it to be like this."

Before she could respond, he was out the door.

And she was alone again.

Chapter 11

She was working at the café. It was exactly where he'd been told she'd be, and he was relieved that his information was accurate. Relieved to see that his wife was okay. And distressed to see her like this. Her beautiful long, dark hair chopped off. Her face pale and bare of makeup. Her slender figure clad in a short black skirt and a low-cut shirt. Serving meals. Cleaning dishes. Flirting with men who were looking down her top.

He felt the rage stir inside him.

Wantonness. Lust. Infidelity. He added to the list of sins for which she would have to atone.

Soon.

For now it was enough to watch. To know that she knew he was watching. And she did. In her heart, in her soul, she knew.

They were linked, after all. Inextricably bound by vows spoken in front of God. Vows that no package of papers delivered by a process server could eradicate.

She turned suddenly toward the window. Her dark eyes

wide, searching. She didn't see him. And she wouldn't recognize him if she did. Still, the coffeepot trembled in her hand.

His lips curved in a satisfied smile as he turned away.

She knew she was being watched.

For now that was enough.

Two days had passed since Riane had found out about her adoption. Two long days in which an uneasy tension had hovered over the Quinlan household like a storm cloud. Her relationship with her parents was strained. Maybe that was understandable, considering recent revelations, but it was unusual.

Would things ever return to the sense of normalcy that had existed before? Or would their family forever be tainted by the lies of the past? Riane had no answers to these questions and no one with whom to share her thoughts and her feelings. No one she could trust with such a secret.

She might have talked to Joel about the situation, but he'd hightailed it back to Pennsylvania after the night they'd spent in the motel. Or the night *she'd* spent in the motel. She still didn't know where, or even *if,* Joel had slept that night, and the short trip from the motel back to her home the following morning had been difficult, the unresolved sexual tension straining through the veneer of polite conversation.

She still blamed him for the upheaval in her life, but she missed him, anyway. He was the one person who knew the truth about her, the one person who hadn't seemed to care that she wasn't who she'd always believed herself to be.

Not knowing where else to turn or what else to do, she kept herself busy at the camp, watching over the construction, catching up on paperwork and doing anything else that would occupy her time. Unfortunately, it wasn't enough to occupy her mind.

So when she came in late on that second night and found her parents together, she shared with them the decision she'd made: "I'm going to Fairweather tomorrow."

"Good," Ryan said. Ellen just nodded.

"I don't know how long I'll be gone," Riane told them.

"Will you call?" Ellen asked.

Riane wanted to refuse, but she knew it would be petty to do so. Instead she nodded.

Ellen forced a smile. "I'm glad you're going."

"Are you?" Riane asked, a deliberate note of challenge in her voice.

"Of course."

"Why?"

Ellen slipped her hand inside her husband's larger one, linking their fingers together. It was a subtle but unmistakable gesture of solidarity, and Riane didn't so much resent it as she resented no longer feeling as if she was a part of that cohesive unit. Since the truth about her parentage had come to light, she'd felt more isolated and alone than ever.

"Because we know you won't stop wondering until you've met your sister," Ryan told her.

"Aren't you worried that I might find something with her that's been missing from my life?"

Riane got no satisfaction from seeing the pain she'd deliberately sought to inflict reflected in her parents' eyes.

"We've thought about almost nothing else since we found out you had a sister," Ellen confessed.

"Then why do you want me to go?"

"Because we've been incredibly selfish for twenty-two years. Because we believe this is something you need to do for you."

"For me?" Riane challenged. "Or for you? Won't it assuage some of your own guilt if I reconnect with the sister I lost?"

"Maybe," the senator acknowledged. "And maybe you've been so dissatisfied your whole life because there's a part of you that hasn't forgotten her."

Riane wanted to believe that could be true, but she'd racked her brain searching for some memory—anything—

that would give her a hint about her sister. Always without success.

"What about my biological parents?" Riane taunted. "Maybe I should look them up, too. We could have a real family reunion."

Ellen paled noticeably, but it was Ryan who responded. "That's enough, Riane." His tone was sharp, commanding. "We know you're hurt and angry, but you don't ever speak to your mother that way."

It was on the tip of Riane's tongue to snap back that Ellen wasn't her mother, but she was tired of the fighting and she knew that hurting her parents wouldn't resolve anything.

Ellen put her other hand on her husband's arm. "If you want to find your biological parents, that's your choice."

Riane sighed wearily. "I don't know what I want anymore."

"Do you want us to go to Fairweather with you?"

The offer shouldn't have surprised her. It did. And what surprised her even more was the urge to accept the offer, to let her parents take control and make everything better—as they always had when she was a child. But she wasn't a child anymore, and this was a journey she had to make on her own.

"Thanks, but I think I need to do this alone."

Ellen nodded, as if she understood. And she probably did. She'd always known what was in her daughter's heart—sometimes before Riane did herself. The realization made Riane feel both petty and ungrateful. She'd been difficult and confrontational since she'd learned of her adoption; her parents had continued to be loving and supportive.

So why couldn't she just forget that she had another family somewhere? Why was she so preoccupied with finding a sister she didn't even remember?

She wasn't sure of the answers to these questions, she only knew that she had to go to Fairweather.

* * *

Now that she was in Fairweather, Riane had no idea how to take the next step.

She drove through the town, propelled by curiosity and indecision, and she was amazed at how much the town reminded her of Mapleview. The tree-lined streets, the classic architecture, the tidy little shops, the friendliness of passersby. Despite the fact that it was more than twice the size of her hometown, it had a similar, welcoming feel. It unnerved her, that someplace she'd never been could feel so much like home.

She parked in front of the Fairweather Courthouse—a beautiful building highlighted with towering white pillars and gleaming, multifaceted windows. Still, she knew it wasn't the architecture that had drawn her to the location, but the possibility that Arden might be inside.

Joel had told her that Arden was a family law attorney, engaged to a criminal defense attorney. She didn't know much more than that, and she wasn't sure where to look or even if she was ready to find Arden. She probably wouldn't recognize her, anyway. The only picture she had of her sister was the one Joel had given to her—a picture taken almost twenty-two years earlier. But she ventured inside and wandered through the halls.

She followed a group of people as they filed back into one of the courtrooms. When the proceedings resumed, Riane quickly realized that Arden was one of the lawyers at the front of the room. The judge never called her by name; the woman never turned around. But somehow Riane knew, and she found it a little disconcerting that she'd happened into this particular room, almost as if drawn by a will stronger than her own.

Determined to banish such nonsensical thoughts from her mind, Riane slipped out before the arguments were finished. The halls were quieter now, and she leaned back against the stone wall and wondered at the fate that had sent her into that courtroom—and the cowardice that had sent her out again.

"Riane?"

She turned, then chastised herself for doing so. She didn't know anyone in this town. The man who had spoken must have been speaking to someone else. But Riane wasn't a very common name, and the speaker was coming straight toward her.

"Riane Quinlan?"

She hesitated briefly. "Yes."

"Shaun McIver." He held his hand out to her, and she accepted it automatically.

It took her a minute to place the name. Shaun McIver was the man who was engaged to marry Arden. The man who had sent Joel to find her. "How did you know who I was?"

"You're kidding, right?"

She frowned.

"The resemblance between you and Arden is unmistakable."

Riane wasn't comfortable knowing she looked so much like the sister she couldn't remember that this stranger had picked her out of a crowd. Okay, so it was a small crowd, but a crowd nonetheless.

"Did you see her?" Shaun asked.

"No. I mean, I think she was in the courtroom, but I didn't talk to her."

"Isn't that why you're here?"

"No, um, I was just passing through."

"Oh." He made no effort to mask his disappointment. "I thought—I hoped—that you'd come to see her. Us."

Riane sighed. "I'm not really sure why I'm here."

"Oh." This time he smiled, as if he understood. "Do you have time for a cup of coffee?"

She glanced at her watch, desperately scrambling for an excuse as to why she didn't have the time, but her brain seemed to have shut down.

"All right," she agreed.

Joel replaced the receiver in its cradle, staring at it warily for several long seconds after he'd terminated the connection.

His instincts were in overdrive again, and he wasn't sure if it was a result of the phone call he'd just completed or because that phone call had brought Riane to mind again.

Again. As if he'd ever stopped thinking about her.

He hadn't seen or heard from her since the morning after the night they'd spent in that dreary little motel room. The night they hadn't made love. The night he'd wished he could go back to ever since and play things differently.

He still believed he'd done the right thing. She'd been vulnerable, half-drunk, and almost engaged to Stuart Etherington III. But he was damn tired of doing the right thing. What he'd wanted to do, what he still wanted to do, was hold her in his arms and spend hours making love with her.

But that wasn't a likely scenario. He'd done his job. His client was satisfied, and Joel had other cases to focus on. But Riane was never far from his thoughts.

Which was why that telephone call bothered him. What possible information could Gavin Elliott have that would be relevant to an assignment already completed?

Still, Joel hated to think that he might have left any stone unturned. Ever since the fiasco that had ended his career with the police department, he'd been diligent in crossing every *t* and dotting every *i*. So he would attend the proposed meeting, and he would find out what the hell was going on.

He made some notes in another file, reviewed the report on a domestic surveillance case and kept himself busy until the sun was finally setting. Mike had left hours ago, but Joel wasn't in a hurry to return to his empty home.

He'd been content with his life before he'd met Riane. After the time he'd spent with her in West Virginia, his life seemed empty somehow. Rationally, he knew nothing had changed. Everything was exactly the way it had been before he'd ever taken that trip. His office was the same. His house was the same—although his houseplants had been in desperate need of watering, his lawn in need of mowing...

The thoughts trailed off as a knock sounded at his door.

He glanced up, surprised that anyone would stop by at this hour. His surprise turned to disbelieving pleasure when he saw Riane in the doorway. He blinked, not certain if she was really there or if his mind had conjured up her image. And what an image: she was wearing a dark purple dress of some clingy fabric that molded to the curve of her breasts—soft, creamy breasts that had filled his palms, centered with luscious pink nipples that responded eagerly to his touch—

"Hello, Joel."

The sound of her voice yanked him out of his reverie, but the blood continued to hum in his veins. "Hi."

"I wasn't sure if you'd still be here," she admitted.

"I had some things to finish up," he said inanely. He wanted to go to her, touch her, but he wasn't sure how she'd respond. Things had been awkward between them the morning after the night at the motel. And he didn't know why she was here, what she was doing in Fairweather.

Riane just nodded.

The silence stretched between them. Tense and uneasy.

"What are you doing here?" he asked at last.

"I was in town." She shrugged, as if her being in town was a usual occurrence. "I thought, if you didn't have other plans, maybe we could have dinner together."

"Tonight?"

She nodded.

"No plans." He closed the file he'd been studying, shoved it on top of the pile on his desk. If he'd had any plans, they were forgotten the moment she appeared in his doorway.

"There's a great Italian restaurant just a few blocks down," Joel told her, finally rising from behind his desk and moving toward her. "We could walk from here."

"That sounds good," Riane decided.

"Okay." He indulged his need to touch her by taking her elbow and guiding her out of the office. He locked up the building.

She walked quietly beside him as he turned onto Queen

Street. "I wasn't sure I'd ever hear from you again," Joel said. "You didn't even say goodbye the last time I saw you."

She smiled wryly. "I suppose I owe you an apology for that. I was hurt and I was angry, and I shouldn't have taken it out on you." She twisted the strap of her purse around her hand, not looking at him.

"I needed you that night. You made me feel things I'd never felt before. Want things I'd never wanted. And when I realized you didn't want me…" Her words trailed off, she lifted a shoulder in a half shrug. "I was hurt. I felt as though I'd been rejected all over again."

"Wait a minute, sweetheart." Joel took hold of her elbow again, forcing her to stop and look at him. "What do you mean, I didn't want you?"

Riane shrugged. "I thought it was pretty self-explanatory."

"How could you possibly think I didn't want you?"

"You wouldn't make love with me. You walked away."

"I walked away because I had to, and it sure as hell wasn't easy. You were engaged to another man."

"I told you that was over," she said, frowning.

"But you hadn't told *him.*"

"So you walked out on me because you were concerned about Stuart's feelings?"

He didn't give a damn about Stuart Etherington III, he never had. "I was concerned about yours. Your life had just been turned upside down. You didn't know what you wanted."

"I wanted *you,*" she said again.

Just the words heated his blood. "You didn't want to be alone," Joel corrected gently, "and I was there."

"Do you think I would have made love with just anyone that night?"

"I didn't know. And I hated to think that you would regret it in the morning."

She shrugged again and continued walking. "It doesn't

matter now, anyway. Nothing happened. There's no reason for either of us to regret anything.''

''I have regrets,'' Joel admitted, falling into step beside her again.

''About what?''

''About not making love with you.''

Riane turned her head, her dark eyes wide. Surprised. Questioning.

''Every night since then, I've lain alone in my bed, thinking about you. Thinking about what might have happened. Wondering why my conscience suddenly decided to make an appearance when I wanted nothing more than to be with you.''

''If you'd really wished things were different, you could have called,'' she reminded him.

''I wanted to call,'' he told her. ''I can't tell you how many times I picked up the phone. But I didn't think you'd want to hear from me.''

''Why?''

''Because I was responsible for all the upheaval in your life.''

''I can't argue with that.''

''As long as you're not still holding a grudge,'' Joel said dryly.

Riane smiled. ''I'm not.''

Their conversation paused when they entered the restaurant and waited to be escorted to their table. Riane ordered the angel-hair primavera, Joel the chicken parmigiana.

''I'm glad you came by,'' Joel said, after the waiter had delivered their drinks.

''Me, too. And I'm glad we cleared the air…about that night.''

''Did we?'' Joel wondered. He wasn't sure they'd accomplished anything except to stir up already vivid memories. Memories of Riane stretched out beneath him on that narrow bed, her skin soft and warm beneath his hands, her body writhing in response to his touch.

Riane picked up her glass of wine. "I thought so."

"What's the situation with you and Stuart?" he asked, needing to know, even if the answer wasn't what he wanted to hear.

"It's over."

He studied her for a moment, wondering about the complete lack of emotion in her response. She didn't sound heartbroken, but maybe she was just hiding her emotions. "Are you sorry?"

"No. Sad, a little, that our relationship didn't mean more to either one of us. He didn't want to accept it at first, but when I hinted that I might be a political liability, he didn't ask any more questions."

The man was an even bigger idiot than Joel had given him credit for being. Regardless of her parentage, Riane was an incredible woman, and Stuart Etherington III obviously wasn't worthy of her. Of course, a bastard child from the wrong side of town could never be worthy of her, either, but Joel wasn't going to think about that now.

"What did your parents say about it?" he asked instead.

"Not too much," she admitted. "They try not to interfere in my personal life, although I know my mother was relieved. She's always been fond of Stuart, but she knew—maybe even before I did—that I wasn't in love with him. She wanted more for me than a political alliance."

"She really does love you."

She nodded. "I know."

"Then you've come to terms with everything?"

"I'm starting to. That's one of the reasons I'm here. I think I want to meet my..." The words trailed off, as if she had trouble saying *sister,* acknowledging the relationship she had with a woman she couldn't remember. "I want to meet Arden."

"Have you contacted her yet?"

"No." She sipped her wine. "But I met her fiancé today."

"How did that happen?"

"Unintentionally."

"And?" he prompted.

"He invited us to dinner tomorrow night."

"Us?"

"Well, me," she admitted. "But he said I could bring a friend. I'm hoping you'll come with me. I-I'm not sure I can go…alone."

"You can," he assured her. "But I'll go with you, if you really want me to."

"Thank you."

Then their dinner arrived, and conversation moved to more neutral topics while they ate. They both refused dessert but accepted the offer of coffee.

"How do you know Shaun?" Riane stirred cream into her cup.

"I've done some investigative work for his law firm in the past," Joel admitted. "Including trying to find the man who was stalking Arden."

"When? What happened?"

"It started just about a year ago. She was getting threatening letters. Then her apartment was torched and a bomb was planted in her office."

"Did you find whoever was responsible?"

"I confirmed who it was. Shaun saved her. Actually, they saved each other. It's a long story," he said. "You'll have to ask her if you want the details."

"And the stalker?"

"A guest at the Lakewood Psychiatric Facility."

Riane shook her head. "I think maybe I should be grateful for my nice boring life."

"I don't think anyone would consider your life boring," Joel mused. "But if you wanted to shake it up a little…"

He let his words trail off, deliberately enticing her.

"What did you have in mind?"

"There's a new country-western bar that we passed on the way here. It just opened a few weeks ago."

Riane grimaced. "Country-western wouldn't be my first choice."

''I don't know,'' he teased. ''It brings back pretty good memories for me.''

''My memories of that night are definitely mixed.''

''Then let's make some better ones,'' he said, pushing his chair away from the table.

Chapter 12

The only thing country-western about the bar Joel took Riane to was the music. There were no horns mounted on the walls, no Stetsons, no cowboy boots. Most of the patrons appeared to be white-collar businessmen just wanting to unwind with a drink or two after a long day at the office, or women in search of such men.

They found a small table on the perimeter of the dance floor and nursed their drinks and watched the crowd mingle. The volume of music made conversation difficult, but Riane didn't mind. She was just grateful for his presence. Grateful for the fact that she wasn't staring at the walls of her hotel room and contemplating the mysteries of her life.

Joel leaned closer. So close she could practically feel the heat radiating from his body. She could still remember the texture of his skin beneath her palms, the warm, musky scent of it. She swallowed, her throat suddenly dry.

"Shall we dance?" he asked.

His voice was low, his breath warm on her cheek.

Riane nodded, even while her heart warned her that it

would be a mistake. But she couldn't resist the opportunity to get closer, to feel his arms around her.

She should have heeded the warning from her subconscious. As soon as he touched her, she was lost. His hand scorched her skin through the fabric of her dress, bringing to mind all-too-vivid memories of the feel of those hard, wide palms on her bare flesh. His thighs, solid and strong, brushed against her, reminding her how they'd clamped down on either side of her hips, holding her immobile while he'd done all kinds of delicious things to her body.

"Relax, sweetheart." He murmured the words gently, his warm breath fluttering the wisps of hair at her temple.

She was trying to relax, but with every second, every movement, her awareness heightened. Her heart was pounding so loudly she couldn't hear the song being played. It was different from the first time they'd danced. So much had happened since that first night. So much had changed. The desire she'd felt from the very beginning was still there, but stronger now. Fueled by the knowledge of his kiss, the memory of his touch.

Still, despite her own yearning, she felt safe in his arms. Protected. She wasn't exactly sure why she felt that way, or why she welcomed the feeling. She'd always prided herself on her independence. She needed to know that she could stand on her own. But his hold didn't restrain, it supported. His strength didn't make her feel weak, only cherished.

She tilted her head to look up at him. His eyes held hers for a long moment, intent, searching, then his gaze dropped to her lips. Riane's breath caught in her throat. Excitement tingled inside her as she waited for his kiss. Waited with breathless anticipation, mounting desire.

But he didn't kiss her.

He pulled back abruptly. "I think we should be going."

"Oh. Okay," she agreed, trying to mask her disappointment.

He took her hand to guide her through the maze of patrons as they exited the bar. The air had cooled a little since they'd first left the hotel, but it was a pleasant evening to walk. Still she shivered when Joel let go of her hand, acutely conscious of the loss of warmth from his touch.

She folded her arms over her chest. "Thank you for tonight," she said.

"I had a good time," Joel said.

Riane nodded. "I wasn't sure if I should stop by your office today. I know it was last minute. You might have had other plans." She knew she was babbling, but she didn't seem able to stop. She didn't know what it was about Joel that unnerved her so much.

"Other plans? You mean a date?" He chuckled.

"Why is that funny?"

He shook his head. "To be honest, tonight is the closest I've come to a date in a long time."

"Oh." She was surprised by this revelation, and strangely pleased. "Why?"

"I don't know. Lack of interest, maybe."

"Still mourning the failure of your marriage?" she suggested.

"Hardly. My marriage was over long before the divorce papers were signed."

"Because of your job?" she prompted.

"Because my wife was sleeping with my partner's husband."

Riane stopped in the middle of the sidewalk and turned to stare at him. "You're kidding?"

"Unfortunately, I'm not." He stuffed his hands into the pockets of his jeans and resumed walking.

"Is that the reason you're so adamant about not becoming involved with anyone who's otherwise committed?"

"One of the reasons," he agreed. "Unfortunate personal experience and a general belief that extramarital affairs are in poor taste. If a relationship is that bad, get out of it."

"Would you…" She hesitated, knowing she had no right to ask the question, but curious anyway.

"Would I what?"

"Would you ever get married again?"

He was silent for a long minute. "I didn't used to think so," he admitted, then shrugged. "But maybe."

Riane wasn't sure what she expected him to say, and she couldn't have said why she was disappointed by his response. But she was, and that unnerved her enough that she decided not to pursue the topic any further.

"Here's your hotel," Joel said.

"Oh." Riane just stood there, staring up at the building and feeling awkward. She could feel Joel shift on his feet beside her, knew he was probably anxious to get back to his own place, but she didn't want to be alone. Not yet.

"Do you want to come in for a drink? Or a cup of coffee?"

Joel shook his head. "I don't think that's a good idea."

"Oh. Okay." She nodded.

He started to step away, hesitated. "Are you going to be okay?"

She forced a smile. Strong and independent, she reminded herself. "Sure."

Joel sighed, wondering why he wasn't able to walk away from her when he knew it was the smart thing to do. "Did you want me to come up for a while?"

Riane turned back to him, her deep brown eyes pleading. God, he was such a sucker for her eyes. "Would you?"

No. *Absolutely not.* The last thing he needed was further stimulation of his fantasies by accompanying Riane to her hotel room. As if the night they'd spent in that shabby motel wasn't torture enough on his libido. But when he opened his mouth, the response that came out was "Sure."

She fell silent again on the ride up to the seventh floor in the elevator. She was probably having second thoughts about inviting him up to her room. And she should be. He'd told her he had regrets about not making love with her before; she had to know how much he still wanted her.

"I know this is going to sound ridiculous," Riane admitted, stepping through the door of her hotel room. "But I don't like being alone. Since I found out about my childhood, I..."

Her words trailed off, her cheeks flushed.

Joel closed the door behind him and moved toward her. He cupped her cheek in his hand, tilted her head so that she had to meet his eyes. "Tell me," he said softly.

"I've been having nightmares," she confessed. "I wake up in a panic, not knowing where I am, who I am."

"I'm sure that's a natural reaction, considering everything you've been through."

"Maybe. And as soon as I open my eyes and recognize my surroundings, I'm okay. But..."

"But nothing's familiar here," he guessed.

She nodded.

"Do you want me to stay with you?" If he'd thought about it, he never would have made such an offer. But the words were out of his mouth before his brain had clicked into gear, and when Riane turned those big brown eyes on him and nodded in gratitude, he was lost.

"Come on," he said, taking her by the hand.

"Where?"

"To bed."

Her eyes widened.

Joel chuckled, even while his hormones were raging at his insanity. "I'm going to lie down with you, not attack you," he told her.

"Oh."

He led her over to the king-size bed that dominated the room. The bed that had been the focus of his attention since he'd walked through the door behind Riane and laid eyes on it. Now, as she willingly followed him, his treacherous mind conjured erotic images of Riane and him rolling over on that mattress, naked, sweaty, panting. He nearly groaned aloud as he desperately tried to banish the images. But his body was on full alert and he didn't know how he was going to get through this night.

"Can I put my pajamas on?" Riane asked as he pulled back the covers.

Joel hesitated, remembering the skimpy camisole top and high-cut panties she'd worn at the budget motel. But that was because she didn't have anything else, and the word *pajamas* brought to mind images of warm, bulky flannel.

"Sure," he agreed, feeling magnanimous. Pajamas had to cover more skin than the dress she was wearing. And he intended to tuck her safely away under the covers, anyway. For his own sanity and self-preservation, he'd sleep on top.

She tugged something out of her suitcase and disappeared into the bathroom.

Joel stretched out on top of the bed and stared at the ceiling, waiting for her to return, envisioning a more enjoyable end to the evening than Riane sleeping peacefully beside him. The images came back with a vengeance: naked, sweaty, panting.

Unfortunately, Riane had made it clear that her interest in him was in the past tense. *I wanted you,* she'd said. Not *want,* but *wanted.* And she'd assured him she had no regrets about that night, about not making love.

He'd never regretted anything more. To hell with his own moral code—she hadn't really been engaged to Stuart. To hell with the rules of consent—she may have been drunk, but she wasn't too drunk to throw herself at him.

Joel sighed and scrubbed a hand over his face, razor stubble rasping against his palm. Yes, he had regrets. He also knew that if he could go back to that night, he'd walk away again. Because he cared about her too much to take advantage of the situation. And that, he knew, would be his downfall. Caring was a weakness; caring for someone like Riane was complete folly. He'd learned that lesson from his ex-wife.

He'd been attracted to Jocelyn, flattered that she'd reciprocated his interest. But when the passion had waned, there had been nothing left. Nothing but bitterness and regrets.

He pushed the memories aside. It was easier to do now.

Jocelyn was part of a past he didn't care to remember, and time and distance had healed the wounds—or most of them, anyway. The pain of those that remained had dulled enough to be tolerable.

He heard the click of the door as Riane stepped out of the bathroom, and all thoughts of his ex-wife were vanquished from his mind.

Maybe, technically, what she was wearing were pajamas, but they were neither bulky nor flannel. The top was less than a camisole, the neckline plunging, the thin straps crossing over her bare back. The bottoms were long, but they sat low on her hips, exposing a tantalizing few inches of creamy skin and the darker hollow of her navel. He wasn't sure what the outfit was made of, except that the material was flimsy and silky and clung enticingly to her curves.

He forced his jaw shut, swallowed. "All set?"

Riane nodded.

"Okay, then." He patted the empty space on the bed beside him. "Let's get some sleep."

Thankfully, it didn't seem to take her long to drift off. But when she rolled over and pillowed her head on his chest, Joel's hopes of getting any shut-eye diminished. It was torture to have her in his arms and not be able to touch her, to watch the rise and fall of her breasts beneath that skimpy top and remember the weight of them in his palms, to listen to her soft, even breathing and recall her throaty moans and whimpers.

He tried to move away, hoping that a little physical distance might cool the heat raging through his body, but the hand she'd tucked under her cheek fisted in his shirt, as if to hold on to him. And Joel resigned himself to staying awake—and aroused—for the duration of the night.

He considered reneging on his promise and just getting the hell out of her hotel room, but he couldn't forget the way she'd looked at him. The embarrassment when she'd admitted to the nightmares. The undisguised gratitude when he'd offered to stay. No one had ever looked at him like that—like he was some kind of hero.

He'd never wanted anyone to look at him like that; he'd never wanted anyone to need him. But he wanted to be there for Riane. He wanted her to know that she could depend on him. He wanted a lot of things where Riane was concerned, and they were all out of his reach.

The circumstances of her adoption had brought them together, but there was nothing to hold them there. She was the cherished daughter in a family of wealth and privilege; he'd grown up in a loveless and impoverished home. She thrived in the spotlight; he abhorred it. There was no way their pasts could be reconciled, no hope for a future together.

He should get out of here—out of her hotel room, out of her life. So what if he'd promised to go to her sister's with her tomorrow? So what if she was depending on him for moral support? He needed to start thinking about self-preservation, because he knew if he spent any more time with Riane, he could fall in love with her. Hell, he was already halfway there.

No, there was no way he could allow that to happen. He had to step back, step away, and never look back. And he would.

Tomorrow.

Riane was relieved when they arrived at Shaun and Arden's house the following afternoon and found there were others in attendance for the barbecue. Arden's cousin, Nikki, and Nikki's husband, Colin—who also happened to be Shaun's brother. And Nikki and Colin's children: Carly, a darling six-and-a-half year old girl, and Justin, a chubby-cheeked little boy who wasn't yet six weeks old.

The boisterous interaction awed Riane just a little. It had been just herself and her parents for so long that she didn't know what to say or do. She felt confident that she could hold her own in any discussion about global politics, but she didn't know the first thing about family dynamics.

Still, everyone made an effort to draw her into the conversation, and Joel was careful not to venture too far from her side. She hated that she needed the reassurance of his presence, and yet she found such immense comfort in his nearness. She'd been working crowds at political functions for years, accustomed to mixing with acquaintances or strangers. But these were people she should know; this was her family.

Carly was a blessing. The child took to Riane immediately, and Riane enjoyed listening to her animated chatter. It was easy to relate to her because she wasn't worried about the little girl's preconceptions and expectations.

Arden, on the other hand, baffled her completely. The elegant professional woman she'd witnessed in court the previous day had dissolved into tears when she'd seen Riane and Joel on the doorstep. Riane had backed away instinctively, having no idea how to respond.

Arden had excused herself tearfully.

"She wasn't sure you'd really come," Shaun said by way of explanation.

And then he'd taken Riane's hands in both of his and kissed her on the cheek. "Thank you."

And that simply, Riane had felt herself drawn—willingly or not—into the chaos that was the McIver family.

A family barbecue, Riane quickly realized, was nothing like a formal evening at the country club. There was plenty of laughter, an abundance of food and a ton of chaos. Conversation flowed as freely as the wine and left Riane equally dizzy. She was glad she'd agreed to come, and relieved that Joel was with her. His was the only familiar face within this group of strangers, and she was comforted by his presence. At least until his thigh brushed against hers under the table, and comfort shifted to awareness to desire.

When Carly piped up from the other end of the table asking for a Popsicle, Riane was quick to offer to get it for her. She'd just sent the child back outside with her coveted cherry treat when Arden came in. It was a decidedly awkward moment as the two sisters faced each other without interference.

Riane cleared her throat, searching for something to say. Something that might, perhaps, break through the polite facade that had governed their interaction.

"Dinner was great," she ventured at last, unable to come up with anything more substantial.

"Good. I mean, I'm glad you enjoyed it. Shaun picked up the steaks, but I know a lot of health-conscious people avoid red meat these days, although try to explain that to a meat-and-potatoes kind of man."

It was while listening to Arden babble about the meal they'd already consumed that Riane considered something she hadn't before: Arden was just as nervous about this meeting as she was. While the realization didn't alleviate any of her own apprehension, it did, at least, level the playing field a little. And it gave her the courage to cut through the polite distance they'd respected throughout the afternoon.

"This is awkward, isn't it?" she asked.

Arden nodded. "I expected it would be, and yet I hoped it wouldn't."

"I'm not sure I understand why you were looking for me, what you expected," Riane admitted.

"I don't know what I expected, either," Arden told her. "I mean, twenty-two years is a long time, and you were little more than a baby the last time I saw you."

"I don't remember you," Riane confessed.

Arden's smile was obviously strained. "The logical part of my brain knows you couldn't. The emotional part wishes you did."

"Why were you looking for me? Why now?"

"That was Shaun's doing," Arden admitted. "Not that I didn't want to find you. But I was afraid."

"Of what?"

Arden folded her hands in front of her, toyed with the large square-cut-solitaire diamond ring on the third finger of her left hand. "I was afraid you'd hate me."

This revelation stunned Riane. Whatever she'd expected, it hadn't been that Arden would be haunted by any of the same doubts and insecurities that plagued her. "Why would I hate you?"

"Because I left you."

"I don't understand," Riane said. "I thought I was the one who was adopted."

Arden nodded. "I guess you don't know as much about everything as I thought you did."

"My parents—my adoptive parents," she amended, "have answered all my questions. But maybe I haven't been asking all of the right ones."

"We share the same mother," Arden told her. "My father died when I was four, and our mother married your father about a year later.

"Our family life wasn't very pleasant. Gavin—your father—was abusive. Verbally at first, but it soon escalated to physical violence. It got worse when our mother got pregnant with you. There's no need to go into all the details," Arden said, "but my aunt—Nikki's mother, my father's sister— came to visit for my ninth birthday. She recognized that it wasn't a healthy environment, and she convinced our mother to let me go live with her.

"She wanted to take you, too," Arden said. "Although I didn't know that at the time. I only remember her telling me that I was going to live with her from now on, and I cried and cried. I didn't want to leave you. I didn't want him to do to you what he'd done—" She shook her head, as if to dislodge the memory, and Riane's stomach churned as her mind thought of countless ways to finish the incomplete thought—none of them pleasant.

"Anyway," Arden continued, her lips curving slightly in response to a happier memory, "I had this doll. It was the last gift my father ever gave me. A beautiful doll with long dark curls and big blue eyes. She was my most prized possession, and you used to look at her and say 'pwetty.'"

Riane shifted, a little embarrassed to hear stories of her

childhood from a woman she didn't remember. Memories she couldn't share.

"When I left, I gave that doll to you. I wanted you to have something to remember me by."

"Ohmygod." Riane clapped her hand over her mouth, stunned. "Eden."

Arden looked at her strangely. "Eden?"

"That's what I called her—I must have been trying to say 'Arden,' but everyone thought it was 'Eden.' I called the doll Eden."

Arden smiled. "You remember it?"

"I still have it."

Riane watched her sister's eyes fill with tears and felt her own throat tighten. She'd been so sure there was nothing left between them, no connection. But she was no longer so certain. The doll she was referring to was old and worn, but she'd still held on to it. After all these years she still had that doll—the doll her sister had given to her.

"I'm glad you kept it," Arden told her.

"I never understood why I was so attached to it," she admitted. "I remember packing up my room as I was getting ready to go away to law school and thinking that maybe it was time to give her up. But I just couldn't do it."

"You went to law school, too?"

Riane shrugged. "It seems to be a family tradition."

"Your parents must be really proud of you."

"Yeah, I think they are." She hesitated, then finally asked the question she hadn't been able to bring herself to ask of anyone else. "Do you have any contact with my biological parents?"

Arden shook her head. "No. Not since—no."

Riane nodded.

"Ask."

"Ask what?"

"Whatever's on your mind but you think you shouldn't."

Riane smiled. "You're very perceptive."

"Being able to read people is an important part of my job."

"You're very good at your job," Riane said.

Arden looked startled.

"I saw you in court yesterday," she explained.

"It's easy when you're always on the side of truth and justice." She grinned. "It's something Shaun and I often disagree about."

Riane laughed, starting to feel a little less awkward.

"You haven't asked yet," Arden reminded her.

"I'm not sure I want to know."

"About our family," Arden guessed.

Riane nodded. "I feel disloyal to my parents—my adoptive parents—"

Arden waved off the proviso. "They are your parents in every way that counts."

"I'm curious," Riane admitted. "About the people who contributed to my DNA. On the other hand, I know I wouldn't have been taken out of their home if they'd been good parents."

"I don't know why they did the things they did, why they made the choices they made. All I can tell you is that I was relieved to know that you didn't have to grow up with them."

"When I first learned I'd been adopted, I just wanted to pretend it wasn't true," Riane confessed. "I was happy with the life I have in West Virginia, with my parents."

"I'm glad you're happy," Arden said sincerely.

"I'm glad you found me," Riane told her.

Arden's smile was luminous. "Me, too."

Somehow Joel found himself back in Riane's hotel room after driving her home from the barbecue. He had every intention of dropping her at the door, but when she'd looked at him with those big, dark eyes and asked if he wanted to come up for coffee—well, he suddenly had an undeniable craving for coffee.

Just coffee, he promised himself as Riane dumped the prepackaged grounds into the coffee filter. One cup and then he was out of there. No way could his body survive another night like the last one.

"Did you have a good time at Arden and Shaun's?" Joel asked.

Riane flicked the switch, set the coffee brewing, and nodded. "Thank you."

"I enjoyed myself," he told her. And he had, despite the flak he'd taken from Shaun about being the "friend" Riane had invited. Even if he'd known that Shaun would question the relationship between his investigator and his soon-to-be sister-in-law, as he should have, he wouldn't have refused to go. Riane had needed a friend, and he'd needed to be there for her.

"The whole family seems very well integrated," she said.

Integrated. Joel smiled. "You fit in well with them, too."

She seemed surprised, but pleased by his observation. "I liked them. All of them."

"Why does that surprise you?"

"I've never made friends easily."

"You didn't seem to have any trouble making the rounds at your charity ball," he pointed out.

"That's different," she explained. "Most of those people aren't friends, they're acquaintances. It's superficial interaction. It's harder with people who could really matter."

"Why?"

She turned away as the coffee finished brewing. She poured two cups, passed one to him.

"I've led a pretty sheltered life. It's not just that my parents were protective, which they were, but I didn't have much privacy. Every family outing was a media event. As a child I didn't mind, really, because I didn't know any different. But as I got older, it made it difficult to cultivate any kind of personal relationships. So I didn't date much through high school, and never anyone exclusively.

"I didn't get my first real taste of freedom until law school.

I met Cameron Davis in my first year. He was a year ahead of me—smart, popular, incredibly sexy.''

"Feel free to edit out any unnecessary details," Joel interrupted dryly.

Riane smiled. "Well, he was. He was the kind of guy every girl wanted to date—and he wanted to date me. I was twenty years old at the time—probably the oldest living American virgin, and determined to change that status.

"And then I found out…I'm still not sure whether or not it was deliberate, but my roommate let it slip that Cameron wanted to get naked pictures of me to sell to the tabloids."

Joel felt all the protective instincts he'd never known he had stir to life inside him.

"He'd never really been interested in me." Riane plunged ahead with the story, but he could tell she was still hurt by this betrayal. "He just wanted to take advantage of who I was to make a quick buck."

"He didn't deserve you," Joel told her.

"I know that now," she agreed. "At the time, though, I was hurt. Angry. Humiliated. I couldn't believe that I'd been so naive. And I was horrified to think how devastating that could have been to my mother's career. I decided, then and there, that if I was ever going to become involved with someone else, it would have to be someone with a similar background and similar interests.

"That same year, when I came home for Christmas vacation, I met Stuart. He was everything Cameron wasn't. He didn't sweep me off my feet or fulfill any kind of romantic fantasies, but I wasn't looking for anything like that after my recent relationship disaster."

Joel shifted uncomfortably. He didn't want to hear the details of her relationship with Stuart Etherington III, but for some reason she felt compelled to share them.

"We started dating. Stuart took me to the finest restaurants and private showings at art galleries and opening nights at the theater. We had a lot in common despite the age difference, and there were no sloppy kisses, no groping, no pressure. There was also no excitement or spontaneity, but I didn't mind.

"And then I met you," Riane said. "And I realized that kisses didn't have to be sloppy, touching wasn't always groping, and I knew that I wanted something more than what I'd previously been willing to settle for."

She lifted her cup to her lips, sipped. "In some ways, finding out that I'm not the biological daughter of Ryan and Ellen Quinlan has been liberating. It's given me the courage and freedom to think about what I want instead of worrying about how my actions will affect anyone else. I want something for me."

He nodded, still not certain where she was going with this conversation.

"I want to make love with you."

He was glad he was already sitting down, because he was pretty sure that statement would have knocked him over.

"If you're not interested," she continued hurriedly, "that's okay. But you indicated that you might be, so I thought that if you were…interested, that is, maybe we could…you know."

Oh, yeah. He knew. He'd spent far too much time over the past few days fantasizing about what it would be like to make love with Riane. Wishing he'd never walked out of that motel room.

Now he was in her hotel room, and she was looking at him with those deep brown eyes, telling him he didn't have to walk away. She was offering him everything he wanted. And still something made him hesitate.

"It's not that I'm not interested, Riane."

"But?"

"But you've just come out of a long-term relationship and—"

"Stuart and I never had sex."

"You—what?" He couldn't believe what she was saying. He knew that she and Stuart had dated for more than three years, they'd talked about getting married. How was it possible that he'd—that they'd—never?

Christ, what was wrong with the guy? He cleared his throat. "Why not?"

She shrugged. "He said he was willing to wait until we were married, if that's what I wanted."

"Is that what you wanted?"

She shrugged again. "I didn't have strong feelings one way or the other." She hesitated, then said, "He didn't make me feel the way you make me feel."

It was her unflinching honesty that undid him. "Don't tell me things like that, sweetheart," Joel practically groaned.

"Why not?"

"Because I'm trying very hard to be noble here, to do the right thing, and you're not making that easy for me."

"What do you think is the right thing?"

"Getting out of here before I take you up on that offer."

"I know what I want, Joel. And I want to make love with you."

She'd said she wanted to get rid of her virginity with Cameron, although she hadn't followed through with it. And she said she'd never slept with Stuart. Somehow he didn't think she'd been having sex with anyone other than her boyfriend, but he needed to know for sure.

"Have you ever, um, been with a man before?"

Her cheeks flushed with color; she shook her head.

A virgin.

He couldn't get his mind past those two words. His brain simply refused to compute anything else. He didn't believe it.

She was twenty-four years old, sexy, sophisticated. There was no way— And yet, he knew it was true. In fact, it explained a lot of things. The intriguing contrast between her hesitation and eagerness, the honesty and uncertainty in her responses to his touch. But there was still one question unanswered.

"Why me?"

''Because I thought if I was finally going to be with someone, it should be someone I trust. You know me, Joel. You know everything there is to know about me, and you're not impressed by who I am or appalled by the details of my life.''

She lifted her chin, met his gaze directly. ''So the only question now is, do you want me?''

Chapter 13

It took every ounce of willpower Riane had to stand her ground and meet Joel's gaze as she asked him that question. Or maybe she was just too paralyzed with fear to move. What if he said no? What if he turned her away—again?

She couldn't bear another rejection. Not from Joel. Not when she wanted him with a depth of desire that seemed to obliterate all else. She didn't quite understand how it was that her body could so desperately crave something it had never known, all she knew was that when she was with Joel, she wanted him.

"Do I want you?" Joel repeated the question slowly. Then he set his coffee down and stood up.

Riane was rooted to the floor. He took a step toward her. Her breath backed up in her lungs. He reached out and pried her mug from nervous fingers, set it aside. Then he cupped her cheek in his palm, stroked his thumb over the curve of her lips.

"Only more than I want to breathe," he said softly.

Riane let out the breath she hadn't realized she was holding and managed a tremulous smile.

"I want you so much it scares me," he admitted. "Especially now, knowing that you've never been with anyone else. I want to touch you, every inch of you, but I'm so afraid of hurting you."

"I'm not afraid," she told him. And she wasn't. Somehow she knew that everything would be okay because she was with Joel.

But Joel still looked as if he needed some convincing, so she rose onto her toes and touched her lips to his.

She wasn't prepared for the wealth of emotions she felt as he took control of the kiss, his mouth moving over hers with masterful purpose, his hands stroking over her body in lazy seduction. No one had ever touched her the way Joel touched her. With every brush of his lips, every caress of his fingertips, she felt cherished.

She didn't really have any expectations about making love. When she'd lived in the dorm, she'd heard other women compare horror stories about their "first time." The one common thread was that it was painful and generally quick. She was prepared for that.

And she thought that once the decision had been made, they'd take off their clothes and go to it. Joel had other ideas.

He did take off her clothes, but there was no haste. Instead, he stripped her garments away with painstaking slowness. First her blouse, lingering over each button, drawing out her anticipation, his eyes never leaving hers. His so dark and intense it made her breath catch in her throat. But breathing didn't seem to matter anymore. Nothing mattered but experiencing the moment, being with this man.

When all the buttons were undone, he slid his hands inside. His fingers skimmed over her collarbone, sending tingles of awareness, currents of desire, through her veins. Anticipation continued to build inside her, crowding out the last remnants of anxiety, any lingering vestige of uncertainty.

He pushed the blouse off her shoulders, slid it slowly down

her arms. Then he lowered his head and captured her mouth in a kiss that she wished would just go on and on forever. His lips were firm and warm, moving over hers with seductive expertise. Her own parted on a sigh, and his tongue slipped inside and mingled with hers. Riane threaded her fingers through the thick silky hair at the nape of his neck, holding him close, closer.

So captivated was she by his kiss that she didn't realized he'd unfastened the clip of her bra until she felt his palm skim up her rib cage to the curve of her breast. Instinctively she arched toward him. His thumb brushed over the distended nipple, and she gasped at the shock of pleasure.

He found the zipper at the back of her pants and slid it down slowly, his fingertips skimming over her buttocks. Then the fabric pooled at her feet and his hands were on the backs of her thighs, moving upward again in a teasing caress that simply melted her bones.

As if sensing her complete and unconditional surrender, he picked her up and carried her over to the bed. He laid her on top of the mattress and disposed of her panties.

Suddenly she was aware of her nakedness, self-conscious. She tried to pull the spread to cover her, but Joel stopped her. His eyes raked over her, appraising, approving. "You're so beautiful."

The husky tone of his voice convinced her that he believed it. And she felt beautiful. Desirable. Desired.

She lifted her arms in silent invitation, and he lowered himself onto the bed. His mouth found hers again, his kiss deeper now, hungrier. She shifted her hips, positioning him at the juncture of her thighs. Joel groaned against her lips, and his hands found her hips, stilling their instinctive movements.

"I'm trying to take my time."

"I don't want you to take your time. I want to feel you inside me."

"We'll get there," he promised her. "Eventually."

"Now." She wasn't sure how much longer she could endure the torturous teasing. She was assailed by so many sensations she thought her system was just going to explode. There was an unfamiliar tightness coiling in the pit of her belly, seeking release, demanding fulfillment.

He chuckled softly. "Let's do this my way, this time."

This time.

She liked the sound of that. She wanted to believe that they would be together like this again. That they could have more than one night.

So she let him have his way, and she had absolutely no regrets. His hands were relentless on her body, stoking the fire that burned inside her. He left no inch of her skin untouched, his lips following the path that his fingertips had traced on her skin until she practically wept with the urgent need to mate her body with his. When Joel's teeth closed over her nipple, his tongue swirling around it, her release came. Hot and fast, it left her gasping and breathless and completely confused. She hadn't expected this. Hadn't expected anything like it. And already the anticipation was building inside her again, and she wanted more.

"Joel. Please." She could feel the wet heat between her thighs, the throbbing ache. The emptiness she needed him to fill, the pressure only he could release.

But he wouldn't be hurried, and she was stunned to realize how much more he could coax from her body. How much more she could give. It seemed like an eternity before he stripped off the rest of his clothes. He took a condom out of his wallet and sheathed himself. Riane had given absolutely no thought to protection and was grateful that he'd done so.

When she felt him part her thighs with his knee, she thought, *Now. Finally now.*

But he didn't immediately rise over her, thrust into her. Instead he drove her up again, higher even than before, and she was still quivering with the aftershocks of her climax when he slipped inside her. Her body was more than ready for the intrusion, aching for the fulfillment. There was a brief—almost imperceptible—stab of pain. She tightened instinctively, and Joel stopped moving, but the pain was already gone, the pleasure overwhelming all else.

"Are you okay?" he asked, holding himself immobile over her.

She lifted her hips off the mattress, pulling him deeper inside, and heard him groan. She smiled. "Much better than okay."

Then he was moving inside her, long, steady strokes that seemed to touch the very center of her soul. And as her body stretched to accommodate his movements, she felt her heart expanding, too, and taking him inside.

The simple beauty of their joining stunned her, and she wished she could just hold on to the moment forever. Then his movements quickened and his thrusts came harder, deeper, faster. Tension coiled inside her; sensation layered upon sensation. And suddenly everything exploded in a shower of heat and light and so much pleasure she wasn't sure she could stand it.

She screamed out with her release, shocked less by the wanton cry emanating from her throat than by the violent shudders that racked her body. Joel's mouth fused with hers, swallowing her cries. And he leaped with her.

When their lovemaking was completed, she *was* afraid. Afraid of feeling so much more than she ever thought she could; afraid of losing her heart to this man who she couldn't ever hope to hold on to.

Joel eased his body slowly from hers and back onto the mattress, tucking her close to his side. "Are you okay?" he asked again.

She nodded and snuggled contentedly against him, determined not to think about anything but the here and now. "I never expected…so much."

"I wanted to make sure there was pleasure before the pain," he told her.

She smiled. There had been so much pleasure she couldn't remember anything else.

"Is it always like that?" she asked, still awed by the whole experience.

He laid his hand on her cheek, gently stroked his thumb over her skin. His eyes were dark, serious. "No."

She frowned, uncertain how to interpret his response.

"But sometimes, if you're very lucky, it can be that good."

Her relief must have shown, because he chuckled softly.

"Of course, that might have been an anomaly. The only way we'll know for certain is if we try it again."

Then he proceeded to prove to her that it wasn't an anomaly at all.

Having accepted his departure from the police force and the failure of his marriage, Joel had built a new life for himself. A new career in a new city. And he'd been content. He hadn't thought anything was missing—until he'd met Riane.

When he awoke in Riane's bed, her body nestled close to his, he felt his heart swell with a feeling of such profound contentment and inexplicable happiness it stunned him for a moment. And that was when he realized he'd done something he thought he'd never do: he'd fallen in love.

The realization almost sent him into a full-scale panic because regardless of the depth of his feelings for her, he knew there was no future for them. She was a Rutherford—that should have been more than enough incentive to keep him the hell away from her. Okay, so maybe it wasn't Rutherford blood running through her veins, but she'd grown up in their world, with all the attendant rights and privileges. He was a Logan—paternity unknown. There was no way her parents would ever approve of him.

Not that he wanted their approval. He'd be damned before he'd try to fit in with the Rutherford-Quinlans of this world. He'd tried to be what Jocelyn wanted, and his failure had hurt them both. He wouldn't do that to Riane. He wouldn't make her promises he couldn't keep. He wouldn't ask for anything she didn't want to give. Which meant that he couldn't hope for anything more with Riane than what they had now.

Despite the warm presence of her sleeping beside him, he suddenly felt alone. Having experienced the joy and fulfillment of making love with Riane, how could he live the rest of his life without her?

There was no easy answer to the question, but he knew that it was what he'd have to do. But not yet. For now she was here. And he intended to enjoy every single minute they had together.

He skimmed a hand over her torso, his fingertips trailing over the silky softness of her skin. Riane murmured in her sleep and snuggled closer, one of her legs sliding between his, her breasts pressing against his chest. He touched his lips to her throat, nibbled gently. Her eyes opened; her lips curved.

"Hi," she said softly.

"Hi." He cupped the fullness of her breast in his hand, stroked his thumb over the pebbled nipple. Her breath caught, her eyes darkened. "Any regrets?"

"Only that I wasted so much time sleeping."

He kissed her, a tender soul-stirring kiss to express the feelings he couldn't put into words. Despite his intention to take things slowly, to spend hours cherishing every inch of her body, their passion escalated quickly.

Her hands roamed over him, boldly, freely. Whatever inhibitions Riane might have had before they'd made love last night had been quickly shed. She was eager and curious and—his eyes crossed when she wrapped her fingers around him—a very fast learner.

She stroked him slowly, teasingly, until his breath grew ragged and he had to remove her hand or risk disappointing both of them. But Riane wasn't deterred. She continued her leisurely exploration of his body, halting only when her fingers found the scar low on his abdomen.

He wondered if it would bother her, this tangible evidence

of his failed career. She traced the puckered flesh slowly, her touch gentle. "Is this where you were shot?"

"Yeah," he admitted.

"Does it hurt?"

"Most of the time I don't even remember it's there."

Her eyes were dark with concern. "Can you tell me what happened?"

He shrugged, as if every second of the incident wasn't permanently etched in his memory. "I got an anonymous tip that there were videotapes in the building. The police had gone over every square inch of the warehouse looking for evidence, but they'd missed the tapes because they were hidden inside a hollow door. On those tapes was evidence of executions that Conroy had ordered. Evidence he kept to ensure the continued loyalty of his executioners and—some members of his inner circle believed—for his own viewing pleasure."

"That's sick."

Joel didn't disagree. "I knew the tip might be nothing more than a trap, an attempt to get rid of me because I'd come too close to exposing the truth about Conroy. But I wanted so badly to make the case against him, and I needed those tapes to do it."

"Did you find them?"

"I found them," he admitted. "They were in my hand when I was shot. But when I came to, hours later in the hospital, no one seemed to know anything about the videotapes."

She rubbed her fingertips gently over the scar again. "I read the newspaper account of your injury. And even though I was furious with you at the time, it terrified me to think how close you'd come to being killed."

"I wasn't."

"Thank God for that." She looked up at him and smiled. "If I'd never met you, I'd still be a virgin."

Joel chuckled, surprised that he could find humor in anything when his body was wound up so tightly with wanting her. But Riane was constantly surprising him, as she did when she slid down his body and touched her lips to the scar. Then she moved lower.

He sucked in a breath and hauled her back up, flipping her onto her back and pinning her to the mattress with his own body.

He paused only long enough to protect her, then slipped into the welcoming wet heat of her body. They moved together, falling into a comfortable rhythm as if they'd been making love for years. He'd never felt as complete as he felt when his body was joined with Riane's, and he never wanted to let her go.

Later that morning Joel convinced Riane to check out of the hotel and go back to his house. Not that it had taken much convincing. It was as if they both knew their time together was limited and didn't want to spend a single minute apart unless it was absolutely necessary. Not that she'd made any mention of leaving, but he knew it was inevitable.

He'd never managed to keep a woman in his life for very long. Not even his mother had stuck around. He and Jocelyn had maintained the illusion of their marriage for almost four years, but the relationship had deteriorated long before their vows were dissolved. So he resolved to enjoy the time he had with Riane and treasure the memories when she was gone.

They spent the day together, wandering through the market and the shops of downtown. They had lunch at a little café overlooking the water, then walked through the botanical gardens and bought ice cream from a street vendor. They held hands and shared kisses on the sidewalk, oblivious to the passersby, oblivious to everyone but each other. Joel couldn't remember the last day he'd spent like this—doing nothing and having the time of his life.

They stopped at a Chinese takeout place on the way home and forgot about the food the minute they stepped through the door. It was a long time later before they bothered to reheat their dinner, and much later still when they finally fell asleep, their bodies tangled together.

When Joel finished his shower Monday morning and stepped back into the bedroom to get dressed, he was disappointed to find that Riane was already out of bed. Not that he had time to slide between the covers with her again, but simply because he liked to see her there.

He found her in the kitchen sipping from a mug of coffee. She was wearing one of his T-shirts and, he could tell by the way the soft cotton molded to her curves, absolutely nothing else. He felt his system snap to attention without the necessity of caffeine.

"I have a meeting this morning," Joel said, after a long, lingering kiss. "But I'm hoping it won't take too long."

"I'll be here whenever you get back," she assured him.

He kissed her again, more tempted than ever to blow off his scheduled appointment. The whole meeting would probably be an exercise in futility, anyway. He couldn't imagine anything that Gavin Elliott might tell him that was more important than taking Riane back upstairs and making love with her again.

He slid his hands beneath the hem of the T-shirt, confirming his earlier supposition that she was naked beneath the garment. She sighed as his fingers skimmed over her skin, pressed herself closer to him, and he completely forgot that he even had an appointment.

It was Riane who finally pulled away. Her cheeks were flushed and her breath came in shallow gasps, but she put her hands on his chest and pushed him toward the door. "You have a meeting."

He glanced at his watch and swore. He was already late. Still, he brushed one last kiss on her lips. "I'll be back soon."

It would be soon, he promised.

He held the society page closer. Studied the picture. It was

a poor quality photograph, but it was her. The last piece of
the puzzle.

This meeting would confirm it. Eliminate any residual
doubt. As soon as he was certain, he could set his plan in
motion.

The door of the diner opened.

He tucked the paper out of sight.

Joel pushed aside his lingering apprehension as he pushed
open the glass door. He wasn't convinced that Gavin Elliott
had anything of interest to tell him, but he couldn't forget
about the phone call. He couldn't stop wondering about the
information Elliott claimed Joel would want.

The only thing Joel wanted right now was to go home—
to Riane. But he knew that she wouldn't be able to move
ahead with her life until she'd dealt with all the ghosts of
her past. Unfortunately, Gavin Elliott was one of those
ghosts.

The breakfast crowd had long since gone, and only a couple of tables were occupied when Joel stepped into the diner.
The scents of burned grease and stale smoke permeated the
air. A female voice crooned from the ancient jukebox in the
corner about love gone bad.

Joel spotted Elliott immediately. He was seated at one of
the green vinyl booths near the back of the restaurant. He
looked better than he had in prison. He was clean shaven and
dressed in a suit. His hair was neatly combed, his eyes clear,
purposeful, the hint of a smile on his lips.

His demeanor unnerved Joel. What did a man recently released from prison have to look so damn pleased about?

He slid into the seat across from Elliott.

"Coffee?" Elliott asked, as pleasantly as if he was enter-
taining in his own home.

Joel wanted to refuse, but Elliott was already waving the
waitress over to their table.

She was young, probably not much more than twenty, Joel
guessed, and her faded pink uniform stretched tightly across

her very pregnant belly. She flipped over the cup in front of Joel and filled it from the carafe she carried in her hand.

"Can I get you a menu?" she asked, offering a tired but pleasant smile.

"No, thanks." Joel wanted to get this meeting over as quickly as possible.

"I'll have the special," Elliott said. "Eggs scrambled with sausage."

The waitress nodded and retreated to the kitchen to place his order.

"Pretty little thing, isn't she?" Elliott commented, watching the woman's retreating form.

Joel sipped at his coffee.

"She'd be about my daughter's age, wouldn't she?"

"I wouldn't know," Joel said.

"You've found her though." It was more a statement than a question, as if Elliott already knew the answer.

"I'm not at liberty to discuss the details of my investigation with you."

"'Not at liberty,'" Elliott mocked, then smiled. "I gave you useful information, didn't I?"

"You gave me the name of a lawyer who passed away several years ago," Joel told him.

"Lawyers keep files," Elliott said.

"Usually they do," Joel agreed, wondering if Elliott had brought him here to seek rather than impart information.

Elliott shook his head. "I thought there was something unusual about the way things were handled."

"What do you mean?"

Elliott turned to the waitress as she set his plate in front of him. "Thank you, darling."

She offered another tired smile. "Enjoy your breakfast."

"I'm sure I will," Elliott responded pleasantly, and proceeded to dig his fork into the mound of eggs.

"Why did you think there was something unusual about the adoption?" Joel demanded.

Elliott sprinkled pepper onto his eggs, slathered grape jelly onto a triangle of toast.

Joel sat back, his fingers clamped tightly around the ceramic mug in his hand. The man was playing him. He knew it. He just didn't know how to end the game. He could walk away, of course, but he couldn't shake the feeling that Elliott was holding back some crucial piece of evidence. And that this meeting was his only chance to get it.

"They took good care of her, didn't they?" Elliott asked, slicing through a sausage link.

Joel was surprised by the question. The last time he'd spoken to Elliott, the other man had shown no interest in the daughter he'd given up more than twenty years earlier.

"Bet she grew up in a big house, with lots of fancy clothes and expensive toys." Elliott continued to eat, not bothered by Joel's lack of response. "The atmosphere in this place leaves a lot to be desired, but the food is phenomenal."

Joel accepted a refill on his coffee. It was strong and a little stale, but he imagined it was better than whatever they served in prison.

"Was there a reason you requested this meeting, Mr. Elliott, or did you just want company over breakfast?"

"Of course there was a reason," Elliott assured him. "I don't believe in wasting time—mine or anyone else's."

"Are you going to share that reason with me?" Joel asked, his patience rapidly dissipating.

"It's about my daughter," he said. "Rheanne."

Joel waited while Elliott dabbed his mouth with his napkin and pushed his empty plate aside.

"I thought you might want to know that they paid us to give up our baby."

Chapter 14

After his meeting with Gavin Elliott, Joel's urgency to return to Riane was superseded by a combination of guilt and confusion. He didn't want any more lies between them, so how could he not tell her what he'd learned? And yet sharing the information without verifying it first would only hurt her more. Intentionally or not, he'd already caused her enough pain.

He couldn't tell her. Not until he knew for certain whether or not what Gavin Elliott had told him was true. There had been a time when he'd wanted, more than anything, to dig up some kind of dirt on the Rutherfords. Riane had changed things for him. But if Ellen and Ryan had paid to adopt her, their actions were very definitely illegal, and Joel would have all the ammunition he needed. He just wasn't sure that he wanted it anymore.

He stopped by the office, hoping to discuss the latest revelation with his partner. Mike was waiting for him, with a copy of the *Fairweather Tribune* in hand.

Wordlessly he passed the paper across the desk. Joel recognized the picture immediately—it was the same one that had been printed in the *Mapleview Mirror* after the charity ball. The caption, however, was new:

Professional Acquaintance or Personal Vendetta?

No one knows why local P.I. Joel Logan has been spending so much time with West Virginia Senator Ellen Rutherford-Quinlan's daughter recently, but speculation is that Logan has finally found a way to avenge his dismissal from the Philadelphia PD. Marcus Rutherford—yes, a relative of the lovely Ms. Riane Quinlan—was the presiding judge in a case that ended Logan's career in Philadelphia. Logan was charged with, although never convicted of, leaking investigative information to the Conroy crime syndicate.

Joel didn't read any further.

"Is this today's paper?" he asked.

Mike nodded. "We could sue for libel. The reporter whose name is on the article obviously didn't even check his facts."

"They'll print a retraction tomorrow," Joel guessed. "A tiny little 'oops' buried somewhere on the back of the last page." He didn't care, really. He didn't believe the article could hurt the business, but he was concerned that it might hurt Riane.

"Does she know about the Rutherford connection in the Conroy case?" Mike asked, somehow following Joel's train of thought.

"Not from me."

"Then maybe you should tell her," Mike advised. "Before she sees it in print."

Joel was surprised by his friend's advice, especially since Mike had made no secret of the fact he disapproved of Joel's personal involvement with Riane. He nodded. "I'll be at home if you need me."

He was almost out the door before his partner spoke again.

"I'll cover for you tomorrow," Mike said, then grinned. "In case you have some extra groveling to do."

"I hope she gives me the chance."

Joel made several stops on the way home, arming himself with the groveling essentials: a bottle of Riane's favorite merlot, a large pizza with extra cheese, pepperoni and hot peppers, and a huge bouquet of fresh spring flowers. Still, as he turned on to his street, he breathed an audible sigh of relief when he found her car still parked in the driveway.

And then he found Riane—in the bathtub. Her hair was piled loosely on top of her head, her body hidden beneath a thick layer of scented bubbles. She had a glass of white wine in her hand, a second glass and the bottle were on the apron of the tub along with about half a dozen flickering candles.

Somewhere in the back of his mind it registered that she must have taken a trip into town, because he was sure she wouldn't have found those romantic trappings around his house. Thankfully, she hadn't picked up a newspaper.

He cleared his throat and she opened her eyes, her lips curving in a slow sensual smile.

"I was hoping you'd be home before the water got cold," she told him.

"I was hoping you'd be naked when I got home."

"I'm not naked."

He took a few steps into the bathroom. "What are you wearing?"

She stood up, her body rosy and glistening from the heat of the water, ribbons of foam adorning her satiny skin. "Bubbles."

All the blood in his head quickly migrated south. "I must be dreaming."

He didn't realize he'd spoken the words aloud until Riane's tentative smile widened.

"I wanted to seduce you this time," she admitted shyly.

"You've succeeded." He dropped the pizza box on the counter, the flowers and wine beside it.

"I haven't even started." She picked up a glass of wine and offered it to him.

Joel stepped forward to take the glass from her fingers and set it back down. Then he lifted Riane out of the tub and into his arms, mindless of the water soaking through his clothes and dripping on the floor as he moved purposefully to the bedroom.

"I'm wet," Riane protested.

Joel grinned down at her. "I hope so."

She laughed softly when he dropped her on the mattress. The humor in her brown eyes quickly turned to desire as she watched him strip off his clothing. He lowered himself onto the bed beside her, muscles quivering, straining. He forced himself to rein in his escalating passion. Less than forty-eight hours earlier he'd taken her virginity—and he'd taken her several times again since then. Both her actions and her words proved that she shared his desire, but he figured her body would be aching, tender.

He touched his mouth to hers, softly. He stroked his tongue over the fullness of her bottom lip, savoring. He trailed kisses over her jaw, nipped at her earlobe, nibbled his way down the slender column of her throat.

He worked his way down to her breasts and lingered. Milky flesh, rosy nipples, dusky peaks. He tasted and teased, tormenting them both before he moved on. His tongue trailed a path to the center of her belly, and lower still.

She squirmed, and he knew he was again leading her into new territory. The realization only heightened his need to explore.

He skimmed his hands over the length of her torso, under her hips, lifting her off the mattress slightly. He felt her hands on his shoulders, her short nails digging into the flesh.

To restrain or encourage?

He didn't know. He only knew that he had to taste her.

He dipped his head between her thighs, heard her gasp, felt her jolt when his tongue plunged into her. And he feasted.

Riane's body quivered and bucked as the climax ripped through her, her passionate reaction causing his own desire to spiral out of control. No, it was more than desire. It was stronger, deeper, undeniable.

He *needed* Riane. He needed her like he'd never needed anyone before. He needed her more than he needed to breathe. With no regard for his earlier thoughts of care and patience, pausing only long enough to protect her, he plunged into her.

She didn't balk at the primitiveness of his possession but rose up to meet him, taking him deeper and harder with each thrust. Her hands raced over him greedily, her fingers burning his flesh, each frantic touch driving him closer to the edge. He captured her mouth, swallowed her trembling sighs and throaty moans. Then her muscles contracted around him, and he plunged into the abyss of pleasure right along with her.

"Not that I have any complaints," Joel assured her later. "But was there any particular reason you wanted to seduce me?"

"I wanted to see if I could," Riane admitted.

"Anytime."

She smiled, but he detected a hint of worry in the endless depths of her dark eyes. "And because I wanted to take your mind off things."

"What things?"

She slid from the bed and pulled a folded newspaper out of the side pocket of her suitcase. "Have you seen this?"

He closed his eyes and silently cursed his hormones for overruling his head. It had been his intention to talk to her about the article as soon as he got home, but then Riane had been naked and he hadn't thought about anything but burying himself inside her.

"Yes, I've seen it." He tensed, waiting for her to vent her outrage and accusations.

But she climbed back onto the bed and wrapped her arms around him. "I'm sorry."

He was speechless for a moment. ''Why are you apologizing?''

''Because I have a pretty good idea who leaked this story to the press.''

''Stuart,'' Joel guessed.

''Probably,'' she admitted. ''He blames you for the end of our relationship.''

''And this is his way of trying to make you question my involvement with you.''

''After three years, I would have thought he'd know me better than that.''

''You're not angry?'' Joel asked. ''That I didn't tell you who the judge was?''

''No. I wish you had told me. But the information was in the file Stuart gave me last week.''

''Why didn't you ask me about it?''

She shrugged. ''Because I don't believe that our relationship is about anything or anyone but you and me.''

He was stunned. Jocelyn would have ranted and raved and likely destroyed something expensive. Riane's calm and unquestioning acceptance forced Joel to acknowledge how different from his ex-wife Riane really was, and how extraordinarily lucky he was.

He cupped her face in his hands. ''You are an incredible woman.''

Riane smiled. ''Of course, if I find out I'm wrong, I'll have to really hurt you,'' she teased.

Joel grinned and dropped a light kiss on her lips. Was it any wonder that he'd fallen in love with this woman?

He pulled back, as if a few inches of physical distance might give him a better perspective. But he could no longer deny the truth of what was in his heart. He did love her. He wasn't sure exactly how or when it had happened, but somewhere along the line, he'd fallen in love with Riane Quinlan.

Unfortunately, loving her didn't change anything: she was still the daughter of a senator, a Rutherford-Quinlan by upbringing if not by blood; he was a kid from the wrong side of town who didn't have a clue who his father was. He'd be a fool to think they could have a future together; he'd be even more of a fool to spoil what they had right now by wishing for something that could never be.

And right now he was starving.

"How does pizza sound?"

Riane lingered in bed while Joel went downstairs to reheat the pizza. She stretched, feeling aches in muscles she didn't even know she had, but she smiled. They were the aches of a woman who had been well and truly loved, and she wished she could hold on to the feeling forever.

Of course, they both knew this wasn't forever. Joel's life was here in Pennsylvania; hers was in West Virginia. Okay, maybe the geographical distance wasn't insurmountable, but it was significant.

She had to go back to Mapleview. She *wanted* to go home. Meeting with Arden and learning more of the details about her biological family had cleared up some of her confusion. She might never understand why her parents had lied about her adoption, but she would be forever grateful for their unconditional love and support.

But the issue with her parents aside, why couldn't she have a future with Joel? She knew he had doubts about whether her parents could accept him, but she didn't. Her parents would love Joel because she did.

She sat up straight, stunned by the revelation that had come so easily from her heart. She loved Joel.

She clutched the bed sheet against her chest, considering. Maybe she wasn't really in love. Maybe she was confusing sex with love. She'd never been intimate with a man before, she'd never experienced the kind of physical connection she'd shared with Joel. Maybe what she was really feeling was just…gratitude, she decided, for his initiation into the rites of lovemaking.

She shook her head, wondering why she was so determined to discount her emotions. She'd given up on falling in love; she'd made a conscious decision to marry for practical reasons rather than emotional ones. Then Joel had walked into the charity ball and her entire life had changed.

And she had no intention of letting go of the best thing that had ever happened to her.

Resolved, Riane pushed herself off the bed. She grabbed a softly worn denim shirt from Joel's closet and hastily fastened the buttons. Now that she'd acknowledged her feelings, she wanted to share them. She wanted to spend the rest of her life with Joel, and she wanted to start now.

The thought brought a smile to her lips and her step was light as she headed downstairs to the kitchen. She could smell the pizza in the oven, the spicy aroma teased her nostrils, caused her stomach to rumble. But Joel wasn't in the kitchen.

There was a light on in the den, so she stepped through the family room and into the open doorway. He wasn't there, either, but something—an instinct she would later wish she could have ignored—propelled her closer to the desk. His agenda was lying open on top of the blotter and beneath the current date was a notation:

> Sam's Diner
> 9:30
> re: Rheanne

She felt a sudden hollowness in her gut that had nothing to do with her want for food. She backed away from the desk, her eyes still glued to the page.

"There you are," Joel came into the room, offering her the glass of wine she'd abandoned earlier.

"Rheanne," she said, surprised that her voice sounded so steady. "R-H-E-A-N-N-E. Is that the name on my original birth certificate?"

Joel hesitated, his gaze dropping to the book on his desk and the easy smile slipping from his face before he answered with a short nod.

"Why is that name in your agenda for today? Did you have an appointment with someone about me?"

"Yes," he admitted.

"Who?"

"I can't talk to you about it right now."

"If it's about me, why can't you discuss it?"

"Because I don't know if there's any truth to the information I was given."

"Does it matter?" she asked. "Your job was to find me. You found me."

"It's not that simple."

"It can be. If you could just let it go." Then she laughed, bitterly. "You're still a cop, aren't you? You just won't stop digging until you have all the answers. Even if it ruins my life."

"It isn't just about you," Joel said gently. "It's about right and wrong."

"It is about me," she insisted. "And if you cared about me at all, you wouldn't do this."

"Damn it, Riane, I'm doing this because I care about you. If we're going to have any kind of relationship, we can't start with lies or deception between us."

"I haven't lied to you about anything."

"Don't you want to know the truth?"

"No." She didn't care that she sounded unreasonable. She wasn't feeling very reasonable at the moment. "Not if it's going to hurt the people who mean the most to me."

"You know I can't walk away from this."

"Well, I can." She walked past him and up the stairs again.

She pulled on a pair of jeans and shoved the rest of her clothes into her suitcase. Not half an hour earlier she'd been euphoric to discover she'd fallen in love. Now she knew that the man she loved was continuing to pursue a personal vendetta against her family, and she couldn't be a part of that. She had to leave, and it was tearing her heart out.

If this really was love, she decided as she wiped a single tear off her cheek, she didn't want any part of it.

Joel stood at the bottom of the stairs, looking stunned and hurt when she came down with her suitcase in hand. "Don't go, Riane. Please."

"You've made your choices. I have to make mine."

She scooped up her purse and keys off the coffee table and walked out the door.

Chapter 15

He walked into the apartment as if he had every right to be there. Which, of course, he did. He was her husband, after all.

"Hi, honey. I'm home."

The magazine slipped from her fingers. She glanced up, her dark eyes wide and haunted. She rose from the chair, stepped behind it. "H-how did you find me?"

"I told you I would."

"You sh-shouldn't be here," she said. Her fingers dug into the back of the chair. Ragged nails on faded upholstery. "They'll send you b-back. To jail. For vi-violating your p-parole."

"Only if they know I'm here."

"P-please, Gav." She swallowed. "You have to go."

"I don't think so, honey. Not until we've settled a few things."

"P-please."

He smiled at the tremor in her voice. Yes, this was going

exactly as planned. She was begging already. Her eyes swimming with tears.

"You let them put me in a cage." He crossed the room to where she stood.

She shook her head in denial. Tears spilled onto her pasty cheeks. "I n-never wanted you to g-go to jail—"

"It doesn't matter what you wanted." His tone was cold. "That's what happened. You stole four months of our life."

"I-I'm s-sorry. I'm s-so s-sorry."

He cupped her chin in his hand. His fingers bit into the flesh. Forced her to meet his gaze. "You were always sorry, Felicia. And I always forgave you. Maybe that was my mistake."

"I am s-sorry."

"Words. Just words." He shrugged.

"Wh-what are you g-going to do?"

"I'm going to make you sorry."

She shook her head again. "N-no. P-please."

Her pleading was more annoying than satisfying now. She was ruining the whole scene with her pathetic whimpering, and that really pissed him off. He lifted his arm and lashed out with a backhand. It sent her flying. Adrenaline surged through him again.

She crashed against the dining room table. Crumpled to the floor. She didn't cover her face or cower. She didn't move at all.

"Get up," he demanded.

She didn't respond.

He bent over, grabbed her by the shoulder.

And saw the blood.

It was already pooling on the linoleum. Spilling out of the side of her head. He stepped back. Stared in disbelief at the smear of red. His wife's blood. On his hand.

Panic trickled into him. A slow and steady stream. This wasn't part of his plan. This wasn't supposed to happen.

She was just lying there.

Lifeless.

Almost like she was dead.

Damn it, this wasn't supposed to happen!

Was she dead?

Had he killed her?

He hadn't intended to kill her. He'd only wanted to hurt her—to make her suffer as he'd suffered.

He scrubbed his hands through his hair. Tried to order his chaotic thoughts. He needed to think. He needed a new plan. Whatever happened, he wouldn't go back to jail.

He'd have to leave the country. He'd go far away. Somewhere that had never even heard of extradition. But to do that he'd need money. A lot of it.

It was close to midnight by the time Riane arrived home. She'd managed to hold back the tears throughout the three-hour drive, but as she sat in her car in the driveway, the sheer relief of being home overwhelmed her and she was no longer able to do so.

She leaned her forehead against the steering wheel and wept. She couldn't believe she'd been such an idiot. *Again.* It had been one thing to make a fool of herself with Cameron Davis, but she wasn't twenty years old anymore. She should have known better. This time, not only had she let her hormones overrule her head, she'd let her heart get involved, too. She'd fallen in love with Joel Logan, and he'd betrayed her.

She sat up straight and swiped impatiently at the tears streaming down her cheeks. She'd managed perfectly well before he walked into her life and she'd do so again. She had her family—both the parents who'd raised her and loved her, and the sister she'd rediscovered—and her responsibilities at the camp. She didn't need anything else.

So why did her heart ache at the thought of never seeing him again?

She was angry with Joel, angrier with herself. He'd never made her any promises. What right did she have to be upset now simply because she'd learned he wasn't the man she'd wanted him to be?

She climbed out of the car and made her way up to the front door. She hadn't even put her key in the lock when the door opened. Ellen Rutherford-Quinlan stood on the other side, wearing a long, silky robe and a hesitant smile. Her hair was tousled, her deep green eyes shadowed.

"How is it that you always know I'm home even before I've opened the door?" Riane asked.

"Mother's intuition." Ellen stepped back so that Riane could enter, her eyes anxiously searching her daughter's face. "I've missed you."

"I missed you, too."

"Any particular reason you chose the middle of the night to venture home?" There was no censure in her voice, just concern.

"We can talk in the morning, Mom. You should get back to bed before Daddy starts wandering around looking for you."

"I'm not worried about your dad, I'm worried about you." And she gently but firmly took Riane's arm and guided her into the den. "Do you want something to drink—a glass of water, a cup of tea, something stronger?"

Riane shook her head. "No, thanks."

Ellen propelled her toward the sofa, sat down beside her. "Tell me."

Those two words were all it took for the last of Riane's resolve to crumble. "I found out that Joel's still digging for information about my adoption." And the tears started all over again.

Ellen held her while she cried, as she'd done so many times in the past. And, as always, her quiet comfort and reassurance soothed Riane. Eventually the sobs subsided, the tears dried, but the ache in her heart remained.

"He's only doing his job," Ellen said gently.

"Why aren't you angry about this?"

"I was never entirely comfortable with the way things

were handled,'' Ellen admitted. ''And I've never stopped worrying that somehow, someday, this would all come back to haunt us. It's almost a relief to know it's going to happen.''

''I know my adoption wasn't handled through all the proper channels,'' Riane said. ''If that information comes out, it could ruin your career.''

''Do you really think that matters to me now?''

''It should.''

''The only thing that matters is you. I made some bad choices, a lot of mistakes, and I regret a lot of them. But I'd do it all again if it was the only way I could have you.''

Riane's tears spilled over again. She'd been so hurt and angry when she found out about her adoption, she hadn't paid enough attention to her parents' feelings. She hadn't really considered how difficult the whole situation was for them, how they must have agonized over the choices they'd made.

Ellen cradled her daughter's face in her palms and brushed away the tears. ''I appreciate your concern,'' she said. ''But somehow I don't think all these tears are for me.''

''I'm tired. I'm confused. I'm not sure what I'm feeling right now,'' Riane told her.

Her mother smiled sympathetically. ''You're in love with him, aren't you?''

Riane hadn't even wanted to admit the truth to herself, to acknowledge that she'd fallen in love with a man who'd used and betrayed her. But she couldn't lie to her mother; she didn't want to. ''Yes,'' she admitted.

''How does he feel about you?''

Riane laughed, bitterly. ''I have no idea. He says he cares about me.''

''You don't believe him.''

''He wouldn't be doing this if he really cared.''

''Love isn't always that simple,'' Ellen told her.

''It should be,'' Riane said, then sighed. ''Why couldn't I have fallen in love with Stuart?''

''Do you think that would have been easier?''

"I don't know. Maybe. All I want is someone to share my life and my dreams. Someone with whom I can share the kind of connection that you and Daddy have."

Ellen smiled. "Do you think it was love at first sight for your father and me?"

"Wasn't it?"

"I didn't even *like* him when I first met him."

"Why not?" Riane felt strangely insulted on her father's behalf.

"Because he was arrogant and rude and much too sexy for his own good."

The explanation appeased Riane somewhat. "What changed your mind?"

Ellen considered. "It wasn't any one thing, really. But we were at law school together—we had classes in common and group assignments to complete, so we were forced to spend a fair amount of time together. And eventually I realized that there was more to him—more substance, more heart—than I'd wanted to believe. And when he first kissed me," she smiled a little at the memory, "I felt as though the ground was actually trembling beneath my feet."

Riane sighed. She knew that feeling all too well. "Is that when you knew you were in love?"

"No, that's when she decided not to speak to me for the next six months."

Riane turned to see her father leaning nonchalantly against the door frame. "I didn't realize you were up, too."

"I didn't want to miss out on all the girl talk," he said, moving into the room to brush a kiss on Riane's temple. "When did you get home?"

"Just a little while ago." But Riane didn't want to rehash her reasons yet again. "Why didn't Mom talk to you for six months?"

"Because as soon as he stopped kissing me, he opened his mouth and reminded me what an arrogant ass he was," Ellen told her.

"Because I told her I was going to marry her," Ryan offered an alternate explanation.

"After that very first kiss?" Riane asked.

"I knew even before then," Ryan admitted. "For me, it *was* love at first sight."

"You're a hopeless romantic," Ellen chided, but she was smiling with genuine love and affection at the man who'd been her husband for thirty-five years.

"And you're practical enough for the both of us," Ryan told her.

And in that moment, Riane realized that her mother was right. Love wasn't easy—it wasn't supposed to be. It was about affection and caring and compromise. And although the realization didn't ease her own heartache, her parents' relationship affirmed for her the power and endurance of love.

"Go back to bed," she told them. "I didn't mean to disturb you."

"Are you going to get some sleep?" Ellen asked.

Riane didn't know if she could with the jumble of chaotic thoughts swirling around in her mind, but she nodded and feigned a yawn to appease her mother. "I'll see you in the morning."

Ryan kissed her again. "I love you, baby."

She blinked away the moisture behind her eyes. "I love you, too. Both of you."

Ellen squeezed her daughter's hand in a silent show of support before letting her husband drag her out of the room.

Riane didn't sleep much, but she felt somewhat better in the morning. Her late-night conversation with her parents the previous evening had reassured her of the constancy of their love despite the uncertainty of everything else at this point in her life. And it had alleviated the strain they'd all been living under since she'd learned of her adoption. Life was pretty much back to normal in the Quinlan household, which allowed Riane to focus her attention on her other concern—the camp.

It was her work at the camp that gave her life direction and purpose, and she desperately needed both right now. So, after a quick breakfast with Sophie, she headed over to the site.

She wandered through the drizzle, mindless of the cold and wet, inspecting the progress on the new cabins. She was excited about the program that already existed and her short- and long-term plans for the camp, and she was proud that her fund-raising efforts had made this current expansion possible. If the progress continued on schedule, and she had every reason to believe that it would, the Quinlan Camp for Underprivileged Children would double its capacity within the next three years.

Why had she felt so compelled to focus on the needs of underprivileged children? It was a question that had been asked of her numerous times over the past few years. Her explanation had always been the same as the one she'd given Joel: that witnessing the plight of impoverished children through her parents' work in the foreign service had motivated her to find a way to help. While she still believed there was validity in that response, she wondered if there wasn't more to it.

Was it possible that her own experiences as a child, experiences that she couldn't even recollect—the neglect by her biological parents, the trauma of being separated from her sister—had subconsciously instilled in her an empathy for children in similar situations? And if there was any truth at all in that supposition, maybe she and Joel had more in common than she'd realized.

She shook her head. Regardless of their similarities or differences, she couldn't get past the fact that she'd been so wrong about him. She'd thought he cared about her. Damn it, he'd made her believe he cared. But it had all been a facade. The whole time he'd been luring her toward his bed, he'd been digging for dirt on her family.

Okay, if she was honest, she had to admit he hadn't lured her into his bed. She'd wanted to be there. In fact, she'd practically pushed him there. But that didn't make his betrayal hurt any less.

"Ms. Quinlan?"

Riane started at the sound of the unfamiliar masculine voice close behind her and hastily wiped the tears from her cheeks. She'd been certain she was alone, that all the workers had left the site for the day because of the inclement weather. Obviously she was wrong. She blinked the remaining traces of moisture out of her eyes before she turned.

And found herself staring into the snub-nosed barrel of a gun.

Chapter 16

It wasn't in Riane's nature to give in to a bully, and she couldn't think of any better way to describe the man who was holding her at gunpoint. Still, she kept her chin up and her resolve firm.

Her resolve faltered just a little when he directed her to his car and ordered her to get in. Even with her rudimentary knowledge of self-defense, Riane knew a victim was never supposed to get into an assailant's vehicle. But he'd seemed ready, even eager, to use the gun he'd waved in her face, and she hated to think that her blood could be spilled on the grounds of her camp. She wouldn't let some madman tarnish the project she'd put so much of her heart and soul into.

So she'd ignored her self-preservation instincts and gone with him. She wasn't exactly sure where, since he'd tied her hands behind her back and blindfolded her when they got to his car. A green midsize vehicle with Michigan plates, she noted. She knew it would be important to give as much information as she could to the police, if she managed to get out of this in one piece.

Her abductor removed the blindfold when they arrived at their destination. It was, Riane realized with a bizarre sense of irony, the same motel where she and Joel had stayed the night she'd run out of gas on Highway 27. It had to be the same motel. She couldn't imagine two different establishments choosing the same horrid shade of orange for their decor.

Still, it didn't do her any good to know where she was unless he let her use the phone to call someone. And she didn't think that was likely.

So she was surprised when he pushed her onto one of the twin beds and said, "I want you to make a phone call.

"You're not going to talk," he continued, eliminating her quick burst of hope. "You're just going to dial. I'll handle the rest."

"Who am I supposed to call?" she asked, forcing her voice to remain level. His request had calmed some of the panic that had been escalating inside her. Whatever this man wanted, it wasn't sexual in nature, and for that she was infinitely grateful.

"You're supposed to be a smart woman," the man taunted. "I'm sure you can figure it out."

"Why don't you enlighten me?" she suggested, unaccountably angered by his smug tone.

"I'm the kidnapper, you're the hostage. The only thing you need to know is that if you don't do exactly what I tell you, I'm going to put a bullet through you."

She was helpless to prevent the instinctive shudder that rippled through her at the threat. He seemed to look forward to the possibility of doing just that.

"If I'm a hostage, it means you think someone is willing to give you something you want in exchange for me. I won't be much good as a bargaining chip if I'm dead," she pointed out.

He smiled menacingly. "Only if they know you're dead."

Okay, he had a point there. "What do you want?"

"Money."

"Why?"

"Why?" He laughed. "Because money makes the world go round."

"Why me?" she asked. "What makes you think anyone would be willing to pay anything for me?"

"I've seen that fancy house on the hill you live in, the car you drive, the jewels you wear." He flicked a grimy finger against the sapphire stud in her ear. "And I figured if they were willing to pay a hundred thousand dollars for you before, who knows how much they'll pay now?"

His lips curved in a sick smile. "I think I'll ask for a million. Yes, that's a nice round number. It'll be enough to get me out of this hick town, out of this stinking country."

Riane was no longer paying attention to his tirade. "What do you mean—they paid before?"

"Your parents," he said. "I don't imagine a hotshot senator will have any trouble finding a lousy million bucks."

"Who did they pay? Why?" She didn't know why she felt compelled to ask the questions; she was certain she wouldn't want to know the answers.

"They paid *me*," he told her, and the slow, obscene curving of his lips made her skin crawl. "Because I'm your father."

Joel's attention was riveted on the side of Felicia Reynolds's face, on the menacing-looking bruise visible just beneath the peak of her baseball cap. "What happened to you?"

She dropped her gaze again and folded her trembling fingers together. "I fell."

He'd heard it before—he'd heard all the excuses before. "He found you, didn't he?"

"I don't know what you're talking about." But her response was belied by the tremor in her voice.

Joel swore viciously under his breath, and Felicia flinched as if struck by a physical blow. He forced himself to rein in his anger. She'd obviously seen enough evidence of temper recently. "Have you been to the hospital?" he asked more gently.

She nodded and pushed her hat back slightly, revealing a neat little row of stitches that disappeared into her hairline.

"How about the police?"

She pulled the cap back down, her eyes wide, terrified. "The cops don't need to know that I'm clumsy."

"They need to know if Elliott was here."

"He wasn't," she insisted.

"Ms. Reynolds, any contact with you is a violation of his parole—he would go back to jail and you'd be safe."

"Only until he got out again," she said bitterly.

"You need to go to the po—"

"No," she interrupted, no longer denying Elliott's involvement. "I'm safe now."

"How can you be sure?"

She hesitated, folding her fingers together again so tightly that her knuckles turned white. "B-because…because Gavin thinks…I'm dead."

"You could have been," Joel agreed, studying the swelling and discoloration on the side of her face more carefully.

"If he goes back to prison, I will be."

"You can't let him get away with this."

"I thought you came here to talk about Rheanne," she reminded him.

Joel nodded. He had, and he knew better than to insist on helping someone who didn't want help.

"Your ex-husband told me the adoptive parents paid for your child," he said at last.

She hesitated for a second, then nodded.

"How much?" The amount didn't matter nearly so much as Felicia Reynolds's admission that she and her husband had signed away their rights to their child in exchange for a sum of money, but he'd gone too far to turn back now.

She didn't look up. "A hundred thousand dollars."

He'd seen and heard a lot in his thirty-three years, but he was still shocked. Not by the figure she'd recited but by the fact that this woman had, without any indication of regret or remorse, sold her two-year-old child. "Whose idea was it to sell her?"

"We didn't sell the kid," she denied. "That's illegal."

Not to mention immoral and unethical and abhorrent.

"What would you call it when you give up your child in exchange for a sum of money?" he challenged, unable to mask his disgust.

She looked up now, lifting her chin in a gesture of defiance. "We were entitled to be, um, reimbursed, Mr. Rutherford said, for our expenses."

He had the truth now, but he still didn't know what he was going to do with it. Mike had been right when he'd accused Joel of using the connection in Arden's sister's case to pursue a more personal agenda. When Judge Rutherford had destroyed his career, Joel had vowed that he would someday have his revenge against the privileged classes who thought their money could buy them anything.

Now he knew without a doubt that Ellen Rutherford-Quinlan had used her money to buy a child, and it was within his power to reveal the truth and bring her down. After five seemingly endless years, revenge was finally within his grasp. He should have been ecstatic. Instead, he felt only growing despair and aching emptiness, because every step he took closer to exposing the secret was a step further away from Riane. There was no way she'd ever forgive him if he used this information against her mother.

He tried to tell himself that it didn't matter. Riane had already walked out of his life, just as he'd known she would. She was a woman, after all, and every woman he'd ever cared about had abandoned him.

Why, then, did her leaving hurt so much? And why did finding a way to win her back suddenly seem so much more important than the revenge he'd sought for so long? So much more important than anything else?

As he reached for his cell phone to call Riane, it started to ring.

* * *

Both Ellen and Ryan Quinlan were in the living room when Joel arrived. Ryan sat on the edge of the couch, his concentration focused intently on the phone, as if he might will it to ring. The senator was pacing. Her usually immaculate hair looked as though she'd repeatedly run her fingers through it, her face was bare of makeup, her eyes red rimmed and filled with anxiety.

Until that moment Joel hadn't been convinced of the gravity of the situation. All Ellen Rutherford-Quinlan had said on the phone was that she needed him to come to the house right away. Joel had sensed the urgency and hadn't asked any questions.

"Thank you for coming, Mr. Logan." It was Ryan who spoke to him, his voice shaky, as if he was holding on to the little control he had by a fraying thread.

It was Joel's first meeting with Riane's father, and not at all the circumstances under which he might have wished the introduction to take place.

"Our daughter's been kidnapped," the older man continued.

Joel felt his heart drop like a stone into the bottom of an empty well. But he shook his head, refusing to believe it. She'd probably just gone for a drive. Or maybe she'd gone to the camp. There were a million possibilities, but kidnapped was not one of them.

"We got a telephone call," Ryan told him. "Just before we called you, from the man who's taken her."

Joel had come right away. Still, the drive from the diner had taken more than an hour, and every minute of it seemed interminable. "You haven't heard anything since then?"

"No."

"Do you have any idea who's taken her? Why?"

Ryan just shook his head. "He only told us that he has Riane."

"Did you speak to Riane at all?"

"He wouldn't let me."

"Then maybe he doesn't have her," Joel suggested, wanting desperately to believe it himself. "Maybe this is some kind of hoax."

That was a better alternative than to believe some nut really had Riane, because even in the movies kidnappers made their hostages say a few words. Proof of life, it was called. If the kidnapper wouldn't give it, the hostage was as good as dead. He shook off the thought. Riane was going to be fine. She had to be.

"We wouldn't have bothered you if we thought this was a hoax, Mr. Logan." The senator's voice whipped across the room like a physical slap. "My daughter is missing. She went to the camp this morning. Her car is still there. She isn't."

"The grounds are pretty extensive," Joel reminded her. "If Riane decided to take a walk or—"

"She didn't take a walk. She was kidnapped. Jared, the camp supervisor, went out there this afternoon to tend to the horses. He found—"

Her voice broke and she turned away, as if ashamed for him to see any hint of her suffering. "He found her Harvard ring on the ground beside her car."

She turned to face him again, her eyes flashing with annoyance, "And before you suggest that it might have slipped off her finger, I can assure you that it didn't. We gave her that ring after law school graduation, and she has never taken it off. She did so now to tell us she didn't go willingly."

"Forgive me for being blunt," Joel said. "But I know that Riane has had a lot to deal with in the past few weeks. Can you really be certain that she didn't just go off somewhere for some time alone?"

"We're certain," Ryan said, slipping his arm across his wife's shoulders in a visible sign of support. "When Riane came home last night, we resolved a lot of things. She wasn't angry or upset when she left here this morning."

Joel scrubbed his hands over his face, surprised by the rasp of stubble against his palm. He'd forgotten to shave this morning. Hell, since Riane had walked out on him last night he hadn't even slept. He felt grossly unprepared to deal with this latest crisis, but he knew he couldn't be anywhere else right now.

Focus, Logan.

He wouldn't be any help to Riane if he didn't keep his mind on the present situation. So, unthinkable as it was to believe that she'd actually been kidnapped, he forced his mind to accept the possibility and gather all the details.

"Did the kidnapper ask for money?"

Again Ryan shook his head. "He said he'd call back. He had some details to take care of first."

Christ, Joel thought with disgust. It was like whoever had kidnapped Riane didn't know any of the rules. There was nothing worse—or more dangerous—than an amateur.

"You need to speak to Riane," Joel said. "Don't agree to anything until you talk to her."

"We'll do anything to get our daughter back," Ellen told him.

And so would he, Joel vowed silently. "I understand that," he told her. "But I don't want the kidnapper to know that until we've heard from Riane."

She looked at her husband, wordlessly seeking his agreement. Ryan nodded.

"Okay," the senator agreed.

"Depending on his reasons for targeting your daughter," Joel said, and he was afraid to even speculate on what those reasons might be, "the kidnapper may want some kind of media exposure."

"No," Ryan said immediately. "We want this kept out of the press."

"Shouldn't your priority be getting Riane back?" Joel asked, his tone cool.

"Riane is, and always has been, our priority," Ellen told him. "That's why we don't want the press getting wind of this. Wackos get ideas—"

"Not to mention the damage to your political career if the details of recent revelations came to light," Joel said.

The senator turned to him, her eyes hot with anger. "Is that what you think—that I'm trying to cover my own ass?"

"Aren't you?"

She gasped. "No. We—"

"Regardless of what you may think of us," Ryan interrupted his wife's outburst, "the only thing that matters here is getting Riane back safely. I agreed to call you because Ellen thought you cared about Riane. If she was wrong, if our daughter doesn't matter to you, then we'll find someone else to track her down and bring her home."

"No," Joel said. "I'll do this."

The senator nodded stiffly. "Then do it."

So Joel made some phone calls and pulled strings with a buddy in the FBI. With the political clout of the senator to back him up, he had the Quinlan telephone lines tapped within twenty minutes without the necessity of any official Bureau involvement.

When the phone finally rang, another agonizingly slow thirty minutes later, he was waiting on the extension.

"Hello?" Ellen's usually controlled voice wavered.

"Mom, it's me."

Ellen closed her eyes, silent tears sliding down her pasty cheeks. Joel's own sense of relief was so overwhelming he had to lower himself into the nearest chair or risk falling down.

"Are you okay, honey?"

"I'd feel better after a few slices of sausage pizza, but I'm fine." Her voice trembled a little, but she sounded strong.

"We'll get you a dozen pizzas," Ellen promised. "Just tell us what we need to do. Whatever it takes, we'll get you home."

Joel should have been annoyed that the senator had so blatantly disregarded his instructions, but he couldn't blame her for promising anything. Right now, he was so anxious to see Riane, to touch her—to know she was alive and well and safe, he would have promised the moon and the stars to bring her home.

"He wants a million dollars," Riane said. "If you don't have the money ready within the next two hours, the price is going up by half a million."

"We'll have the money," the senator promised, heedless of the tears that continued to fall. "Just tell us where to deliver it. We'll make sure it's there."

"He hasn't told me where he wants it dropped off," Riane said.

The next voice over the line wasn't Riane's, but Joel recognized it anyway.

Gavin Elliott.

"I'll call you in half an hour with more details," Elliott said, then disconnected.

Joel's stomach clenched. He was responsible for this. For everything. He'd gone to see Elliott, he'd started asking questions about Riane, he'd set this whole thing in motion. And if anything happened to Riane, he'd never forgive himself.

Joel dropped the receiver back into its cradle and looked at the tracing equipment. He shook his head. He hadn't expected the call would be long enough, but he'd had to give it a shot.

"I don't understand Riane's comment about pizza," the senator said, wiping at the wet streaks on her face. "Why wouldn't he feed her if she's hungry? Aren't kidnappers supposed to show good faith or something like that?"

"I don't think she was saying she was hungry," Joel admitted. "I think she was trying to tell us something."

"What?"

"That I'm not sure." He stood up and paced the length of the room, trying to kick-start his brain. He couldn't think straight. He was so tied up in knots worrying about Riane that he was barely functioning. But he knew she was depending on him. Her comment about the pizza proved that. She, at least, seemed to be thinking clearly.

She must have known her parents would contact him after

they received the first call. She had to know he'd be listening in to the conversation. But still, her comment didn't make any sense to him. She didn't even *like* sausage pizza.

And that suddenly, he knew what she was trying to tell him. Riane was at the motel where they'd stayed the night he'd found her at the country-western bar. The night she'd eaten, with a reluctance exceeded only by hunger, three slices of sausage pizza.

Clever girl, he thought, his heart swelling with pride. She'd given him an invaluable clue about her location without tipping off Elliott to the fact that she knew where she was. She was beautiful and brilliant and brave, and if he hadn't already been head over heels in love with her, he would have fallen right then.

"I think I know where she is," Joel said.

"Where?" Ellen and Ryan demanded in unison.

He glanced at his watch. Elliott said he'd call back in half an hour. If he remembered the location of the motel correctly, it would take him almost that long to get there. And if he was wrong—

No. Riane had definitely been telling him that she was at that motel. In fact, he should have suspected Elliott would take her there. It was off the beaten path, yet close enough to facilitate a quick exchange of money for hostage. Elliott certainly wouldn't expect that Riane had ever been there before. She was a senator's daughter; it was one step above a fleabag motel.

"I'm not positive," Joel cautioned them. "But there's someplace I need to check out."

"I want to go with you," Ellen said.

"No."

"She's my daughter."

"And if she's there, you could blow everything by rushing in."

"I want to be there. I need to see her. To know that she's okay."

"I'll bring her home," Joel promised.

"But—"

Again, it was her husband's wordless communication—a simple touch of his hand on her arm—that silenced the senator's further protests. "Let him go," Ryan said. "We have to get the money together and we need to be here when Riane calls back."

Ellen nodded reluctantly.

Ryan exchanged a look with Joel. A plea. A promise.

Then Joel was gone.

He tied her up. He bound her wrists and stuffed a washcloth in her mouth. To keep her quiet and out of the way. He wouldn't let another woman screw this up for him.

Rheanne had always factored into his plans. Anyone who'd paid a hundred grand to buy a baby would pay again—and pay dearly—to keep that secret. And the woman who'd bought his baby was now a bona fide U.S. senator. It was almost too perfect. Any scent of a scandal would ruin her career, shame her family. He never doubted that she would pay.

The money he'd get from the senator would have given Felicia and him a new start. Felicia had ruined that part of his plan. And he'd been forced to take immediate action. To upgrade his strategy from blackmail to kidnapping.

He glanced at the woman on the floor. She was restrained, helpless. But she glared at him with fire in her eyes. He almost smiled. She had spirit—like her mother and her sister. He felt a pang of sorrow over losing Felicia. Fury for Arden's role in all of this. She'd been the one to turn her mother against him.

But maybe he should thank Arden. Her desire to be reunited with her little sister had led Joel Logan to Rheanne. And Rheanne was his ticket out of this whole mess.

The senator hadn't even balked at the million-dollar price tag. He should have asked for more. Two million. Five million. She would have paid anything.

He smiled. Maybe next time.

* * *

When it came down to the crunch, it was almost too easy. That realization sent a fresh wave of panic through Joel. It was the same thought he'd had before he'd taken a bullet in the gut, before his life had unraveled in front of his eyes. This time there was so much more at stake. This time it was the woman he loved.

He recognized the car as soon as he pulled into the parking lot. The dirty green Malibu with a patch of rust on the rear fender and Michigan plates. Joel swore and checked the clip in his gun. Gavin Elliott was a smart man, but taking Riane had obviously been an act of desperation, and that made him much more dangerous.

Joel picked up the empty pizza box he'd tossed onto the passenger seat. It was a prop—a reason to knock on the door. He hadn't planned any further than to get inside. He needed to know that Riane was okay. God help Gavin Elliott if she wasn't.

He pulled his Yankees baseball cap lower over his forehead and marched up to the door of room six. He'd already verified Elliott's registration with the desk clerk. He'd given a false name—John Smith—and paid cash, but he'd noted his license plate number on the registration card. That was proof enough for Joel.

Snatching Riane had obviously been an impulse, or Elliott wouldn't have used his own car in the act. Which made Joel realize that Felicia Reynolds was right: Elliott thought he'd killed her. No doubt he needed the ransom money from Riane's kidnapping to get him out of the country. And it was further proof of how far gone the man was that he actually thought he would get away with it.

Joel knocked boldly, as if he was expected. As someone delivering a pizza would be. He saw the curtains flutter, heard the slide of the chain being drawn back. Then Gavin Elliott was at the door.

"I didn't order any pizza," he rasped, his eyes shifting

from the flat cardboard box to Joel's face, widening in recognition and alarm. "What the hell are you doing here?"

Joel's only response was to plow his fist solidly into Elliott's jaw. The older man staggered backward and crumpled into a heap on the orange shag carpet. Joel was almost disappointed that he didn't get to throw more punches. But as much as he would have enjoyed going a few rounds with Elliott, his concern was for Riane. He flexed his fingers, his eyes desperately searching the shabby room for any sign of the woman he loved.

He found her, kneeling on the floor behind the dresser. Her wrists tied together in front of her, a rag of some kind stuffed into her mouth. Her hair was tangled and her eyes were smudged with shadows of fatigue, but she was there. And despite the way they'd parted at their last meeting, he could tell she was relieved to see him.

He knelt beside her, carefully removing the cloth from her mouth, murmuring softly to her as he brushed away the tears of relief and gratitude that tracked slowly down her cheeks. "Are you okay, sweetheart?"

She nodded, although she couldn't seem to stop trembling—or crying. "B-better now."

There was so much he wanted to say to her, so many feelings warring for expression inside him. But the most important thing right now was to get her out of there. "Let's get you home."

He started to fumble with the knot binding her wrists together, stunned to see that his own hands were shaking. In all his years as a cop, even in that final showdown, he'd never been as terrified as he'd been when he'd learned of the danger Riane was in. God, he loved this woman, and if he hadn't already screwed things up too badly, he was going to spend every day of the rest of his life showing her how much he loved her.

"He's g-got a gun," Riane said, her voice shaky, frantic.

So preoccupied was he with Riane that it took a moment for her words to register, and that moment—probably not more than a fraction of a second, was a fraction of a second too long. He turned just as the gunshot exploded.

He never saw how Riane managed to launch herself from her position on the floor and throw herself in front of him. But he did see, as if in slow motion, her body jerk back as the bullet slammed into her.

Chapter 17

Joel's response was automatic. He wasn't aware of his own gun in his hand, his finger on the trigger. He didn't hear the discharge; he didn't feel the recoil; he didn't see Elliott fall.

He only saw Riane—and he watched in horror as she fell back against the wall, slid slowly to the floor.

"Christ, Riane." Blood was seeping from her shoulder, the dark crimson stain spreading over the shirt, soaking it. "What the hell were you thinking?"

It was easier to be angry than to think that she could be dying. The rational part of his brain knew it wasn't likely. The bullet didn't seem to have hit any major arteries and a .22 caliber handgun didn't have a lot of firepower. But her skin was clammy, those beautiful dark brown eyes wide and glazed, and she was losing a lot of blood.

He propped her up a little higher, trying to keep the injured shoulder above her heart. He knew he should get a towel to stanch the flow of blood, but he'd have to go into the bathroom for that and he couldn't bear to leave her. Not even for a few seconds. So he pulled his own T-shirt over his head and pressed it into the wound. She didn't wince, and he knew then that she probably couldn't even feel the bullet hole in her shoulder. But the blood continued to flow.

She licked her lips, blinked several times. He knew she was going to lose consciousness, and he couldn't stand the thought of her slipping away, even for a moment. He dug his cell phone out of his pocket and managed to dial 911, tersely explaining the situation and requesting immediate ambulance assistance.

Then he disconnected the call and began to pray. He'd never been a particularly devout man, but he found himself seeking divine assistance now. The words and pleas and promises tripped over one another, jumbled together in his head, with only one consistent thought: *Please, God. Let her live.*

He cradled her in his arms, still applying pressure to the wound. "Stay with me, sweetheart. Please, stay with me. The ambulance is on the way. Just hold on a little longer."

Riane managed a slight nod, then closed her eyes.

"Come on, Riane. Talk to me."

Her eyes flickered open slowly, and she blinked, as if trying to bring his face into focus. "Sorry about your shirt."

Riane spent four days in the hospital. Four torturously long days. As if the pain in her shoulder wasn't excruciating enough every time she moved, her parents never seemed to leave her room. She knew they'd been worried about her, and she appreciated their concern, but she was starting to feel smothered by their love.

And forgotten by the man she loved.

She had a vague recollection of Joel riding in the ambulance with her, holding her hand on the way to the hospital. She'd found comfort in his presence and the steady reassuring murmur of his voice. She wasn't sure she clearly remembered anything he said, but she thought—or maybe she just hoped—he'd told her he loved her.

It was those words—real or imagined—that had given her

hope. But since she'd regained consciousness, she hadn't so much as caught a glimpse of him. When she finally gathered up the courage to ask about him, her mother admitted that he'd gone back to Pennsylvania.

His apparent indifference hurt so much more than the residual pain in her shoulder. The scar from the bullet was insignificant compared to the scars on her heart.

She didn't really blame Joel for not wanting to stick around. They'd each understood that their relationship wasn't for the long term, and she'd reiterated that statement, clearly and finally, by walking out on him. So she shouldn't have been surprised that he hadn't stayed; she had no right to feel hurt. They lived in different worlds, wanted different things. Or so she'd honestly believed. Right now all she wanted was Joel.

She was released from the hospital on Thursday, with strict instructions from her doctor to get plenty of rest. Ellen and Ryan continued to hover over her bed, as if afraid to let Riane out of their sight. Sophie fluffed pillows and baked cookies and brought magazines Riane never got a chance to read.

News of the abduction, the shooting, and the death of her abductor, had been plastered all over the news. For three days it was the lead story on the local stations—things like that just didn't happen in Mapleview. The incident even garnered national coverage because the victim was Senator Ellen Rutherford-Quinlan's daughter. Despite the media frenzy, no one seemed to have made the connection between Riane and Gavin Elliott, which was at least something for which she could feel grateful.

Arden and Shaun came to visit the day after she arrived home from the hospital. The second reunion between the two sisters had been more natural, and more emotional, than the first.

"I was so afraid I'd found you only to lose you again," Arden said tearfully.

Riane had cried, too, feeling incredibly blessed despite recent events. It wasn't so hard, she realized, to open up her heart to this extended family that she'd never known she had. And both Ellen and Ryan had seemed genuinely pleased to meet their daughter's older sister and Arden's fiancé.

Still, Riane couldn't help feeling as though there was something left unfinished.

Three days later she was in the solarium, stretched out on a wicker chaise lounge with both sets of French doors open to allow the cool breeze and the scent of spring flowers into the room. Her arm was still in a sling, and although the pain had lessened somewhat, her sense of restlessness had not.

Sophie brought her a glass of fresh-squeezed lemonade and a plate of oatmeal-raisin cookies. "I can't just sit around eating all day," Riane complained. "I'll get fat."

"You need to put on a few pounds," Sophie told her, fluffing the pillow from the end of the lounger, replacing it beneath Riane's feet. "If that wind picks up any, it'll blow you away."

"I hardly think that's likely."

Sophie huffed. "You haven't eaten a decent meal since you've been home. Since Mr. Logan left town."

"My lack of appetite has nothing to do with him," Riane said firmly.

"And he calls here every day for a report on the local weather," Sophie muttered sarcastically.

"He called?" Riane asked, annoyed at the sudden flutter of excitement in her belly.

"Every day since you've been home."

Riane paused with the glass of lemonade halfway to her lips. "Why?"

Sophie shook her head. "Why do you think? Because the man's in love with you."

"If he loves me, why hasn't he come to see me?"

"Because men are idiots. Men in love are even worse. And that's just what I told him, too."

Riane couldn't help but smile at the assessment. Sophie had strong opinions, strong emotions, and she never hesitated to express either one. She didn't doubt that Sophie had told

Joel exactly that. Riane's smile faltered. Regardless of what Sophie might have said, Joel was still in Pennsylvania and she was here.

"He nearly wore a hole through the floor in the waiting room while you were in surgery," Sophie said, shaking her head. "As if we didn't know that you could survive a little gunshot wound."

"Little gunshot wound?" Riane said indignantly. "I could have been killed."

Sophie shook her head again. "Not my girl. She's tough. Too stubborn to let a bullet take her down."

Riane laughed. It felt good to return to some sense of normalcy after the craziness of the past couple of weeks.

"Now that's a sound I haven't heard around here in far too long," Ryan said, coming into the solarium from the family room.

"What are you doing home in the middle of the day?" Riane demanded.

"Just came by to check on my favorite girl," he said, bending to kiss her cheek. "How's the arm?"

"Stiff."

Sophie snorted. "How much longer are you going to let her play up that scratch?"

Ryan grinned and sat on the lounger beside his daughter, taking her uninjured hand and squeezing gently. "As long as she wants."

Sophie retreated into the main part of the house, shaking her head the whole way.

"What *I* want," Riane told him, "is my files from the camp. I'm going crazy just sitting around here day after day."

"Everything's on schedule," Ryan assured her. "You have a very capable staff who are finally getting a chance to prove themselves because you're not around to do everything."

"I like doing everything," Riane said mutinously.

"I know. You're a control freak, just like your mother." Ryan's tone was affectionate.

"I'm not a control freak," Ellen denied, following her husband's path into the room.

Ryan chuckled.

Riane turned to her mother, eyed the red silk dress and jacket Ellen was wearing. The suit Riane knew she wore whenever she was about to tackle a controversial issue in the Senate or just generally needed to boost her self-confidence. "Where have you been?"

"I had a press conference this morning."

"Why? Why didn't you tell me?"

"Because I didn't want you to worry."

"Control freak," Ryan said again.

But this time Ellen smiled at him, and in her eyes was a wealth of emotion—gratitude, affection, relief.

"I resigned my seat in the Senate."

Riane sat up abruptly, winced at the resultant pain that lanced through her shoulder like a hot blade. She swore under her breath and sank back into the thick cushion. "Because of me," she said weakly.

"No," both Ellen and Ryan denied in unison.

Riane wasn't convinced.

Ellen sat down on the end of her husband's lounge chair. "Because it was what I needed to do."

"You think Joel will take the information about my adoption to the press?"

"My decision had nothing to do with Mr. Logan."

"But you love your job," Riane protested.

Ellen shrugged. "Now I'll find another job to love."

Riane couldn't help looking skeptical.

"I happen to know of a law firm that has an opening," Ryan said. "There's even a corner office with a pretty good view."

"*My* office?" Riane asked.

Ryan smiled. "It's not *your* office until you take the job, and we both know you're not going to."

"But—"

"No 'buts,'" her father interrupted. "I've already given your job—and your office—away."

Riane blew out a frustrated breath.

Ellen reached over to take Riane's hand, cradling it between both of her own. "You have to decide what *you* want to do," she said gently. "Not what you think *we* want you to do."

"I don't know what I want," Riane admitted.

"Do you want Joel?"

Riane looked down at their joined hands, drawing strength from the unquestioning support of her family. Even now, after everything that had happened, neither of her parents was trying to influence her decision. Whatever mistakes she'd make in her life would be her own, but she knew they would always stand by her. And it was that knowledge that gave her the courage to answer her mother's question.

"Yes."

"Then go get him."

"Why should *I* have to go after *him?*" Riane demanded sulkily.

"Because you're the one who walked out," Ellen reminded her.

"He's the one who hightailed it back to Pennsylvania."

"I think he blames himself for what happened," Ryan said. "And believing that, he wouldn't think he was welcome to stay."

It was something Riane hadn't considered but realized she should have. Joel had been instrumental in uncovering the truth about her adoption, and in doing so he'd brought Gavin Elliott into her life. Rational or not, she knew him well enough to know he'd feel responsible for the events that had followed.

The realization gave her hope. Maybe he wasn't staying away because he didn't want her but because he felt guilty about what had happened in that motel room. And he wouldn't feel guilty if he didn't care about her.

"Do you love him?" Ellen asked gently.

Now Riane smiled. "The first time he kissed me, I felt as though the ground was actually trembling beneath my feet."

Ryan shook his head. "I don't need to hear these things about my little girl."

Ellen only smiled back at her. "Go get him."

"Now?" Riane asked, startled.

"Why not? If you sit and think about it, you'll think of a hundred reasons why you shouldn't go. Follow your heart."

"You're really okay with this?"

"I think the one thing I've learned over the past couple of weeks is that I have an incredible daughter. She's beautiful and strong and exactly the kind of woman I hoped she'd be someday." Ellen leaned forward and took both of her daughter's hands in hers—a gesture of support, a symbol of unity. "It takes a very special man to appreciate a woman like you, and I think you've found him."

So Riane went to Pennsylvania to find him.

Eight days had passed since the incident in the motel room. Eight nights in which Joel watched over and over again as Riane threw herself in front of the gun. He awoke from those dreams with the warm stickiness of her blood on his hands.

In a futile attempt to banish the torturous memory, he worked harder and longer and slept less. But he couldn't forget the image of Riane on that stretcher. Pale, almost lifeless, the blood continuing to spill out of the hole in her shoulder.

When the doctor had come out after the surgery to tell Riane's parents that she was going to be okay, he'd done something he couldn't ever remember having done before. He'd put his head in his hands and he'd wept.

He'd experienced loss before. His mother, his grandmother, his sister. His career. His wife. Max. He'd never felt the heart-wrenching agony he'd experienced every single moment that Riane was behind the closed doors of that operating room.

Even when they'd told him that she'd be okay, he wasn't convinced. He wouldn't believe it until he saw her with his own eyes. And so he'd waited until visiting hours were long over, and he'd sneaked into her room.

She'd been sleeping—sedated. Her hair dark against the pristine white pillowcase, her face pale. Her shoulder was bandaged, an IV protruded from the back of her delicate hand.

He'd reached out tentatively, brushed her hair away from her face, rubbed his knuckles gently across her cheek.

It wasn't enough. That single glimpse, that single touch, wasn't nearly enough. But he forced himself to be satisfied—to walk away. She was going to be all right. He had no right to ask for anything more.

And so he got into his car and came back to Pennsylvania.

Back to a home that was empty without her. Back to a bed that carried a lingering trace of her scent no matter how many times he changed the sheets.

Damn it—even now, even in his office, he could smell her. That slightly musky scent that clouded his senses. He shook his head, scrubbed his hands over his face, rubbed his tired eyes.

Maybe he needed a vacation. Mike had been on his case since he'd come back from West Virginia to take some time off—to get away. But there was nowhere he wanted to go without Riane.

He opened his eyes again, and she was there.

He blinked, certain she would disappear as quickly as she'd appeared, but the image remained.

"Hello, Joel."

He ignored the sudden rush of his pulse, the tightening around his heart. He'd promised himself that he could get over her, but he needed more time. It had only been a few days. He hadn't even started to heal.

"Riane." Her name was little more than a whisper on his lips. Or maybe it was a plea.

She stepped into his office, closed the door behind her.

She was so beautiful, even with her arm in a sling and her face tired and pale, she was the most beautiful woman he'd ever known.

He swallowed, searching for something to say, finally settling upon, "What are you doing here?"

"I needed to see you. I need to know why you left."

"My job was done."

"Is that all I ever was to you?" She sounded casual, as if it was simply idle curiosity that prompted the question, as if his response didn't really matter.

He wished he could be as cool, but his heart was breaking all over again just looking at her. "You know better than that."

"I thought I did." She shrugged. Again, very casual. "But I didn't think you'd take off without saying goodbye, either."

"Is that why you're here—because I didn't say goodbye?"

"I'm here because I never got a chance to thank you."

"Thank me?"

"For saving my life."

"Saving your life?" Joel wondered briefly if he was having some out-of-body experience because nothing she was saying made any sense to him.

"You came after me...you found me. Even though I walked out on you. And I wanted to thank you for that."

"Christ, Riane. He shot you. He could have killed you, and it was all my fault."

"How was it your fault?"

"I led him to you," Joel said, even now horrified by the realization that she'd nearly died because of him. That the life of this precious, beautiful woman could have ended because he'd been unable to put aside his personal quest for vengeance.

Joel shook his head, guilt gnawing at his insides. "He probably hadn't even thought of you in the past twenty years until I started asking questions." He broke off, appalled. "I'm sorry. I keep forgetting—"

"That he was my father," Riane finished for him.

"He was your father," Joel repeated. "And I killed him." Even if she could somehow forgive him for everything else, how could she ever get past that fact? How could *he* ever get past it?

"He would have killed you," Riane said. "And me. I wish I could forget it. I wish I could pretend it wasn't true." She managed a wry smile. "It was devastating to learn that the people who raised me weren't really my parents. Although I know now that I was wrong to ever have thought that. They are my parents—in every way that counts."

"I'm glad you worked things out with them."

"There are a lot of things in my life that I still need to resolve, but I'm working on them."

He just nodded.

"That's the real reason I'm here," she admitted softly. "To see if we can resolve what happened between us."

"I didn't realize it was *un*resolved."

"When we were in the ambulance—on the way to the hospital—I thought you said you loved me."

Joel didn't respond. There wasn't any point in admitting his feelings, opening up his heart.

But she wouldn't accept his silence. "Did you say it?"

He swallowed. "Yes."

"Did you mean it?"

"Why are you bringing this up now?"

"Because I need to know if it's really over between us or if maybe we could start again."

"It's over."

She looked away quickly, but not before he saw her eyes fill with tears. He hated himself for hurting her, for doing so callously and deliberately. But he knew it was for the best. So he braced himself, prepared to watch her walk out the door. To walk out of his life, taking his heart with her.

Riane stopped in front of the door, hesitated.

Just go, he pleaded silently. *Now. Don't make this any more difficult.*

She turned back abruptly, her eyes glittering. Not with

tears now, but anger. "Do you really expect me to believe it's over?"

She retraced her steps across the room until she was standing in front of him again. "My life has been turned completely upside down over the past several weeks, and even though there were times I wanted to pretend none of this really happened, I never wished it away because through all of this chaos I found you.

"You made me believe that everything that's happened doesn't change who I am. And if I'd never found out I was adopted, I would never have known how desperately my parents wanted a child—how much they cherish me because they couldn't have children of their own. They gave me love and security. They taught me to be confident in who I was and what I wanted.

"You taught me to accept who I am, to be proud of who I am. And, damn it, you made me love you."

He didn't have time to catch his breath, to even think of a response, before she was plunging ahead again.

"So if you can look at me and tell me that you don't care about me—that you don't love me, I'll believe you. And I'll go. But don't you dare tell me you don't want me because you think you know what's best for me.

"Maybe you're not the kind of man I envisioned myself spending my life with. I'd be willing to bet I'm not the type of woman you were looking for, either. But the fact of the matter is that I think we've found something pretty special together, and I'm not willing to throw it away because you have some warped sense of nobility."

If he'd had any doubts before, he didn't now. She wasn't the type of woman he'd been looking for. He hadn't wanted anyone; he hadn't wanted to admit he needed anyone. It wasn't until that moment—when she'd looked him in the eye and practically shouted that she was in love with him, almost daring him to dispute it—that he realized she was exactly what he needed.

And the tightness that had settled into his chest when he'd driven away from West Virginia finally began to ease.

Joel wasn't sure if she'd finished her speech or if she'd just run out of breath, but she was silent now. He'd never loved her more.

"Are you done?" he asked, pushing his chair away from the desk and rising to his feet.

Riane nodded.

"Then maybe you'll shut up for a minute so that I can say something."

She glared at him and opened her mouth to speak.

He held up a hand. "You had your turn, now it's mine."

Her jaw snapped shut, but the mutinous look was still in her eye. He finally gave in to the urge to touch her, reaching out to take her free hand in his, linking their fingers together. The skin-on-skin contact reassured him that she was real and gave him the courage to say what was in his heart.

"First of all, I *do* love you. I meant it when I said it the first time. I love you even more now."

The clenching in her jaw eased, the set of her mouth relaxed.

"You're not the kind of woman I envisioned spending the rest of my life with," he admitted. "I didn't want to share my life with anyone. I was perfectly happy to be alone and independent, until you came along. You're everything I never knew I wanted, and so much more."

He watched her eyes fill with tears even as her lips curved.

"Don't start crying," Joel warned. "I'm not good with tears, and I'm not finished yet."

"I'll wait," she promised.

"I want to be with you. For now. Forever. But only if you promise not to throw yourself in front of any more bullets. Because if you do anything that stupid again, I'll kill you myself."

She laughed. There were tears spilling onto her cheeks, but she was laughing. Then she was in his arms and they were kissing.

Joel savored the taste of her, relished the softness of her curves pressed against him, marveled at the way she fit so perfectly in his arms. Nothing had ever felt better than holding her, and he knew he couldn't let her go.

He'd tried to do the right thing, he'd tried to walk away, but she'd come back to him. He'd been deceitful and dishonest—he knew he didn't deserve her. But by some miracle he didn't dare question, she'd fallen in love with him. And as he'd vowed that fateful day when he'd found her bound and gagged in the motel, he was going to spend every day of the rest of his life showing her how much he loved her.

He lifted her off her feet and sat her on his chair, kneeling beside her. He could feel a single bead of sweat trickle down his back as he prepared to take the biggest risk of his life. A life that was empty without Riane in it.

"I didn't plan this," he admitted. "I didn't think I'd ever get a chance to do this, but you're here and you claim to love me, so I'm going to take this chance and grab it with both hands."

He took her hands in his and held on tight. "I don't have a lot to offer, and I don't make promises I can't keep. But what I have I want to share with you. And I can promise my love and my loyalty forever."

"That's all I ever wanted," Riane told him.

* * * * *

Don't miss Brenda Harlen's next exciting
Silhouette Sensation book, Extreme Measures,
available from the shops in February 2005.

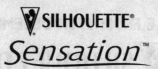

SILHOUETTE®
Sensation™

AVAILABLE FROM 17TH DECEMBER 2004

SURE BET Maggie Price

Line of Duty

In order to solve a series of murders, rookie officer Morgan McCall and police sergeant Alex Blade pose as newlyweds. Though reluctant to act on the attraction flaring between them, danger led to desire, and soon their fake marriage felt all too real.

CROSSFIRE Jenna Mills

Bodyguard Hawk Monroe wanted to break Elizabeth Carrington's cool society façade. She'd walked away from him before, but now a threat to her life brought her back. Despite the danger, Hawk planned to recapture the passion they once shared.

SHADOWS OF THE PAST Frances Housden

A stalker had taught Marie Costello to trust no one, but when a gorgeous stranger asked her to dance, she broke all the rules and said yes to CEO Franc Jellic. But would her newfound happiness with Franc trigger another deadly attack from her past?

SWEET SUSPICION Nina Bruhns

Witness Muse Summerville knew agent Remi Beaulieux would keep her safe—but locked away in a cottage under his protective custody, she found him impossible to resist. Yet before long, they had to face the crime boss threatening to tear them apart…

DARKNESS CALLS Caridad Piñeiro

Shivers

Powerful, dangerous and the key to catching a psychotic killer, Ryder Latimer was everything FBI agent Diana Reyes couldn't have—and everything she wanted. But once she learned his secret, would his sensual promises of eternal love be enough?

IN THE ARMS OF A STRANGER Kristen Robinette

Police Chief Luke Sutherlin knew better than to fall for a prime suspect, but the loving way Dana Langston held the unknown baby in her arms made it hard for him to believe *she* could have murdered the child's mother. Luke knew he had to uncover the truth—before he lost his heart forever.

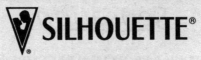

Published
17th December 2004

M394

A spell-binding novel of heart-racing
suspense and heated passion

SHARON SALA

MIMOSA GROVE

ITS BEAUTY WAS SEDUCTIVE — YET DANGEROUS...

4 Books
and a surprise gift!

We would like to take this opportunity to thank you for reading this Silhouette® book by offering you the chance to take FOUR more specially selected titles from the Sensation™ series absolutely FREE! We're also making this offer to introduce you to the benefits of the Reader Service™—

- ★ FREE home delivery
- ★ FREE gifts and competitions
- ★ FREE monthly Newsletter
- ★ Exclusive Reader Service offers
- ★ Books available before they're in the shops

Accepting these FREE books and gift places you under no obligation to buy, you may cancel at any time, even after receiving your free shipment. Simply complete your details below and return the entire page to the address below. You don't even need a stamp!

YES! Please send me 4 free Sensation books and a surprise gift. I understand that unless you hear from me, I will receive 6 superb new titles every month for just £2.99 each, postage and packing free. I am under no obligation to purchase any books and may cancel my subscription at any time. The free books and gift will be mine to keep in any case.

S4ZEF

Ms/Mrs/Miss/Mr ....Initials.................................

BLOCK CAPITALS PLEASE

Surname ....

Address...

....

....Postcode...

Send this whole page to:
UK: FREEPOST CN81, Croydon, CR9 3WZ